HPBooks

Hotter than Hell

Hot & Spicy Dishes from Around the World

Jane Butel

JANE BUTEL

A native of New Mexico and now a resident of New York, Jane has a successful career in a hot business—hot and spicy foods! An expert in foods and spices from the Southwest, she has two cooking schools—Southwestern Cooking School in Santa Fe and Santa Fe East in Woodstock, New York. In addition she owns and manages Pecos Valley Spice Company and is a prolific writer. She has previously authored nine cookbooks including *Jane Butel's Tex-Mex Cookbook, Chili Madness, Favorite Mexican Foods Cookbook, Hot & Spicy Barbecue* and *Fiesta.*

DEDICATION

To Brennan, my husband, who was always at hand to create, taste and assist in the development of all the recipes, and to Amy, my daughter, who was always helpful and supportive. And to my father, who inspired it all—he's the one who taught me to like it hot! A special thanks to Lori Greene and Anne Gumina, among others, who were always ready to help put this book in its final form. Last, but not least, to my dear agent Sidney Kramer, who along with Elaine Woodard at HPBooks has played a vital role in getting this book into print.

Another Best-Selling Volume from HPBooks

Illustrations by Terry Medaris

Published by HPBooks, a division of Price Stern Sloan, Inc.
360 N. La Cienega Blvd.
Los Angeles, CA 90048
©1987 Jane Butel
Printed in U.S.A.
9 8 7 6 5 4 3 2

Library of Congress Cataloging-in-Publication Data

Butel, Jane.
 Hotter than hell.

 Includes index.
  1. Cookery, International.   2. Spices.
3. Condiments.   I. Title.
TX725.A1B865   1987   641.6'384   87-17795
ISBN 0-89586-646-3
ISBN 0-89586-542-4 (pbk.)

Contents

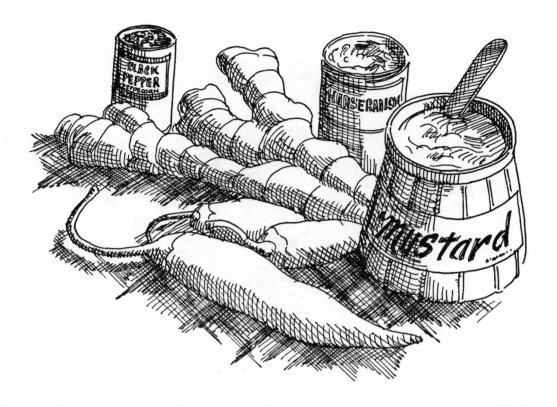

Introduction

The zingly, tingly, singularly exciting flavors of piquant spices thrill the palate like nothing else. Ginger, horseradish, mustard, pepper—if you like your food hotter than hell, you know how these spices can liven up dishes of every kind. And for really punishing, pervasive heat, nothing surpasses chiles.

In putting this recipe collection together, I've used these ingredients liberally. You'll find fired-up favorites of all kinds, from appetizers to soups to salads to main dishes. And since all but the most asbestos-mouthed occasionally crave relief from the heat, I've also included some mild-mannered selections: soothing beverages, side dishes and desserts.

If your passion for heat is a recent one, you may want to begin by reviewing the basic information on ingredients given in the next few pages. But if you're a long-time aficionado of all things fiery, turn right to page 13 and start cooking!

A GUIDE TO INGREDIENTS

Chiles

More than 7,000 varieties of chiles grow throughout the world, differing greatly in size and ranging in flavor from pleasantly spicy to downright satanic. Even the spelling of the word varies. I prefer the Spanish spelling, with a final -e, but you'll also see chili (to me, that's strictly the name of the dish, as in *chili con carne*), chillie, even chilly or chilley. Another point of confusion concerns the frequent use of the word "pepper" to describe chiles—"hot pepper," "chile pepper" and so forth. Chiles are in fact completely unrelated to true pepper (*Piper nigrum*); they belong to the genus *Capsicum,* which in turn falls into the larger family encompassing potatoes, tomatoes and eggplant. There's a simple explanation for the "pepper" designation, though. When Spanish explorers first sampled chiles in the Caribbean islands, they likened the pungent flavor to the black pepper they knew—and named the spicy chile pods accordingly.

Chiles, like bell peppers, turn from green to red (or sometimes yellow or purple) as they ripen; flavor changes, too, from tart and sharp to sweeter and more mellow. In recent years, fresh green chiles have become increasingly available throughout the United States, but ripe, red ones are still sold only regionally and only in autumn. You're far more likely to encounter red chiles in dried form—whole pods, crushed, or ground.

Choosing & handling chiles. When you're buying fresh chiles, remember this: no two chiles have the same heat level, even if they were plucked from the same plant. Chile bushes cross-pollinate freely, and that can result in variation—up to 35 different piquancies in the fruits on a single stalk. The most reliable key to a chile's nature is its size and shape. Small, narrow-shouldered, deep-colored chiles with pointed tips tend to be the hottest; larger chiles that are broad across the shoulders are typically milder in flavor.

In buying dried chiles, there's one important rule: go for the real thing! When purchasing crushed and ground chiles, look for lightproof, airtight packaging and, when opened, a fresh, sinus-clearing aroma. And avoid commercial "chili powder"! Often hot and rank-tasting, it usually contains a mere 40% crushed chiles, with salt, garlic, cumin, oregano and even corn flour making up the remaining 60%.

Because chiles contain volatile oils that can really burn your skin, you should never tackle them bare-handed. It's especially important to take precautions when you're handling fresh chiles, but the rules apply to dried chiles as well: wear rubber gloves when you prepare chiles, and wash both the gloves and your hands thoroughly with soap and water after you're done.

Never, never rub your eyes, nose or mouth while you work; the tissue in these areas is extremely sensitive to chile oils.

Types of chiles. Throughout this book, I've called for only the few types of chiles described below. Some are available in supermarkets, though you'll probably find the best selection in specialty produce stores and Mexican markets. If you can't find the ingredients you need, order them by mail (see the listings on page 195) or use the substitutes suggested.

New Mexico chile. These hybrid chiles are fairly hot and fairly large—about 1 to 2 inches wide at the shoulders, 5 to 7 inches long. For best flavor, parch and peel the fresh chiles before use (see "Parching fresh chiles," opposite). If fresh New Mexico hot green chiles are unavailable, you can generally use canned whole or diced green chiles. (In a few recipes, I've suggested substituting pickled jalapeños to keep the heat level up.)

Dried New Mexico chiles are pulverized, seeds and all, to make the *ground pure New Mexico hot red chile* called for frequently in my recipes. If you can't find it, substitute commercial crushed hot red pepper. Or make your own ground chile from whole dried pods: toast the pods in a 325F (165C) oven just until they begin to darken, then rinse, dry and stem them. Process the pods, 4 to 6 at a time, in a blender or food processor until finely ground. It's best to prepare only as much ground chile as you need for immediate use; if you have some leftover, freeze it or store airtight in opaque containers.

California (Anaheim) chile. Another hybrid chile, the California type looks much like the New Mexico variety, but it's milder in flavor. The fresh chiles should be parched and peeled for use (see opposite) and can be replaced by canned green chiles in cooking. *Ground pure California mild red chile* is simply powdered dried California chile pods; the seeds are often removed before grinding to assure a milder flavor. Very, very fresh paprika is an acceptable stand-in for ground mild chile used as a garnish; in cooking, though, it's too hot to successfully replace the real thing. For best results, try grinding whole dried mild chiles as directed for New Mexico chiles, above.

Jalapeño chile. These fiery, small to medium-size monsters are beloved by those who like eye-watering heat. When fresh, they're firm, round, dark green in color and about 2-1/2 inches long and 1 inch in diameter. If you can't find fresh jalapeños, use the pickled type; they're widely available in most supermarkets.

Serrano chile. Tiny (just 1 to 1-1/2 inches long), skinny and hot enough to make you cry! Serrano chiles aren't always easy to find fresh, but you can always use jalapeños in their place.

Poblano (ancho, pasilla) chile. Fresh poblanos look much like bell peppers, though rather more heart-shaped, but their flavor is much spicier. They're blackish green when fresh, nearly black when dried. Because they may be difficult to find, I've suggested an alternative in each recipe calling for poblanos—green bell peppers or Italian frying peppers in place of the fresh chiles, dried whole New Mexico red chiles in place of dried ones.

Caribe chile. Grown in northern New Mexico, the caribe is a little larger than the pequin (see opposite). It's a hot chile with a characteristic sweet, spicy flavor. I call only for crushed dried caribe chile, available by mail order and in some specialty stores. You may substitute commercial crushed hot red pepper for caribe, but the flavor will be milder and less rich.

Pequin chile. Extra-tiny (just 1/2 to 1 inch long) and devastatingly hot, these chiles grow wild along the Mexican border. They're potent enough to intimidate all but those with fireproof palates—chiles any more fiery than pequins are too hot to have any recognizable chile flavor! I have called for them in their crushed dried form, *pequin quebrado.* Look for pequin quebrado in specialty stores or buy it by mail order; or use cayenne pepper.

Other chiles. In addition to the seven types just discussed, a few other chiles are mentioned in this book. *Fresh Oriental hot green chiles,* available in Asian markets, are small, thin and very hot; you may see them sold as Thai, Szechwan or Hunan chiles (among other names). Jalapeño or serrano chiles are a good substitute. Tiny *Chinese dried hot red chiles,* only about 1 to 1-1/2 inches long, are thin and hot. They're quite widely available, both in Asian markets and well-stocked supermarkets. If you can't find them, you can generally substitute an equivalent amount of pure crushed dried hot red chile. Aromatic, reddish brown *dried Szechwan peppers* are tiny—about the size of peppercorns—and encased in flowerlike husks. Toasting brings out their fragrance and flavor (see Hot Salt, page 141). You can buy them in Asian markets. *Pickled Tuscan peppers* (peperoncini) are sold in almost every supermarket. They're small yellow-green chiles, very mild in flavor. By *Italian crushed hot red pepper,* I mean the crushed red pepper marketed by major spice companies all over the United States. This product is made from any one of a number of hot chiles, so the heat level may not be consistent from bottle to bottle. Store it in lightproof containers to maintain freshness longer.

Parching fresh chiles. The true flavor of a chile resides in the flesh of the pod. The ribs and seeds are the source of most of the chile's heat; you can remove them if a milder flavor is desired. The tough skins of large chiles (New Mexico, California and poblano types) should also usually be removed before use, but I don't feel that this is generally necessary with smaller chiles such as jalapeño and serrano. These have thinner skins, and are usually so finely sliced or minced that the skins aren't noticeable in any case.

To parch chiles, begin by dampening a cloth towel and refrigerating it for 30 minutes (or just wrap crushed ice in the towel to chill it). Rinse and drain the chiles, then pierce each one once near the stem with a sharp knife. If the chile is quite large, pierce it a second time, near the tip. Spread the chiles on a baking sheet covered with foil; broil, turning often, until skins brown and blister.

As soon as the chiles are evenly browned, remove them from the baking sheet and wrap them in the cold, damp towel. Let them steam about 10 minutes. If you're using the chiles right away, peel off the skin in long strips.

Otherwise, seal the unpeeled chiles in plastic bags and freeze them; the skin will come off easily when the chiles are thawed.

Pull the stem off each peeled chile. To remove the seeds, hold the chile point up, then squeeze the pod from the point downward; the seeds will squirt out.

Ginger

Long an important part of Asian cuisine, this spicy-hot root was also prized by the ancient Romans, who used it lavishly and set its value at 15 times that of pepper. Today, fresh ginger is sold all over the United States, but if it's not consistently available in your locale, you may want to preserve some to guarantee a supply. Just place the root in a jar, add enough dry sherry to cover, and refrigerate. The wine keeps the root from spoiling. (You can use the ginger-flavored sherry in cooking, too.)

Crystallized ginger is also generally available; you can eat it straight, as a sweet-hot confection, or chop it for use in desserts like Butterscotch Peach Crisp, page 191.

In a pinch, you may substitute ground ginger for the fresh or crystallized root—the taste won't be as fresh or hot, but will still have a pleasant zip. As a rule of thumb, use about half as much ground ginger as fresh or crystallized. (Employ this rule only when fairly small amounts are involved. If a recipe calls for 1/2 cup crystallized ginger, don't shovel in 1/4 cup ground; wait until you have the real thing on hand.)

Horseradish

There's some dispute over the origin of horseradish; some say this pungent root first grew in Europe, in the area that is now Germany, while others claim it originated in Asia. But no one argues over its value in cooking—it's a marvelous condiment, a zippy addition to sauces, a delightful garnish for seafood and meats.

My father, a genuine horseradish nut, always bought the fresh root and grated it himself, complaining that purchased brands were often extended with turnips and tasted bland and dull. If you cannot find fresh horseradish (or if you're disinclined to grate it yourself), buy the freshest, purest local brand available. Though commercial preparations are almost always blended with vinegar and salt, with care you should be able to find a pungent, well-flavored one.

Mustard

Mustard has been known since Biblical times for both its peppery-hot greens and its tingly seeds. Originally, the seeds may have been eaten whole—a few seeds with each bite of meat—but today, we typically enjoy them ground and blended with vinegar and other seasonings in prepared mustard.

A great number of commercial mustards are available, varying from sweet to bitingly hot, from smooth to crunchy. Flavors differ greatly, thanks to a wide range of added ingredients, including herbs, honey, horseradish and various vinegars. If you really like your mustard hot, you may want to make your own—just mix dry mustard to a smooth paste with beer, wine, diluted vinegar or water. Or doctor up prepared mustard to taste with dry mustard and even whole mustard seeds.

In this book, I have usually called for Dijon-style mustard, which has a sharper, more subtle flavor than the yellow "ballpark" type. But feel free to substitute another favorite mustard, if you like—prepared mustards are really interchangeable in cooking.

Pepper

When Christopher Columbus discovered the New World, he was searching not for a new land, but for a new and shorter route to the source of black pepper. In Columbus's day—and for many centuries before then—pepper was as negotiable a currency as gold and silver, even preferred over those precious metals in some nations. Today, of course, pepper is no longer expensive, nor is it legal tender! Nonetheless, it's an indispensable seasoning in every kitchen, still prized for the liveliness it lends to all manner of foods.

There are over 2,000 varieties of pepper worldwide. The type most familiar to many of us is *Piper nigrum,* the source of black, white and green peppercorns, grown in the hot regions of the world near the equator. To make black pepper, the berries ("corns") are plucked from the vines just before they start to redden, then sun-dried. For white pepper, the berries are prepared a different way: the black skin is loosened by soaking, then rubbed off, leaving only the hot white center. Green peppercorns are berries picked while still soft and green. They're generally sold pickled or dried, in small jars or cans.

For the best, freshest pepper flavor, buy whole black or white peppercorns and grind them yourself. The flat-tasting dust of commercial brands simply can't compare with the sweet-hot spiciness of freshly cracked or ground pepper!

Other Ingredients

Onions and *garlic* are integral to good cooking—especially to good HOT cooking. I prefer the hard, round, hot-flavored yellow onions ("Spanish" onions); the flatter, sweeter, softer-textured Bermuda type isn't really emphatic enough. The garlic of choice is the Mexican variety widely sold in supermarkets. Its fairly large cloves are white outside, purplish inside, with a good hot, pungent taste. Don't use giant-size elephant garlic—it's too mild.

A few recipes call for *Mexican oregano.* This herb tastes sweeter, milder and muskier than the Greek or Italian oregano commonly sold by major spice companies. Though Mexican oregano isn't yet widely available, you can buy it by mail and at some spice shops, greengroceries and gourmet stores. Especially in Tex-Mex and Mexican dishes, it's best not to substitute regular oregano for the Mexican type; the flavor is too harsh.

Mexican vanilla, stronger (by about 1-1/2 times) and more flavorful than our domestic brands of vanilla extract, is unsurpassed for use in beverages and desserts. Unfortunately, it's currently sold only in Mexico because it is not a standard product and does not meet the Food and Drug Administration's guidelines, but it may become available in the United States in the near future. Use it if you can get it!

ABOUT THE RECIPES

Cooking with hot seasonings is obviously a matter of taste: one man's pain is another man's pleasure. In preparing the recipes in this book, it's a good idea to start with the lowest suggested amount of chiles, horseradish and so forth, then slowly work your way up. If you have a number of palates to please, I suggest keeping the heat level relatively low in the dish itself and providing a dish of crushed chiles or other hot seasoning at the table. The real fire-eaters can keep adding until they're satisfied!

The chiles I've used in this book range from mild to searing. The American Spice Trade Association uses "heat units" to rate chiles; on this scale, ground pure mild chile comes in at 5,000 units, ground pure hot chile at 8,000, caribe at 12,000 and pequin—hottest of them all—at 40,000. You may find this information helpful when you're deciding how to adjust each recipe.

A final word: If your mouth is singed from "too much, too hot," ease the pain with dairy fats such as sour cream, butter, cheese or milk. Sweets are effective, too—there's a good reason why ice cream is the traditional finale to a meal that's hotter than hell!

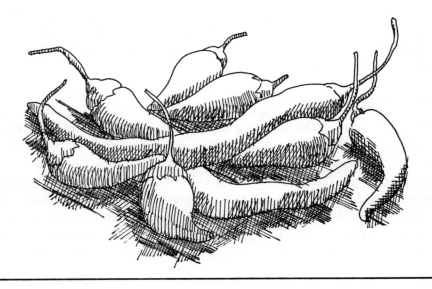

Appetizers
—— *& First Courses* ——

What better way to perk up weary appetites than with a spicy, innovative array of appetizers or a zippy first course? From Zappo Avocado Appetizers to Crunchy Hot Crab Bites to Instant Bloody Marias, these recipes provide an exciting range of flavors—and most can be prepared with little effort. But even those that require a little more of your time, such as Fluffy Greek Cheese-Chile Pastries, taste so delicious that you just might find yourself making them again and again.

You can adjust the spiciness of all these recipes, making them feistier for chile lovers, milder for "tender-mouthed" guests. Go up or down on the ground chile and hot-pepper sauce in Cold & Hot Cucumber Canapés, increase or decrease the amount of green chiles in Guacamole—it's up to you. A sure way to please a range of palates is to serve fiery salsa on the side, so guests can heat up their own servings as they choose.

For a party, offer several different appetizers—some cold, some hot. You might also try serving the main course in one room, appetizers or first course in another. In good weather, start out on the deck or patio; in bad, cozy up to a warm fire.

Hot to Trot Tarts

Fun to make and fun to serve, these spicy yet subtly-flavored tartlets make great party appetizers. You can bake them ahead, then refrigerate or freeze.

> **2 tablespoons lard**
> **1 cup lard (or more—enough to fry tortilla quarters)**
> **6 (10- to 12-inch) flour tortillas, cut in quarters**
> **3/4 pound chorizo**
> **6 eggs**
> **1-1/2 cups light cream**
> **1-1/2 tablespoons chopped fresh cilantro**
> **1 teaspoon ground pure New Mexico hot red chile**
> **3/4 teaspoon salt**
> **1-1/2 cups grated Monterey Jack cheese**
> **1 small red onion, very thinly sliced, separated into rings**
> **12 small fresh hot green chiles such as jalapeño or serrano,**
> **seeded, each cut lengthwise in 8 thin strips**

Generously grease 24 muffin cups, using 2 tablespoons lard. Then heat 1 cup lard in a large, heavy skillet over medium-high heat and lightly fry tortilla quarters until golden, but still pliable. Quickly drain each quarter and place in a "curl" in each muffin cup. Remove casings from chorizo, cut sausage in 1/2-inch slices and fry in another skillet until well browned. Drain well; set aside. In a bowl, whisk eggs until blended; whisk in cream, cilantro, ground chile and salt until well blended. Set aside. Preheat oven to 375F (190C). Evenly divide chorizo among tortilla-lined cups; top evenly with egg mixture, then with cheese and onion rings. Place 4 chile strips on each tart, with tips together in center and strips radiating out to edges. Set tarts on center rack of oven and bake 15 to 20 minutes or until egg mixture is firm. Makes 2 dozen tarts.

Chile-Cheese Surprises

Make these as feisty or as tame as you like. Rosy cheese pastry, flecked with confetti dots of green chile, surrounds stuffed olives, nuts or shrimp, making festive-looking treats that are great for holiday get-togethers and just as good at any other time of year. They freeze well, too.

> **2 cups grated sharp Cheddar cheese**
> **1/4 cup unsalted butter, room temperature**
> **2 tablespoons ground pure New Mexico hot red chile**
> **1/2 teaspoon salt, if desired**
> **2 tablespoons seeded, de-ribbed, finely minced fresh or pickled**
> **jalapeño chiles (or to taste)**
> **1 cup all-purpose flour**
> **2 tablespoons milk**
> **12 pimento-stuffed green olives**
> **12 pecan halves**
> **12 medium cooked shrimp, shelled, deveined, tails removed**

To prepare pastry, combine cheese, butter and ground chile. Taste; add salt, if desired. Work in minced jalapeños until evenly distributed; mix in flour and milk. Preheat oven to 400F (205C). Roll out pastry about 1/8 inch thick. Cut pastry into squares, rectangles or triangles to fit around olives, pecan halves and shrimp; wrap fillings in pastry. Place on ungreased baking sheets and bake 10 to 12 minutes or until pastry feels firm when pressed. Makes 3 dozen appetizers.

A Molded Dome of Cauliflower

A snowy white dome of cauliflower makes a perfect base for a slather of snappy salsa. Guests just pluck off the tender, saucy florets one by one, making this an ideal choice for a cocktail party.

1 medium, perfectly shaped head cauliflower
6 to 8 leaves green or red leaf lettuce
1/2 cup extra-virgin olive oil
1/4 cup fresh lime juice
1/4 cup hot salsa, such as Margarita Jalapeño Salsa, page 143
3/4 teaspoon salt
1/2 teaspoon cayenne pepper
2 tablespoons chopped capers
1 tablespoon chopped parsley
1 small bunch watercress, rinsed well, stemmed, coarsely
**   chopped**
1 cup pitted ripe olives, thinly sliced
1 red bell pepper, parched (see page 9), peeled, seeded, cut in
**   1/2-inch squares**

With a sharp knife, cut leaves and stem from cauliflower. Divide cauliflower into florets about 1-1/2 inches in diameter. Drop florets into boiling salted water; boil about 12 minutes or until tender when pierced. Drain florets and rinse well under cold running water to arrest cooking. Press a layer of florets, stems in, onto sides and bottom of a 1-quart bowl. Pack center of bowl with more florets, stems up, until all florets have been used. Place a plate and a 1-pound weight (such as canned goods) on packed cauliflower. Let stand for 15 minutes; then, holding plate and weight in place, tip bowl to drain off water. Refrigerate weighted cauliflower at least 2 hours. Remove weight and plate; invert a serving dish over bowl, then invert bowl and dish together. Lift off bowl and garnish dish with lettuce leaves. Whisk together oil, lime juice, salsa, salt and cayenne; stir in capers, parsley, watercress, olives and bell pepper. Spoon some of the sauce over cauliflower; place remaining sauce in a bowl and set alongside cauliflower. Once the outer layer has been eaten, guests can dunk florets in sauce in bowl. Makes 4 to 6 servings.

Instant Bloody Marias

Really too easy to be so good . . . and always a favorite with guests. I like to serve them festively, in my most elegant crystal—or, if going Mexicano, I use fine handmade pottery, setting three matching or somewhat similar dishes on a handsome platter.

> **1 pint cherry tomatoes**
> **1/2 cup tequila (or more, as needed)**
> **1 small head leaf lettuce or 1 small bunch watercress, separated**
> **into leaves or sprigs, rinsed well; or use grape leaves**
> **1 (3/4- to 1-oz.) package dry Italian or blue cheese salad**
> **dressing mix; or about 1 tablespoon seasoned salt and/or**
> **pepper**
> **1 teaspoon pequin quebrado**

Rinse tomatoes, then pierce each with a wooden pick. Place in a single layer in a dish; pour in enough tequila to make a shallow layer. Let stand at least 30 minutes at room temperature. To serve, cover a large platter with lettuce leaves, watercress or grape leaves; center the platter with a small glass of tequila, a small glass of wooden picks and a small dish containing salad dressing mix (or seasoned salt and/or pepper) mixed with pequin. Arrange tomatoes atop greens. To eat, spear a tomato with a wooden pick; dip in tequila, then dip lightly in salad dressing mixture. Makes 8 to 12 servings, depending on the rest of the menu.

Quatro-Peppered Goat Cheese Log

Very easy and quick to make, this is a bit out of the ordinary.

> **2 teaspoons whole black peppercorns**
> **2 teaspoons whole white peppercorns**
> **2 teaspoons dried or pickled green peppercorns**
> **1 teaspoon caribe (crushed Northern New Mexico red chile)**
> **2 tablespoons finely minced flat-leaf parsley**
> **1 (7- to 8-oz.) log Montrachet or other similar goat cheese**
> **Thin, plain white crackers, such as Carr's Water Crackers**

In a spice grinder or a blender, grind black, white and green peppercorns together. Combine with caribe and mix well. Spread pepper mixture on a sheet of waxed paper. On a second sheet of waxed paper, spread parsley in an even layer as long as cheese log. Roll cheese in pepper mixture, using all pepper mixture and taking care to coat cheese uniformly. Then lightly roll and press log into parsley. If made ahead, wrap in plastic wrap and refrigerate up to 3 days. Serve at room temperature on an attractive board or plate, accompanied with crackers. Makes 8 servings.

Crunchy Hot Crab Bites

Simple to prepare and serve. If you like, use tuna, small cooked shrimp or even deviled ham in place of the crab.

1-1/2 cups crab meat, drained, all bits of shell removed
1 tablespoon fresh lime or lemon juice
1/2 teaspoon grated lime peel
1 green onion, minced
2 tablespoons minced parsley
1 teaspoon Worcestershire sauce
1 teaspoon hot prepared mustard (or to taste)
Several dashes of liquid hot-pepper sauce (or to taste)
2 tablespoons unsalted butter, melted
16 Melba toast rounds
1/2 cup grated Swiss or sharp Cheddar cheese

Preheat broiler. Combine crab, lime or lemon juice, lime peel, green onion, parsley, Worcestershire sauce, mustard and hot-pepper sauce. Taste and adjust seasonings. Brush melted butter on toast rounds and arrange in a single layer in a broiler pan. Top each round with a portion of the crab mixture, then with 1-1/2 teaspoons cheese. Broil until cheese is melted and crab mixture is hot. Makes 16 appetizers.

Cold & Hot Cucumber Canapés

Very unusual! Few guests will guess what these canapés are made of until they've taken several bites. I particularly like serving these in warm weather, though they're terrific any time.

1 cucumber, about 2 inches in diameter and 5 to 6 inches long
Kosher or sea salt
1 (3-2/3-oz.) can smoked oysters, drained
1 teaspoon fresh lime juice (or to taste)
2 tablespoons mayonnaise
1 teaspoon dry mustard (or to taste)
Several drops of liquid hot-pepper sauce (or to taste)
7 thin slices firm-textured white bread
Mayonnaise
2 teaspoons ground pure New Mexico hot red chile

Slice ends from cucumber, then score sides with the tines of a fork. Cut 28 perfect, very thin crosswise slices from cucumber; set remaining cucumber aside. Sprinkle a large, flat, paper-towel-lined plate generously with salt. Then carefully place cucumber slices in a single layer on salt. Sprinkle tops of slices with salt and cover with another layer of paper towels. Weigh down with a plate and let stand about 2 hours at room temperature. Then rinse slices and pat dry. In a food processor or blender, combine oysters, lime juice, 2 tablespoons mayonnaise, mustard, hot-pepper sauce and remaining cucumber (cut in chunks). Process until well chopped but not pureed. Taste and adjust seasonings. (The mixture can be made as hot as you can handle it.) Using a biscuit or cookie cutter, cut 28 small rounds of bread; or, if lacking a cutter or short on time, quarter each slice of bread. Spread each round or quarter with mayonnaise, then with smoked oyster mixture. Cut each cucumber slice almost in half, leaving halves attached just by the rind and a bit of cucumber next to it. Roll each half-round around your index finger, curling 1 half-round forward, the other half-round backward; set a curled cucumber slice atop each canapé. Sprinkle canapés with ground chile. Makes 28 appetizers.

Chile con Queso

My very favorite formula for this traditional, cheese-fondue-like dip. I was commissioned to develop the recipe for a major chain of fast-food Mexican restaurants. It keeps in the freezer for 6 months and doubles as a great sauce for vegetables and eggs—see Chile-Cheese Onions, page 161, and Sombrero Jalapa, page 127.

> 1/3 cup soybean oil (other vegetable oils don't work as well)
> 1/2 cup finely chopped onion
> 1 clove garlic, minced
> 1 tablespoon all-purpose flour
> 3/4 cup evaporated milk
> 3/4 cup chopped red-ripe tomato
> 1 pound process American cheese, cut in cubes
> 1/4 cup grated sharp Cheddar cheese
> 1/4 cup grated Monterey Jack cheese
> 1/4 cup finely minced pickled or fresh jalapeño chiles with
>   juice (or to taste)

Heat oil in a heavy saucepan, fondue pot or chafing dish. Add onion and garlic and cook until onion is clear. Then stir in flour. Gradually stir in evaporated milk and cook until mixture is thickened; then stir in tomato, cheeses and jalapeños. Cook, stirring, about 5 minutes or until cheeses are melted and flavors are well blended. Taste and adjust hotness. Makes 2 cups.

Guacamole

Everyone likes guacamole, a lively avocado dip that can double as a salad or topping. In addition to serving it the traditional way, with warm tortilla chips, I use it as a topping or filling for a variety of dishes—burgers, chops, omelets, tacos and Southwestern dishes such as Flaming Fajitas, page 102.

> 2 ripe Hass avocados
> 1/2 red-ripe tomato, chopped
> Juice of 1/2 lime
> 1/4 cup finely chopped onion
> 1 clove garlic, finely minced
> 2 tablespoons parched (see page 9), peeled, seeded, chopped
>   fresh New Mexico hot green chiles; or 1 medium pickled
>   jalapeño chile, finely minced
> 3/4 teaspoon salt (or to taste)

Halve and pit avocados and scoop flesh into a bowl. Using 2 knives, cut flesh into 1/2-inch cubes. Then add tomato, lime juice, onion, garlic, chiles and salt; lightly toss together. Taste and adjust seasonings. Serve immediately. Makes 4 to 6 servings.

Brennan's Clams

These are so much fun, so easy and terrific, I'm sure they'll become a favorite appetizer whenever you're barbecuing!

24 cherrystone or other small clams
2 tablespoons cornmeal or fine dry bread crumbs
1/2 cup unsalted butter or Hot Pepper Butter, page 142
1/2 lemon, cut in 2 wedges
1 recipe Very Hot Shrimp Cocktail Sauce, page 143, if desired

Thoroughly rinse clams, then place in a single layer in a baking pan. Add water to a depth of 3 inches; sprinkle on cornmeal or crumbs. Let soak at least 30 minutes so clams will exchange the sand in their shells for the meal or crumbs. Meanwhile, ignite coals in a barbecue grill. Melt butter or Hot Pepper Butter in a saucepan; squeeze lemon wedges into butter and keep warm. To cook clams, place directly on hot coals, 3 or 4 at a time; cook just until shells pop open. (If coals aren't yet hot enough for cooking your steaks, chops or other main-course meat, you can leave them mounded to cook clams.) To eat, remove clams from shells with a fork; dip in lemon butter, then in Very Hot Shrimp Cocktail Sauce, if desired. Makes 2 dozen appetizers.

NOTE: Discard any clams that don't open—DO NOT eat them!

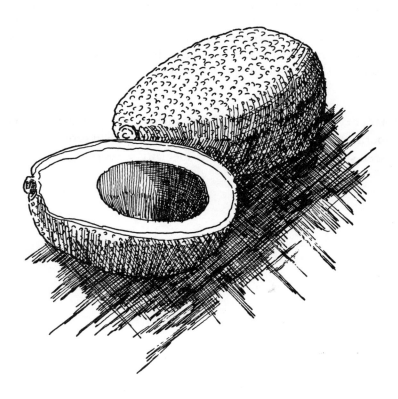

Fluffy Greek Cheese-Chile Pastries

Inspired by the popular Greek appetizers, these melt-in-your-mouth delicacies, spruced up with zesty green chiles, are guaranteed to please most everyone. Be prepared to make many! The filo pastry keeps well in the freezer; the appetizers, either baked or unbaked, can be frozen at least 3 months. (To bake frozen pastries, increase baking time by about 15 minutes.)

Melted unsalted butter
2 eggs
1 pound small-curd cottage cheese (2 cups)
1 pound feta cheese, crumbled
1/4 cup chopped parsley
Pinch of salt
8 to 12 ounces filo pastry (strudel leaves), thawed if frozen
1/2 cup parched (see page 9), peeled, seeded, chopped fresh
    New Mexico hot green chiles or 1/2 cup canned diced green
    chiles (or to taste)

Preheat oven to 350F (175C). Brush baking sheets with melted butter. Beat eggs, cheeses, parsley and salt together until well blended. Stack 2 pastry sheets; cut stacked sheets lengthwise in 3-inch-wide strips. Brush each 2-layer strip with melted butter on both sides, then place a spoonful of cheese filling at 1 end of each strip. Top with a few pieces of chile. Fold 1 corner of strip over filling to create a triangular end; then fold triangle over on itself. Continue to fold triangle from side to side until you reach end of pastry strip; you should have a triangle-shaped pastry. Pierce top of pastry with a wooden pick and place on buttered baking sheet. Continue making pastries to use remaining filo sheets, cheese filling and chiles. Bake 30 to 40 minutes or until golden and flaky. Makes about 4 dozen pastries.

TIP
If you prefer a milder flavor, substitute Münster cheese for the feta. Feta cheese is available from many supermarkets, delicatessens and specialty or Italian grocery stores; filo pastry is often sold in well-stocked supermarkets and specialty grocery stores.

Quesadillas

Simple to prepare, quesadillas are traditionally made from flour tortillas filled with Monterey Jack cheese spiked with jalapeños. But other fillings are equally good—try any taco filling or any mixture of meats, chiles, sour cream and/or cheeses. Dollop a fluff of Guacamole to one side of each serving.

>**6 (9- to 10-inch) flour tortillas**
>**1 cup grated Monterey Jack cheese**
>**1/4 cup thinly sliced fresh or pickled jalapeño chiles (or to taste)**
>**1 egg white, slightly beaten, if necessary**
>**Vegetable oil or lard for deep-frying**
>**6 small leaves red leaf lettuce**
>**1 red-ripe tomato, diced**
>**Guacamole, page 20**

Put 3 tortillas on a work surface near range. Distribute 1/3 cup cheese over each tortilla, leaving a 1-inch margin around edges. Sprinkle tortillas evenly with jalapeños. Top each tortilla with another tortilla. Seal edges, using a fork to crimp about 1/2 inch around entire perimeter. If tortillas are not fresh and moist, you may need to brush bottom edges with egg white to make them stick together. In a heavy skillet at least 12 inches in diameter, heat 1/2 inch of oil to 375F, 190C (or melt enough lard to make 1/2 inch; heat to 375F, 190C). Fry tortilla "sandwiches," 1 at a time, until golden on both sides; use 2 spatulas for turning to avoid spattering. Drain well. Cut each "sandwich" in sixths and serve immediately on warm plates; garnish each plate with a lettuce leaf and accompany quesadillas with tomato and Guacamole. Makes 6 servings (1-1/2 dozen appetizers).

NOTE: Do not prepare tortillas until you are ready to fry them, or they will dry out.

Red Pepper Baskets with Crudités & Rosy Creamy Salsa

Grand enough to kick off a multicourse meal, this pretty appetizer is a lovely choice for any outdoor party. If you wish, group the baskets together on a lettuce-lined platter for a buffet table.

4 red bell peppers
1 bunch fresh broccoli
1/3 pound fresh green beans
12 small fresh asparagus spears
1/4 pound fresh snow peas
1/2 cup dairy sour cream
1/2 cup mayonnaise
1/3 cup Margarita Jalapeño Salsa, page 143, or other hot red
salsa

Slice stem ends from bell peppers; pull out seeds and ribs. Divide broccoli into florets with stems about 4 inches long. Cut tips from green beans. Trim asparagus spears to 6 inches long; pare skin from stalks. Pull strings from snow peas. Parboil each vegetable (except peppers) separately in boiling salted water just until tender-crisp. Broccoli, green beans and asparagus each take about 3 minutes; snow peas take about 30 seconds. When each vegetable is done, transfer it to an ice-filled dish to cool. While vegetables are cooling, combine sour cream, mayonnaise and salsa; spoon 1/4 of mixture into each pepper cup. Stand broccoli, green beans, asparagus and snow peas in pepper cases. Makes 4 servings.

Zappo Avocado Appetizers

So delightfully flavorful! The creaminess of the avocado contrasts with the crunchy corn batter and smooth chile-cheese filling, making a very special and unusual appetizer.

2 avocados
1 large fresh jalapeño chile, cut in thin strips
1/2 cup coarsely grated mixed Monterey Jack and Cheddar
   cheeses
Vegetable oil for deep-frying
1 cup all-purpose flour
1 teaspoon baking powder
1/2 teaspoon salt
3/4 cup cornmeal
1 cup milk
2 eggs, slightly beaten
Margarita Jalapeño Salsa, page 143, or other hot or mild salsa

Halve, pit, and carefully peel avocados. Place strips of jalapeño in each cavity, then pack cavities with cheeses. In a deep, heavy saucepan, heat 2 to 3 inches of oil to 375F (190C). Then, in a bowl, stir together flour, baking powder, salt and cornmeal. Beat in milk and eggs until blended. Dip each filled avocado half into batter to coat completely; fry in hot oil until golden brown. Serve hot, with a side dish of salsa. Makes 4 servings.

Lebanese Grape Leaf Rolls

In Albuquerque, I planted a whole vineyard just to harvest the leaves for this dish! If you're lucky enough to have fresh grape leaves at hand, just pick new leaves that are still thin and tender, then wilt them briefly in a steamer. Use immediately; or freeze flat, with plastic wrap between the layers, in an airtight, moisture-proof container.

These rolls are wonderful lots of different ways—with Greek avgolemono sauce, spicy, aromatic tomato sauce or a sweet-hot sauce such as I'm sharing with you here. Make the rolls small for appetizers, larger for an entree.

1 (12- to 16-oz.) jar grape leaves (3 to 4 dozen small or 2 dozen large leaves); or use fresh leaves, wilted as directed above
Several lamb bones
3 cloves garlic
1 pound ground lamb
1/2 cup uncooked long-grain white rice
1/2 teaspoon ground cinnamon
1 teaspoon salt
1/2 teaspoon freshly ground black pepper
1 tablespoon caribe (crushed Northern New Mexico red chile)
Juice of 1 lemon
1/4 cup sugar
1 (28-oz.) can whole tomatoes

Rinse bottled grape leaves. If necessary, soak bottled or fresh leaves in hot water just until pliable. Place lamb bones and garlic in bottom of a large saucepan. In a medium bowl, mix ground lamb with rice, cinnamon, salt, pepper, caribe, lemon juice and sugar. Place a spoonful of lamb mixture on each leaf and roll up, tucking ends in. Place rolled leaves on top of bones in pan. Drain liquid from tomatoes into pan; coarsely chop tomatoes and add. Then add enough water to come just below tops of rolls. Bring mixture to a boil over high heat. Reduce heat, cover and simmer about 30 minutes or until rice in filling is tender. Makes 3 to 4 dozen small or 2 dozen large rolls.

Exciting Escargots

The sassy flavors of caribe chile and Margarita Jalapeño Salsa make for a spanking new version of this always-elegant appetizer. Serve in small ovenproof earthenware casseroles.

> 1 cup unsalted butter
> 3 tablespoons minced garlic
> 36 large canned escargots
> 1 cup Margarita Jalapeño Salsa, page 143
> 2 tablespoons caribe (crushed Northern New Mexico red chile)
> 12 flour or corn tortillas or 1 small loaf French bread

Preheat oven to 425F (220C). Melt butter in a skillet; add garlic and sauté until garlic barely begins to turn golden. Place 6 escargots in each of 6 individual casseroles; drizzle evenly with garlic butter. Spoon 2 heaping tablespoons salsa evenly over escargots in each casserole; sprinkle 1 teaspoon caribe over each. Bake 15 to 20 minutes or until sauce sizzles. Meanwhile, warm tortillas (or slice and warm French bread). Serve escargots with tortillas or bread for dunking. Makes 6 servings.

Oyster Hot Shots

Tuck these peppy, luxuriously sauced oysters back in their shells after baking (or bake them in the shells, if you wish—just place them on a bed of rock salt in a baking pan). If you prefer, you can serve them on toast rounds or in patty shells or tortilla shells. Or, for a regal first course or light main dish, serve the oysters in scallop shells surrounded with a border of mashed potato.

> 1 cup unsalted butter, room temperature
> 16 medium, fresh oysters, shucked (reserve oyster shells)
> 1 cup dry white wine
> 1/2 cup fresh lime juice
> 1 tablespoon minced garlic
> 3 tablespoons finely minced onion
> 1/3 cup whipping cream
> 4 to 6 fresh jalapeño chiles, cut crosswise in very thin slices, seeded
> 1 teaspoon caribe (crushed Northern New Mexico red chile)

Preheat oven to 375F (190C). Using some of the butter, generously butter a 9-inch-square baking pan. Place oysters in pan and set aside. In a medium, heavy saucepan, combine wine, lime juice, garlic and onion. When mixture just begins to bubble, reduce heat; simmer gently, uncovered, until mixture is reduced to about 1/4 of its original volume. Whisk in cream and remaining butter until butter is completely incorporated. Taste and adjust seasonings. Spoon sauce over oysters and bake about 6 minutes or until edges of oysters just begin to curl. Spoon each oyster into a half-shell, then decorate with jalapeño slices and a sprinkle of caribe. Serve immediately, or keep hot in a warm oven or on a warming tray until ready to serve. Makes 16 appetizers.

Picante Pesto-Topped Oysters on the Half-Shell

These juicy oysters are topped with a fiery version of the familiar Italian sauce; chiles, not the traditional basil, make the pesto base. Select the heat of chiles you prefer, keeping in mind that oysters are quite bland and set off spicy toppings perfectly.

> **1/3 cup freshly grated Romano cheese**
> **3 large fresh green chiles (as hot as you like), parched (see page 9), peeled, seeded**
> **2 dried Chinese hot red chiles**
> **4 cloves garlic**
> **1/4 cup piñon nuts (pine nuts)**
> **3 tablespoons freshly grated Parmesan cheese**
> **3 tablespoons chopped fresh cilantro**
> **Freshly grated nutmeg to taste**
> **1/2 cup unsalted butter, melted**
> **2 to 3 cups rock salt**
> **16 large fresh oysters on the half-shell**
> **2 limes, each cut lengthwise in 6 wedges**
> **2 teaspoons caribe (crushed Northern New Mexico red chile)**

Preheat oven to 400F (205C). Set aside 2 tablespoons Romano cheese. In a food processor or blender, combine remaining Romano, green and red chiles, garlic, piñon nuts, Parmesan cheese, cilantro and nutmeg. Process until pureed. With motor running, add butter in a thin stream, processing until well blended. Line 4 pie plates or rimmed ovenproof plates with rock salt. Place 4 oysters atop salt in each plate; top each oyster with a spoonful of chile pesto. Bake 6 to 8 minutes or until pesto is bubbly. Remove oysters from oven; sprinkle evenly with reserved 2 tablespoons Romano cheese. Broil just until cheese is melted. Garnish each serving with 3 lime wedges, rubbing center edge of each wedge in caribe. Makes 4 servings.

Soups & Salads

Bubble, bubble . . . bubble and brew . . . a steaming pot of soup satisfies like nothing else. Most of the soups in this chapter are sizzling-hot and spicy, like Mexican Papas Sopa and Szechwan Hot & Sour Soup. As always, though, you can adjust amounts of chiles and spices to suit your palate. And if you're looking for a real break from the heat, try Soothing Leek Soup. Mild, creamy, and perfect for a light luncheon entree, it's also a great beginning for a spicy-hot meal.

The salads in these pages are good partners for soup, and creative seasoning makes all of them distinctly out of the ordinary. Holiday Salad of Peppers & Endive is refreshingly crisp, snappy with a chile vinaigrette; minted Tropical Fruit Salad is cool, sweet and soothing. And sassy Acapulco Salad, Thai Hot Beef Salad and the other main-course choices offer a sure-fire way to brighten any meal.

Brazilian Black Bean Soup

Make this soup as feisty as you like; it's easy to temper the heat by adjusting the amount of chiles. A topping of cheese or sour cream and a float of rum help soothe the fire of the brew. Serve as a first course or as a luncheon or light supper entree.

2 cups dried black beans
8 cups cold water
3/4 pound cooked ham, diced
1 ham bone, if desired
4 cloves garlic, crushed
2 teaspoons salt
1/2 cup diced onion
2 whole cloves
1/2 teaspoon ground cumin (or to taste)
1 tablespoon ground pure New Mexico hot red chile or 1
    tablespoon caribe (crushed Northern New Mexico red chile),
    or to taste
Juice of 1 lime
1/4 cup rum
4 green onions, finely chopped
1/2 cup grated Monterey Jack cheese or dairy sour cream
Lime wedges, if desired

Sort and rinse beans, then soak overnight in water to cover. (Or place in a large saucepan and add water to cover; bring to a boil. Remove from heat, cover and let stand 1 hour. Simmer 1-1/2 hours, then proceed with recipe.) Drain beans; place in a large saucepan and add 8 cups cold water, ham, ham bone (if desired), garlic, salt, diced onion, cloves, cumin, ground chile or caribe and lime juice. Bring to a boil; reduce heat, cover and simmer 2 hours or until beans are tender and soup is thick. Taste and adjust seasonings. To serve, remove ham bone, if used. Lace soup with rum; spoon into bowls and top with green onions, cheese or sour cream and lime wedges, if desired. Makes 4 to 6 servings.

Hot Garlic Sopa

One of my Uncle Harry's favorite soups, a delightful dish he learned to make while living in Mexico. Serve it as hot as you can handle it!

1/4 cup olive oil
4 large cloves garlic, minced
4 corn tortillas, cut in sixths, or 1 cup tortilla chips (it's OK to
**   use broken pieces)**
4 cups beef broth
1 or more large fresh New Mexico hot green chiles, parched
**   (see page 9), peeled, seeded, chopped (if fresh green chiles**
**   are unavailable, substitute pickled jalapeños)**
2 teaspoons ground pure New Mexico hot red chile
4 eggs
1 cup grated Monterey Jack cheese
2 tablespoons finely minced fresh or pickled jalapeño chiles

Heat oil in a 3-quart saucepan with a close-fitting lid. Add garlic and cook briefly; then add tortilla pieces or chips and cook until lightly browned, crushing chips with the back of a wooden spoon. Stir in broth, green chiles and 1 teaspoon ground chile. Bring to a simmer. Meanwhile, preheat oven to 450F (230C). Break 1 egg into a small bowl to check for quality. Stir soup rapidly in a small circle, then slide egg into center of circle. Repeat with remaining 3 eggs, working quickly. Cover 2 to 3 minutes to soft poach. Set 4 heated ovenproof bowls on a baking sheet. Spoon soup into bowls, placing 1 poached egg in center of each bowl. Sprinkle each with 1/4 cup cheese. Set in oven just until cheese is melted. Sprinkle each bowl of soup with 1/4 teaspoon ground chile. Depending on your guests' tastes, either top each serving with 1-1/2 teaspoons minced jalapeños or serve jalapeños separately, to be added to taste. Makes 4 servings.

Cream of Broccoli Soup, Caliente

So smooth and flavorful, this basic soup is versatile, too—it can be made with almost any green vegetable (you might try asparagus, spinach, Swiss chard or zucchini). The "caliente" character comes from fresh green chiles; use one or more, to make the soup as tame or zesty as you wish.

For the best, most special flavor in this and other soups, use homemade chicken broth. You'll get the richest taste if you "recycle" your broth: after stewing a chicken, store the broth in the freezer until you're ready to cook another bird. Then use it again, adding extra flavor with vegetables and herbs ... and again, freeze until the next use.

2 cups double-strength chicken broth
1 cup chopped fresh broccoli or frozen chopped broccoli,
**   thawed, drained**
2 tablespoons unsalted butter
1 medium onion, coarsely chopped
1 or more medium, fresh jalapeño or serrano chiles, finely
**   minced**
Salt to taste, if desired
1 cup whipping cream
2 egg yolks
1 tablespoon caribe (crushed Northern New Mexico red chile),
**   or to taste**

Place broth in a medium, heavy saucepan. Add broccoli, cover and bring to a simmer. Meanwhile, melt butter in a small skillet, add onion and cook until lightly browned. Add onion mixture to broccoli-broth mixture, cover and simmer about 30 minutes or until onion is very soft. While mixture is still hot, process it in a food processor or blender until smoothly pureed. Add jalapeño or serrano chiles, taste and adjust seasonings, adding salt, if desired. Return soup to pan and place over very low heat. Beat cream and egg yolks together; pour into soup in a very thin stream, stirring constantly. Cook, stirring, until soup coats a wooden spoon in a fine film; do not let soup boil, or it may curdle. Immediately pour soup into soup cups, sprinkle with caribe and serve piping hot. Makes 4 servings.

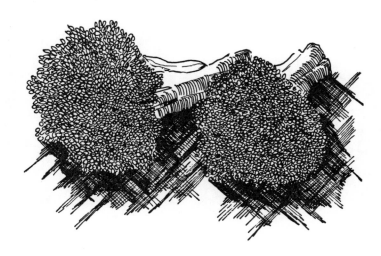

Szechwan Hot & Sour Soup

This very popular spicy-yet-sour soup is a wonderful warm-up on cold days, especially after an afternoon of skiing or skating. As a first course, it's a terrific starter for any Oriental menu. Look for the tigerlily buds and dried mushrooms in Asian markets and well-stocked supermarkets.

> 6 dried cloud ear mushrooms
> 6 dried Chinese black mushrooms
> 6 dried tigerlily buds
> 4-1/2 cups double-strength chicken broth
> 1 tablespoon peanut oil
> 1 tablespoon sesame oil (or 1 more tablespoon peanut oil)
> About 1 tablespoon light soy sauce
> 1/3 pound lean, boneless pork or skinned, boned chicken
>   breast, cut in long, thin strips
> 1 (about 4-oz.) cake fresh bean curd, cut in thin strips
> 1/4 cup bamboo shoots, cut in thin strips
> 2 eggs, slightly beaten
> 2 tablespoons Chinese red rice vinegar
> 2 teaspoons thinly sliced green onion (including some green
>   top)
> 2 teaspoons sesame oil
> 1 teaspoon freshly ground white pepper, Hot Hot Oil, page 141,
>   or purchased chile oil
> Sugar to taste, if desired

Pour boiling water over cloud ears, black mushrooms and tigerlily buds. Let soak 15 minutes. Drain; cut off woody parts of mushrooms and hard tips of buds, then slice mushrooms and buds very thinly. Set aside. Heat broth in a large saucepan. Meanwhile, heat peanut oil and 1 tablespoon sesame oil in a wok or large skillet; when oil is hot, sprinkle on 1 tablespoon soy sauce. Add pork or chicken and stir-fry just a few minutes or until crisp on edges. Add sliced mushrooms and tigerlily buds and stir to brown edges lightly. Then add meat-mushroom mixture to broth and stir well; stir in bean curd and bamboo shoots. When soup comes to a gentle simmer, pour in beaten eggs, stirring soup with a swirling motion. As soon as eggs start to cook, remove soup from heat. Rinse 4 to 6 individual soup bowls or 1 large serving bowl with hot water. Then mix vinegar, green onion, 2 teaspoons sesame oil and white pepper, Hot Hot Oil or chile oil. Divide mixture equally among individual bowls or place all of it in large bowl. Taste soup and adjust seasonings, adding more soy sauce or perhaps a pinch of sugar if a less sour flavor is desired. Stir to mix the cloudlike shreds of egg evenly, then pour into individual bowls or serving bowl. To eat, bring soup spoon up from the bottom of bowl to mix hot and sour flavors into each bite. Makes 4 to 6 servings.

Soothing Leek Soup

Because this smooth soup is not hot, it's a comforting starter to serve before very hot entrees. When you want a change from spicy fare, perhaps you'll enjoy this as much as I do.

> **2 tablespoons unsalted butter**
> **2 tablespoons finely chopped onion**
> **1 large leek, rinsed very well, sliced crosswise (about 1 cup sliced leek)**
> **2 cups double-strength chicken broth**
> **1 cup diced peeled potato**
> **1-1/2 cups whipping cream**
> **3/4 teaspoon salt (or to taste)**
> **Freshly ground black pepper to taste**
> **Freshly grated nutmeg to taste**
> **1/4 cup crumbled blue cheese or freshly grated Parmesan cheese**
> **4 shots dry white wine**

Melt butter in a heavy saucepan. Add onion and leek and cook slowly, stirring often, until soft. Stir in broth, then add potato; cover and cook until potato is tender. Cool, then process in a food processor or blender until pureed. In another saucepan, bring cream to a gentle simmer; cook until slightly reduced, then stir in leek mixture and heat until very hot (do not boil). Season with salt, pepper and nutmeg. Serve hot; sprinkle 1 tablespoon cheese over each serving and offer a shot of wine on the side. Makes 4 servings.

Great-Grandma's Louisiana Gumbo

My Swedish grandmother's mother got this recipe from one of her helpers whose home was in Louisiana. The original recipe was a real kick—it called for a 10-cent soup bone, a sack full of freshly picked okra and so on—but I tested and retested it with modern measurements, finally achieving the true flavor of Grandma's gumbo. To please those who like their gumbo searing hot as well as those who don't, I recommend seasoning it only lightly with hot-pepper sauce, then serving additional sauce at the table. Filé powder, crucial for an authentic flavor, is quite strong-tasting; I have developed the recipe with only a small amount, but those who enjoy the flavor (as I do) can add more to taste. Serve the gumbo over fluffy steamed long-grain rice.

3/4 pound boneless beef chuck (or use pork shoulder, chicken, seafood or any combination)
2 tablespoons all-purpose flour
3 tablespoons bacon drippings
1 pound fresh okra, cut in 1-inch slices, or 1 (12-oz.) package frozen sliced okra, thawed, drained
2 large red-ripe tomatoes, peeled, cut in wedges about 3/4 inch thick, or 1 (1-lb.) can whole tomatoes, drained
2 medium onions, chopped
1 small green bell pepper, cut in large squares
1 large clove garlic, minced
1 teaspoon filé powder (or to taste)
3/4 teaspoon salt (or to taste)
Liquid hot-pepper sauce to taste
Hot cooked rice

Cut meat in 1-inch cubes, then dredge in flour. Melt bacon drippings in a large, heavy saucepan, then add floured meat and cook until browned. Remove meat from pan; add okra and cook until browned (browning prevents the okra from taking on the somewhat slimy texture that many find unpleasant). Return meat to pan, then stir in tomatoes, onions, bell pepper and garlic. Add water to cover. Bring to a boil; then reduce heat, cover and simmer 1-1/2 to 2 hours or until meat is tender and mixture has the consistency of thick soup. Add filé powder, salt and hot-pepper sauce. Simmer 30 minutes longer. Adjust seasonings, then serve over rice. Makes 4 servings.

Mexican Papas Sopa

Traditionally only moderately spicy, this hearty *sopa* is substantial enough to serve as a light lunch or supper; smaller servings also make a nice first course for a light meal. If you enjoy fiery flavors, just include more chiles—the addition of seven or eight will really turn up the heat!

> **1/4 pound salt pork, cut in 1-inch cubes**
> **3 large or 4 medium potatoes, peeled, diced**
> **1/2 cup chopped onion**
> **6 cups chicken broth**
> **2 to 8 fresh jalapeño chiles, finely slivered**
> **Salt to taste**
> **1/3 pound Monterey Jack cheese, coarsely grated**
> **Caribe (crushed Northern New Mexico red chile)**

Brown salt pork in a large, heavy, flat-bottomed pot. Add potatoes; cook until browned. Add onion and cook until clear; stir in broth and jalapeños. Bring to a boil; then reduce heat, cover and simmer 1 hour or until potatoes are very soft. Remove salt pork cubes, if desired. Taste; add salt and more chiles as desired. To serve, preheat broiler. Set 4 to 6 heated soup bowls on a baking sheet. Spoon soup into bowls; top each serving with a circle of cheese centered with a sprinkle of caribe. Broil just until cheese is bubbly, then serve. Makes 4 to 6 servings.

Wicked Watercress & Potato Soup

Simple to make, yet elegantly flavored! Though spiced, this soup is kind to the stomach. It's a great first course or light luncheon entree.

> **4 cups chicken broth**
> **2 medium potatoes, peeled, diced**
> **1 tablespoon instant minced onion**
> **1 cup coarsely chopped watercress, leaf lettuce or fresh spinach**
> **1/2 teaspoon salt (or to taste)**
> **1 teaspoon freshly ground white pepper**
> **1 cup skim milk**
> **Freshly ground black pepper to taste**

Place broth in a medium saucepan. Add potatoes, onion and watercress, lettuce or spinach. Bring to a boil over high heat. Reduce heat to low, cover and simmer about 20 minutes or until potatoes are tender. Pour vegetables and some of the broth into a blender or food processor; process until smoothly pureed, then return to pan. Add salt, white pepper and milk; heat until steaming. Ladle into soup bowls; sprinkle generously with black pepper. Makes 4 servings.

Acapulco Salad

Seafood of the Mexican waters, a palette of fresh, colorful vegetables and a Mexican-inspired dressing add up to a delightful salad—a perfect choice for a light entree. It's best to use Spanish olive oil in the dressing, but if you can't find it, substitute any other good-quality olive oil.

1 cup beer
2 cups water
2 bay leaves
12 whole black peppercorns
1/2 teaspoon salt
1 pound red snapper fillets
3 ears fresh corn or 1-1/2 cups cooked, drained frozen or
   drained canned whole-kernel corn
1 large or 2 medium red-ripe tomatoes, cut in thin wedges
1/2 yellow bell pepper, 1/2 sweet yellow wax pepper or 1 whole
   green bell pepper, cut in thin strips
1/2 fresh poblano chile or green bell pepper, cut in thin strips
1 or more small fresh hot green chiles such as jalapeño or
   serrano, finely minced
3 green onions (including some of green tops), thinly sliced
1/4 cup hot green salsa or chopped canned tomatillos (see Note
   below)
2 tablespoons fresh lime juice
1/4 cup extra-virgin Spanish olive oil
Juice from pickled jalapeño chiles
2 tablespoons minced fresh cilantro, if desired

In a large saucepan, combine beer, water, bay leaves, peppercorns and salt. Bring to boil; add fish, then cover and turn off heat. Allow to cool, covered, about 15 minutes or until fish is opaque throughout. (Fish cooks as liquid cools; this extra-gentle method of cooking keeps the flesh intact.) Meanwhile, cook fresh corn in boiling water until tender; drain, then cut kernels from cobs. Combine corn, tomatoes, bell pepper, poblano chile, hot chiles and green onions; set aside. Then prepare dressing: whisk together salsa or tomatillos, lime juice and oil. Taste and adjust heat; if not hot enough (or if you used tomatillos), add jalapeño juice to taste. Toss dressing with vegetables and place mixture in a large salad bowl. Drain fish; gently flake and scatter around edge of bowl. Sprinkle with cilantro, if desired. Makes 4 servings.

NOTE: If you have fresh tomatillos on hand, you may use them in place of the canned variety. Remove the husks and stems, then steam fruit about 5 minutes or until soft; chop enough to make 1/4 cup.

Grilled Tuna Salad

What could be more soothing than seafood and salad? The combination somehow makes summer seem cooler—even when you include a spirited helping of Tuscan peppers. Crisp garlic toast makes a nice accompaniment for this salad.

> **1 pound fresh tuna steak, cut 1 inch thick**
> **1/3 cup extra-virgin olive oil**
> **2 cups quartered cherry tomatoes**
> **1 cup pickled Tuscan peppers**
> **1 medium-hot red onion, thinly sliced, separated into rings**
> **2 sprigs thyme**
> **2 cloves garlic, minced**
> **2 tablespoons red wine vinegar**
> **1 tablespoon hot prepared mustard**
> **2 teaspoons mustard seeds**
> **2 teaspoons Worcestershire sauce**
> **Salt and freshly ground black pepper to taste**
> **1 head romaine lettuce**

Prepare a bed of hot coals or heat a griddle or heavy skillet over very high heat until very hot. Brush tuna on both sides with some of the oil. Brush barbecue grill or griddle with oil; cook tuna 2 to 3 minutes on each side or until browned on outside but still very rare in center. Cool tuna briefly, then cut it in 1-inch squares. Combine tuna, tomatoes, peppers, onion and thyme. Set aside. Combine garlic, remaining oil, vinegar, mustard, mustard seeds and Worcestershire sauce; whisk to blend, seasoning with salt and pepper. To serve, line a platter or 4 individual plates with lettuce. Fold dressing into tuna mixture; then arrange salad on platter or individual plates. Makes 4 servings.

Hot Spinach Salad with Smoked Salmon

This light yet succulent salad is a great choice when you want to serve something different for brunch, lunch, or a late-night treat.

2 pounds fresh spinach
1 cup extra-virgin olive oil
1 teaspoon chopped fresh ginger (or to taste)
1 tablespoon caribe (crushed Northern New Mexico red chile)
1/3 cup raspberry or red wine vinegar
1 tablespoon sugar
3 tablespoons Dijon-style mustard
3/4 teaspoon salt (or to taste)
1/2 cup whipping cream
1/3 cup chopped fresh dill
1/2 pound smoked salmon, very thinly sliced
6 very thin slices red onion, separated into rings

Rinse spinach very well and discard stems and any tough or wilted leaves. Heat 1/4 cup oil in a large, heavy skillet or wok. When oil is hot, add spinach, ginger and caribe. Cook over medium-high heat, stirring, just until spinach is wilted but not fully cooked. Set aside. In a small saucepan, combine remaining 3/4 cup oil, vinegar, sugar, mustard, salt and cream. Heat until almost simmering, then remove from heat and stir in dill. Divide hot spinach (reheat if necessary) among 6 plates; top with smoked salmon slices. Divide dressing evenly among salads, drizzling it uniformly over each. Garnish with onion rings and serve. Makes 6 servings.

Thai Hot Beef Salad

The Thais are masters in achieving subtle flavor combinations, even with the hottest chiles and spices. Whenever in Thailand, I can never get enough of their hot, spicy dishes. This one is an unusual entree salad.

1 small head romaine lettuce
1 small head red leaf lettuce
1 head Belgian endive
3/4 cup peanut oil
1/4 cup fresh lime juice
3 tablespoons dark soy sauce
1 pound sirloin (cut 1 inch thick), cut in 3-inch-long,
    1/4-inch-wide strips
1 (1-inch) piece fresh ginger, peeled, finely grated
1 tablespoon packed dark brown sugar
2 large cloves garlic, minced
2 or 3 fresh jalapeño chiles, finely minced
1/2 cup coarsely chopped fresh cilantro
3 red-ripe tomatoes, cut in wedges
2 green onions, finely chopped
4 green onions, "butterflied" (onions left whole, green tops
    shredded lengthwise with a sharp knife for 2/3 of their
    length)

Tear romaine and leaf lettuce leaves in bite-size pieces. Carefully remove whole endive leaves from stalk. Enclose greens in plastic bags and refrigerate. In a shallow dish, combine 2 tablespoons each oil, lime juice and soy sauce. Add beef strips to this marinade, stir well and let stand at least 1 hour at room temperature. To make dressing, in a blender or food processor, combine 1/2 cup oil, remaining 2 tablespoons lime juice, remaining 1 tablespoon soy sauce, ginger, brown sugar, garlic and jalapeños. Process until pureed. Set aside. In a heavy skillet, heat remaining 2 tablespoons oil. When oil is hot, drain beef strips (reserve marinade); add beef to skillet and quickly stir-fry just until browned on outside. Mix reserved marinade into dressing. To serve, place chilled greens in a large heatproof salad bowl; top with hot beef strips. "Rinse" out hot skillet with dressing, scraping down sides and bottom to get any remaining browned bits. Pour over beef, then add cilantro, tomatoes and chopped green onions; toss. Garnish with butterflied green onions and serve immediately. Makes 4 servings.

Red Hot Warm Potato Salad

A great way to celebrate the arrival of early spring's delicately pink baby potatoes. We first made this in the country and enjoyed it outside on the patio with Hotter than Hell Buffet Barbecued Chicken, page 71.

8 small red thin-skinned potatoes
3 eggs
1/4 cup unsalted butter
2 tablespoons minced fresh parsley or 1 tablespoon dried
    parsley flakes
1 tablespoon finely minced pickled or fresh jalapeño chiles
1 tablespoon juice from pickled jalapeño chiles (or to taste)
2 green onions, thinly sliced
4 red radishes, thinly sliced
1 teaspoon prepared mustard
1/4 cup mayonnaise
Salt and freshly ground black pepper to taste

Scrub potatoes and cut in halves or quarters, depending on size. Cook in boiling water about 20 minutes or until tender. Meanwhile, hard-cook eggs 15 minutes, then drain. When potatoes are done, drain well; then immediately add butter to saucepan with potatoes. Cover and set aside until butter is melted; then stir until butter is thoroughly combined with potatoes. Add parsley, jalapeños, jalapeño juice, green onions and radishes; shell and chop hard-cooked eggs and fold in. Stir in mustard, mayonnaise, salt and pepper. Taste and adjust seasonings. Makes 4 servings.

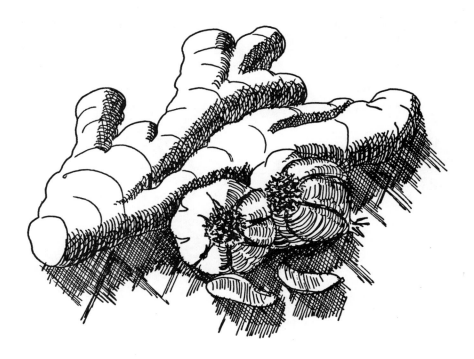

Holiday Salad of Peppers & Endive

This salad is unbelievably pretty, with pale, pale green endive and scarlet bell peppers cut in ever-so-skinny slivers. The salsa can be made hours or even days in advance.

Salsa Vinaigrette, see below
3 small heads Belgian endive, cut lengthwise in 1/4-inch-wide
    strips (see Note below)
2 large red bell peppers, cut in long, 1/4-inch-wide strips
1 small head Boston lettuce

Salsa Vinaigrette:
1/4 cup red wine vinegar
1 clove garlic, minced
2 tablespoons minced onion
1 small fresh mild green chile, parched (see page 9), peeled,
    seeded, minced; or 1 ounce canned diced green chiles
1 small tomato, finely chopped
1/2 cup extra-virgin olive oil

Prepare vinaigrette and let stand at least 30 minutes at room temperature. To serve, toss endive and bell peppers with vinaigrette. Line a salad bowl with lettuce leaves and top with dressed endive and peppers. Makes 6 servings.

Salsa Vinaigrette:
In a jar, combine all ingredients and stir or shake until well mixed.

NOTE: If Belgian endive is not available, you may substitute 3 cups green bell pepper strips, jicama strips, or sliced fresh mushrooms.

Rio Party Salad

Simple to prepare and lovely to look at, with a flavor that enhances any spicy-hot entree. I'm especially fond of serving this salad at buffets, as an accompaniment to two or more casseroles. It makes for a cozy, lingering evening; guests can eat as often and as much as they wish, and the hostess can relax, since nothing wilts or gets cold (just keep the hot dishes warm on a warming tray).

2 (1-lb.) cans hearts of palm, drained
1 pint cherry tomatoes, halved
2/3 cup extra-virgin olive oil
1/4 cup sherry wine vinegar
1 clove garlic, finely minced
1/2 teaspoon salt (or to taste)
1 teaspoon caribe (crushed Northern New Mexico red chile)
1 head Boston lettuce
1 head red leaf lettuce

Place hearts of palm and tomatoes in a medium bowl. Combine oil, vinegar, garlic, salt and caribe; pour over vegetables and stir gently to coat evenly. Let stand at room temperature throughout the day, stirring often and spooning dressing over vegetables. About 2 hours before serving, cover and refrigerate. To serve, arrange Boston and red leaf lettuce leaves around edge of a large platter. Place hearts of palm spoke-fashion around edge; place tomatoes in center. Drizzle all with dressing and serve. Makes about 10 servings.

Watercress-Mushroom Salad, Santa Fe Style

I developed this favorite salad dressing to go over my very favorite combination of salad ingredients—watercress, Belgian endive and mushrooms. Since all of us prefer this dressing over any other, I make tons of the base and keep it constantly in our refrigerator. When I want to use it, I just remove the jar from the fridge and run it briefly under hot water to warm the oil. (For space reasons, I add only about half the oil to the herb-mustard mixture, then add fresh oil when combining the salad ingredients.)

The "Santa Fe" part of this salad is the watercress—we always used our own fresh, peppery, spring-grown sprigs—and the dash of crushed Northern New Mexico caribe chiles.

> 1/2 cup extra-virgin olive oil or walnut oil
> 2 large cloves garlic, finely minced
> 1 teaspoon minced fresh rosemary or 1/2 teaspoon dried leaf
>   rosemary
> 1 teaspoon minced fresh tarragon or 1/2 teaspoon dried leaf
>   tarragon
> 1 teaspoon minced fresh thyme or 1/2 teaspoon dried leaf
>   thyme
> 2 teaspoons minced fresh basil or 1 teaspoon dried leaf basil
> 1 tablespoon Dijon-style mustard
> 1 medium bunch watercress, rinsed well, stemmed (about 2
>   cups sprigs)
> 1 large head Belgian endive, leaves removed from stalk
> 2 cups fresh white button or brown-skinned French
>   mushrooms, very thinly sliced
> 1 teaspoon caribe (crushed Northern New Mexico red chile)
> 2-1/2 tablespoons fresh lime juice

Combine oil, garlic, herbs and mustard and let stand at least 30 minutes (or longer) at room temperature while you prepare the salad ingredients. Arrange watercress, endive and mushrooms in a wooden or glass bowl; refrigerate until cold. To serve, sprinkle with caribe, then add dressing and lace with lime juice. Toss and serve. Makes 4 servings.

Calabacitas Salad

Summer squash of any kind are great in this; I prefer a combination of baby zucchini and small yellow crookneck squash. The piñon nuts make this very New Mexican—piñon trees abound in the nearby mountains.

1/3 cup fresh basil leaves
2 cloves garlic
1/4 teaspoon pequin quebrado (or to taste)
1/2 cup extra-virgin olive oil
3 tablespoons balsamic vinegar (or to taste)
2 small zucchini, thinly sliced
2 small yellow crookneck squash, thinly sliced
1 pint cherry tomatoes, halved
1/3 cup piñon nuts (pine nuts)

Combine basil, garlic, pequin, oil and vinegar in a blender or food processor; process until very well blended. Then place zucchini, crookneck squash and tomatoes in a gaily colored salad bowl. Toss together with dressing and sprinkle with piñon nuts. Refrigerate about 1 hour before serving, time permitting. Makes 4 servings.

Tropical Fruit Salad

Tingled with fresh mint and a honeyed lime dressing, this salad is a great accompaniment to any hot, spicy dish. If fresh mint leaves are unavailable, substitute a good-quality mint jelly and decrease the amount of honey by about 2 tablespoons.

1/2 cantaloupe, cut in balls
1/2 honeydew melon, cut in 1-inch cubes
1 mango, peeled, sliced
2 cups cubed watermelon
1/3 cup honey
1/3 cup fresh lime juice
1/4 cup minced fresh mint leaves
1 small, perfect head Boston or romaine lettuce

Combine cantaloupe, honeydew, mango and watermelon. In a blender, process honey, lime juice and mint until well blended. Drizzle over fruit. Line a clear glass bowl or any pretty salad bowl with lettuce leaves; spoon in fruit mixture. Makes 4 to 6 servings.

Peppy Pasta Salad

You can vary this salad in dozens of ways. The following combination is a favorite of mine, but you may wish to substitute any seasonal vegetables for the artichoke hearts, peas, spinach and peppers.

1 pound dried mostaccioli, twists or other substantial pasta

1 cup Chile Mayonnaise, page 148

3 large or 6 small cloves garlic, chopped (minced, if not using a food processor)

1-1/2 tablespoons fresh lime juice (or to taste)

2 teaspoons Dijon-style or hot German mustard

2 cups well-rinsed, stemmed, lightly packed fresh spinach leaves, cut in narrow ribbons

1 fresh or pickled jalapeño chile, finely slivered

1 red bell pepper, cut in long, thin strips

6 pickled red cherry peppers, halved

1 cup fresh snow peas, cut in diagonal slivers

1 cup marinated artichoke hearts (three 6-oz. jars), drained; or 1 (1-lb.) can artichoke hearts, drained, marinated overnight in Italian dressing

Following package directions, cook pasta in boiling water just until tender to bite. Drain and set aside. Combine Chile Mayonnaise, garlic, lime juice and mustard in a food processor; process until smooth. Combine pasta, spinach, jalapeño, bell pepper, cherry peppers, snow peas and artichokes. Add dressing and toss lightly. Taste; adjust seasonings. Before serving, refrigerate until cool, at least 2 hours (or as long as overnight). Makes 6 servings.

Sauerkraut Soup

A close friend of mine, Janet Pugh, lived in Bavaria for many years. While there, she discovered this hearty, sour-hot soup tamed with sour cream.

1/2 cup unsalted butter
1 pound lean, boneless pork, cubed
1 small smoked ham hock
1 pound lean hot link sausage, halved lengthwise (if the hot
   Bavarian type is not available, use link breakfast sausage and
   add an additional 1/2 teaspoon cayenne pepper to soup)
3 onions, coarsely chopped
1 cup dry white wine
3 cups chicken broth
1 (1-lb.) can sauerkraut or 1 pound fresh sauerkraut, undrained
1 tablespoon anise seeds
1/2 teaspoon cayenne pepper (or to taste)
1/4 cup chopped parsley
2 cups dairy sour cream

Melt 1/4 cup butter in a large, deep pot. Add pork, ham hock and sausage; cook until browned, turning as needed. Remove meat and set aside. Melt remaining 1/4 cup butter in pot, add onions and cook until clear. Add wine and stir about 3 minutes or just long enough to deglaze pan. Stir in broth, sauerkraut, anise seeds, cayenne, parsley and meat. Bring to boil; then reduce heat to low, cover and simmer about 1-1/2 hours or until flavors are well blended and ham hock, pork and fresh sauerkraut (if used) are tender. Remove fat and bones from ham hock; cut or tear meat in bite-size pieces, leaving skin on, if desired. Also cut sausage in bite-size pieces. Skim and discard fat from soup; return ham and sausage to soup. Spoon soup into large bowls. Offer sour cream alongside and let guests spoon as much as they like into their soup. Makes 6 to 8 servings.

Seafood

Succulent seafood earns star ratings when spiced. Pepper, mustard, chiles, horseradish and ginger subtly enhance the mild, slightly sweet flavor of fish and shellfish—and make for terrifically tempting fare. This chapter offers an exciting array of choices, from Sumptuous Swordfish, served with a chile-spiked orange salsa, to golden, buttery Sole with Peppered Macadamia Nuts. Testy Tempura is sure to satisfy both fire-eaters and those who can't take the heat; shrimp and vegetables are deep-fried in a mild lacy batter, then dipped at the table in searing Hot Tempura Sauce.

Most of the recipes in this collection are easy to make. Many have an international flavor, but others—Turbot Leek Martini, Brennan's Red Hot Baby Lobster Tails, Batter-Dipped Poppy Seed Crabs and more—were developed and perfected in my own kitchen to suit "hotter than hell" tastes!

Zesty Szechwan Salmon

This flavorful sauce works pure magic on just about any seafood. We especially enjoy it with stronger-flavored fish and seafood—salmon or clams, for example, as opposed to sole or shrimp. You can make the sauce ahead and store it in the refrigerator; leftover sauce can be refrigerated indefinitely, too.

2 teaspoons cornstarch
2 tablespoons dry sherry
1 tablespoon peanut oil
2 tablespoons fermented black beans
1 teaspoon minced fresh ginger
1 teaspoon minced garlic
2/3 cup chicken broth
1 tablespoon oyster sauce
2 teaspoons dark soy sauce
6 (4-oz.) salmon steaks, cut 1 inch thick
1/4 cup vegetable oil
1/4 cup thinly sliced (1/8-inch) green onions (including some green tops)

Combine cornstarch and sherry; then add peanut oil, black beans, ginger, garlic, broth, oyster sauce and soy sauce. Stir until well blended. (Or process ingredients in a blender or food processor until blended.) Set aside. Prepare a bed of hot coals or preheat broiler. Adjust barbecue grill 4 to 5 inches above coals; position oven rack so fish will be 4 to 5 inches below heat source. Lightly grease barbecue grill or rack in broiler pan. Brush salmon steaks with vegetable oil and place on grill or rack. Cook about 3 minutes, then rotate a quarter turn and cook 2 to 3 minutes longer to create a crisscross pattern. Turn fish over; cook other side the same way (total cooking time is 10 to 12 minutes). To check doneness, pierce center of salmon with a fork; if flesh is opaque and flakes readily, fish is done. Do not overcook! Place salmon on warmed plates and top each steak with a few spoonfuls of sauce, letting sauce run over sides. Garnish with green onions. Makes 6 servings.

Hawaiian Sesame Salmon

Vary this simple-to-prepare salmon dish in myriad ways—use finely chopped macadamias, walnuts or almonds in place of sesame seeds, or top with a favorite hot sauce, such as mustard-dill, pickled pepper or sweet-and-sour.

2 eggs
1/2 teaspoon salt
1/2 teaspoon freshly ground white pepper (or to taste)
1/4 cup sesame seeds
17 whole black peppercorns, coarsely crushed or cracked
4 (4-oz.) salmon steaks, cut 1 inch thick
1/4 cup unsalted butter, melted
4 lime wedges
Liquid hot-pepper sauce

Preheat broiler. Beat eggs lightly; beat in salt and white pepper. Mix sesame seeds and black pepper. Dip salmon steaks in egg mixture, then press into sesame seed mixture to coat completely on both sides. Lightly oil broiler pan, then arrange steaks well apart in pan. Broil 4 to 5 inches below heat source 5 minutes or until browned; turn and broil 5 minutes longer or until fish is opaque in center and flakes readily when pierced with a fork. Arrange on a warmed platter. Top with melted butter, garnish with lime wedges and serve with hot-pepper sauce. Makes 4 servings.

Turbot Leek Martini

Teased with vermouth and slivered hot chiles, delicate-flavored turbot offers a treat for the tastebuds—and arranged on a bed of sautéed leeks, it's a feast for the eyes as well. We first enjoyed this dish with a nice bottle of white wine for an *al fresco* luncheon.

2 large leeks
6 tablespoons unsalted butter
Freshly grated nutmeg to taste
Freshly ground black pepper to taste
3/4 pound turbot
1/3 cup all-purpose flour
1/2 teaspoon salt
2 tablespoons minced fresh parsley or 1 tablespoon dried
   parsley flakes
2 fresh jalapeño or serrano chiles, finely slivered
1/3 cup dry vermouth
Mild red salsa, homemade or bottled, if desired
Lemon wedges

Cut off tops of leeks, leaving about 3 inches of green leaves. Cut leeks in half lengthwise; rinse well, separating layers to wash out dirt. Then cut leek halves in long, thin slivers. Melt 3 tablespoons butter in a skillet over medium heat. Add leeks. Grate nutmeg generously over leeks; also grind a little pepper over top. Cook about 5 minutes or until leeks begin to brown; then turn and stir leeks and grate nutmeg and pepper over them again. While leeks are cooking, melt remaining 3 tablespoons butter in another skillet. Lay turbot out flat. Combine flour, salt, pepper to taste and parsley. Dust turbot evenly with flour mixture; add turbot to butter and cook, turning once, about 5 minutes per side or until light golden brown. Then sprinkle chiles evenly over fish, pour vermouth into skillet and quickly bring to a boil; remove from heat. Arrange leeks spoke-fashion on a platter; set turbot on top. Garnish turbot with spoonfuls of salsa, if desired, and top with lemon wedges. Makes 3 or 4 servings.

Sumptuous Swordfish

"Luscious" is the word for this fresh, elegantly flavored swordfish. Don't compromise on the fresh dill and cilantro, if at all possible. Fresh cilantro is crucial for the flavor; if you can't find it at your regular supermarket, try an Asian greengrocer or specialty store. Kirby cucumbers are delicious small, tender pickling cucumbers; if they're unavailable, use regular cucumbers.

3 small or 2 medium green onions, thinly sliced
1/3 cup fresh or reconstituted frozen orange juice
1/3 cup walnut oil
1/4 cup minced fresh dill
2 pounds swordfish, cut crossgrain as a steak
Salsa de Naranjas, see below
2 tablespoons vegetable oil
8 Kirby or regular cucumber slices
1/2 orange, unpeeled, thinly sliced
4 to 6 sprigs fresh cilantro

Salsa de Naranjas:
1 large red-ripe tomato, cut in 1/4-inch cubes (1 to 1-1/4 cups)
Juice of 1/2 orange (at least 1/4 cup)
1 teaspoon grated orange peel
4 green onions, thinly sliced
1/4 cup coarsely chopped fresh cilantro
2 fresh Oriental hot green chiles, finely minced

Two hours (30 minutes, if in a rush) before planning to serve, combine green onions, orange juice, walnut oil and 2 tablespoons dill in a shallow glass or stainless steel bowl. Place fish in marinade and lightly press into liquid. Turn fish over; spoon more marinade over top and let stand at room temperature until ready to cook, turning fish and spooning marinade over top every 15 to 30 minutes. At least 30 minutes before serving, prepare salsa. *To grill fish*, prepare a bed of medium-hot coals. Set grill in place about 4 inches above coals; lightly brush grill with vegetable oil. When grill is sizzling hot, place fish on grill; cook 2 to 3 minutes, then rotate a quarter turn and cook a minute longer to create a crisscross pattern. Turn fish over; drizzle with some of the marinade and cook 3 to 4 minutes longer or until fish tests done, rotating a quarter turn after about 2 minutes. *To pan-broil fish*, heat a heavy skillet; add vegetable oil. When oil is sizzling hot, add fish. Cook about 5 minutes or until well browned on bottom; turn over, drizzle with some of the marinade and cook until second side is browned and fish tests done. *To check doneness*, insert a knife in thickest part of circular grain of fish; if flesh is moist but not shiny, fish is done. (If fish is cooking slowly, cover it after the first turn.) *To serve*, place fish on a platter and drizzle with remaining marinade; spoon a mound of salsa to 1 side of fish. Press remaining 2 tablespoons dill evenly into cucumber slices, then arrange cucumber slices and orange slices along other side of fish. Top fish with cilantro sprigs. Makes 4 to 6 servings.

Salsa de Naranjas:
Combine all ingredients. Let stand at least 30 minutes, tossing and stirring often to blend flavors.

Hot Socks Snapper with Olive-Anchovy Topping

A sassy topping greatly enhances the mild, moist flesh of snapper—whether red snapper or any other local type. If perchance some "mild mouths" are present among your guests, omit the jalapeños and offer crushed or ground pequin chiles at the table, so those who have a passion for painfully hot foods can please themselves. Do be sure to use only pure chiles for adding at the table, though—commercial "chili powder" just doesn't have the same fresh, clear, fiery-hot flavor.

1/4 cup unsalted butter
1/4 cup olive oil
2 large or 4 small cloves garlic, finely minced
4 (6- to 8-oz.) red snapper fillets
1/2 medium red onion, very thinly sliced, separated into rings
1/2 cup pimento-stuffed green olives, thinly sliced crosswise
1 tablespoon finely chopped flat anchovy fillets
1/2 cup parched (see page 9), peeled, finely chopped fresh
jalapeño chiles (you may substitute pickled jalapeños, but the
flavor will not be as fresh)

In a large, heavy skillet, melt butter in oil. When butter is melted and hot, add garlic and let sizzle, but do not allow to brown. Add fish and reduce heat to medium-low. Cook, turning once, about 5 minutes per side or until light golden brown. Meanwhile, combine onion, olives, anchovies and jalapeños. Set cooked fillets on warmed plates; top evenly with olive mixture and serve. Makes 4 servings.

Huachinango en Salsa Verde

Tart tomatillos are a key ingredient in this luscious, lovely Mexican dish. These little fruits look like green cherry tomatoes with whitish, papery husks—but despite their name and appearance, they're not related to tomatoes. Because fresh tomatillos may be hard to find, I've called for the canned version (available in Mexican markets and some supermarkets). If you can't find canned tomatillos, you may use chopped fresh green tomatoes or even canned red ones—though you won't end up with an authentic *salsa verde*!

1/2 cup coarsely chopped onion
2 tablespoons chopped fresh cilantro
2 fresh jalapeño chiles, stemmed
1 (13-oz.) can tomatillos, well drained, rinsed
6 fresh green chiles (as hot as you like), parched (see page 9),
    peeled, seeded, de-ribbed
1/4 cup unsalted butter (or more, as needed)
1/2 cup all-purpose flour
1/2 teaspoon salt
Freshly ground black pepper to taste
6 (6- to 8-oz.) red snapper fillets
Hot cooked rice

To make salsa verde, place onion, cilantro, jalapeños and tomatillos in a blender or food processor and process until very smoothly pureed. Set aside. Cut each green chile lengthwise; open out to make a flat sheet. Set aside. Preheat oven to 350F (175C). Melt butter in a skillet; meanwhile, combine flour, salt and pepper in a shallow, flat-bottomed dish. Dip fillets in flour mixture, then cook in butter, turning once, about 5 minutes per side or until light golden brown. Wrap each fillet in a green chile "blanket"; arrange wrapped fillets on an ovenproof platter and top with salsa verde. Place in oven just until salsa and chiles are hot; then serve on warmed plates, accompanied with rice. Makes 6 servings.

Sole with Peppered Macadamia Nuts

The mild, rich flavors of sole and macadamia nuts take happily to a sassy sprinkle of crushed caribe. If you like, substitute other dried hot red chiles or even finely chopped fresh green jalapeños for the caribe.

> 3/4 cup macadamia nuts
> 2 tablespoons caribe (crushed Northern New Mexico red chile),
>   or to taste
> 1/4 cup vegetable oil (or more, as needed)
> 8 (6-oz.) sole fillets
> 2 tablespoons unsalted butter
> Juice of 1/2 lemon
> 1 lemon, cut lengthwise in 8 wedges
> 1 tablespoon minced parsley mixed with a sprinkle of caribe
>   (crushed Northern New Mexico red chile)

Crush macadamia nuts with a rolling pin or chop in a food processor, using on-off pulses. Evenly mix nuts with caribe and spread on a large sheet of waxed paper. Heat oil in a large, heavy skillet. Meanwhile, lightly press both sides of each fillet into nut-caribe mixture, using all mixture and coating each fillet as uniformly as possible. Gently place as many coated fillets in skillet as will easily fit. Cook over medium heat until golden on bottom; turn gently, being careful not to break fillets. When second side is golden, turn each fillet out onto a warmed plate and keep warm. Repeat to cook remaining fillets, adding more oil as necessary to prevent sticking. Add butter to nut coating left in skillet; cook, stirring, until golden brown (do not scorch). Turn off heat and stir in lemon juice; then evenly spoon nut-butter sauce over fillets. Dust center edge of each lemon wedge with parsley-caribe mixture; garnish fish with lemon wedges. Makes 8 servings.

NOTE: For those who like it really hot, you can offer additional caribe at the table.

New Mexican Monkfish

With its firm flesh and lobster-like flavor, monkfish is ideal for this richly sauced dish—but if it's unavailable, any dense-fleshed ocean fish (cod, for example) will do nicely.

> 1-1/2 pounds monkfish fillets, rinsed well
> 1/2 cup whole milk
> 2 cups grated full-cream sharp Cheddar cheese
> Hot salsa, such as Margarita Jalapeño Salsa, page 143

Preheat oven to 350F (175C). Place fish in bottom of a large, covered casserole, preferably one with a nonstick finish. (If not using a nonstick casserole, butter lightly before adding fish.) Pour milk evenly over fish. Top uniformly with cheese and 1/4 cup salsa, cover and bake 15 to 25 minutes or until fish is tender but not overdone. Serve hot, with more salsa on the side. Makes 4 servings.

Testy Tempura

Tempura is flexible. You can serve it numerous ways, choosing a variety of vegetables, seafood and/or meats to coat with the delectable batter. A hot, zippy sauce adds extra fun. Here's an assortment of vegetables and shrimp that my friends and family have always liked.

> 1 tiny eggplant, cut in 1/2-inch cubes or 1/2-inch-thick fingers; or 1 medium zucchini, cut in 1/4-inch-thick slices
>
> 6 green onions, "butterflied" (onions left whole, green tops shredded lengthwise with a sharp knife for 2/3 of their length)
>
> 2 (1/4-inch-thick) slices red onion, separated into rings
>
> 6 small spears fresh asparagus
>
> 12 sprigs parsley
>
> 6 fresh mushrooms, halved
>
> 1 medium sweet potato, scrubbed, unpeeled, cut in 6 diagonal slices, each slice halved
>
> 1 pound medium shrimp, shelled, deveined, butterflied
>
> Hot Tempura Sauce, page 142
>
> 2 quarts vegetable or peanut oil for deep-frying
>
> 1 cup all-purpose flour
>
> 1 cup cornstarch
>
> 1/2 teaspoon baking powder
>
> 1 egg yolk
>
> 1 cup cold water
>
> 1/2 cup crushed ice

Prepare vegetables and shrimp as noted in ingredient list above. (I like to leave the eggplant or zucchini and sweet potato unpeeled, but you may peel them if you wish.) Prepare Hot Tempura Sauce. In an electric wok, deep-fat fryer or deep, heavy saucepan, heat about 4 inches of oil to 375F (190C). When oil is hot and all ingredients are ready, prepare batter: place flour, cornstarch and baking powder in a bowl. Whisk egg yolk and water just until blended; add to dry ingredients and mix only until blended. Stir in crushed ice. To fry, dip pieces of food into batter 1 at a time, then lower into hot oil; cook only a few at a time, to keep batter lacy and to avoid crowding pan. Cook foods until golden, then keep warm in a 250F (120C) oven on a paper-towel-lined baking sheet until all are done. Serve warm, with sauce for dipping. Makes 6 servings.

Sizzling Beer-Batter-Fried Shrimp

A crisp, hearty herb-and-spice coating makes these fried shrimp especially right for any occasion where all the guests have good-sized appetites. I like to serve them after a long day spent out of doors, when the hungry horde won't allow me lots of time to fuss around in the kitchen! You do have to plan ahead, though: mix up the batter at least 3 hours ahead and, if possible, clean the shrimp and make the Hot Beer Mustard beforehand, too. French fries and a salad really taste terrific with these shrimp, but you can round out the meal with any dishes of your choice.

>**3/4 cup all-purpose flour**
>**1/2 cup beer**
>**1/2 teaspoon salt**
>**1 teaspoon vegetable oil**
>**Hot Beer Mustard, see below**
>**2 quarts vegetable oil for deep-frying**
>**1 egg, separated**
>**1 tablespoon chopped fresh cilantro**
>**1 tablespoon chopped flat-leaf parsley**
>**2 fresh jalapeño chiles, seeded, de-ribbed, finely minced; or 2**
>**   teaspoons pequin quebrado**
>**1 teaspoon finely chopped chives**
>**1-1/2 pounds medium-large shrimp, shelled, deveined, tails left**
>**   on**
>
>*Hot Beer Mustard:*
>**1/3 cup dry mustard**
>**2-1/2 tablespoons beer (or more, as needed)**
>**Salt, if desired**

At least 3 hours ahead of time (or early in the day), prepare batter: place flour in large, shallow bowl. Then stir in beer, salt and 1 teaspoon oil until smooth. Cover and set aside at room temperature. When ready to fry, prepare Hot Beer Mustard and set aside. Then, in a deep, heavy saucepan, heat 4 inches of oil to 375F (190C). Meanwhile, stir egg yolk, cilantro, parsley, jalapeños or pequin and chives into batter. When oil is hot, beat egg white until stiff and fold carefully into batter. Dip shrimp into batter, lower into hot oil and fry until golden; drain well. Keep cooked shrimp warm in a 250F (120C) oven on a paper-towel-lined baking sheet until ready to serve. Accompany with Hot Beer Mustard. Makes 6 servings.

Hot Beer Mustard:

Vigorously stir together mustard and beer (add more beer, if necessary, to achieve desired consistency). Let stand about 20 minutes before serving. Taste; add a bit of salt, if desired.

Devil's Shrimp

For a super quick, palate-pleasing, devilishly hot dish—serve this! It's great any time, especially on those warm nights when no one really feels like bothering with cooking (but everyone who tastes these shrimp will be glad the cook did "bother" a bit).

1/4 cup unsalted butter
1/4 cup olive oil
6 large or 12 small cloves garlic, finely minced
2 pounds medium shrimp, shelled, deveined, tails left on
2 tablespoons caribe (crushed Northern New Mexico red chile)
1 teaspoon salt (or to taste)
1/2 cup freshly grated Parmesan cheese

Melt butter in oil in a large, heavy skillet. When butter is melted and hot, add garlic and let sizzle, reducing heat before garlic starts to brown. Add shrimp and sprinkle with half each of caribe and salt; cook about 3 minutes or until shrimp barely begin to turn pink on bottom. Then turn shrimp over, sprinkle with remaining caribe and salt and cook 2 to 3 minutes longer or until shrimp are pink but still juicy. Taste and adjust seasonings. Sprinkle with cheese; let stand until cheese starts to melt, then serve at once, on warmed plates. Makes 4 servings.

Camarones Rancheros

These highly flavorful shrimp make for a terrific party dish, since much of the preparation can be done ahead. You can make the sauce early in the day, then reheat it and cook the shrimp just before serving. For a spectacular presentation, serve *camarones rancheros* in a rice ring: cook 1-1/2 cups long-grain rice according to your usual recipe, but add 1/4 cup chopped parsley, 1 clove garlic, minced, and 1 cup parched (see page 9), peeled, seeded, chopped mild green chiles (or use canned diced chiles). When rice is done, press it into a generously buttered ring mold; if prepared in advance, cover mold and keep warm in a low oven until serving time. To serve, just turn rice ring out onto a platter. A salad of grapefruit sections and onion rings, tossed with a honey and poppy seed dressing and served on a bed of lettuce, nicely rounds out the meal.

1/4 cup virgin olive oil
2 large white onions, thinly sliced, separated into rings
2 large green bell peppers, cut crosswise in thin rings
2 cups peeled, quartered red-ripe tomatoes or 2 cups canned whole tomatoes
3 or more fresh jalapeño chiles, finely minced
3/4 teaspoon salt (or to taste)
Freshly ground black pepper to taste
1/2 cup unsalted butter
1/3 cup virgin olive oil
8 to 10 large cloves garlic, minced (2 tablespoons)
3 pounds jumbo shrimp, shelled, deveined, butterflied
1/2 cup dry white wine (or to taste)
1 ripe Hass avocado
Hot cooked rice, if desired
2 tablespoons minced parsley

To make sauce, heat 1/4 cup oil in a large skillet. Add onions and bell peppers; cook until onions are clear, but not browned. Add tomatoes and cook only until they are warm and beginning to release their juice. Add jalapeños, salt and pepper and simmer briefly—just long enough to blend flavors, but not so long that tomatoes, onions and bell peppers become overly soft and shapeless. Set aside. To serve, melt butter in 1/3 cup oil in a large, shallow skillet. When butter is melted and hot, add garlic and cook until slightly golden. Add shrimp; cook quickly, turning as needed, just until shrimp turn pink. Stir in tomato-pepper sauce. When sauce is heated, stir in wine and simmer briefly, just long enough to marry flavors. Meanwhile, pit, peel and slice avocado. Spoon shrimp mixture into center of rice ring (see recipe introduction) or over rice, if desired; or serve as is. Arrange avocado slices around edge of shrimp mixture and sprinkle parsley over top. Makes 6 servings.

Batter-Dipped Poppy Seed Crabs

Double blue and crunchy too! The rich, nutty flavors of blue cornmeal and poppy seeds beautifully complement sweet, tender crab; spicy Margarita Jalapeño Salsa adds just the right surprise. Serve with your favorite vegetable side dish and a simple, tartly dressed salad.

1 cup all-purpose flour
1 teaspoon baking powder
1/2 teaspoon salt
3/4 cup blue cornmeal
3 tablespoons poppy seeds
2 eggs
1 cup milk
1/2 cup unsalted butter
8 small (2- to 3-oz.) soft-shell crabs
Margarita Jalapeño Salsa, page 143

In a bowl, mix flour, baking powder and salt; stir in cornmeal and poppy seeds. In another bowl, lightly beat eggs; blend in milk, then combine milk mixture with dry ingredients and stir until well blended. Add a little more milk, if necessary, to make a smooth batter that will cling to crabs. Melt butter in a large, shallow skillet over medium heat. Dip crabs in batter to coat; add to skillet and cook until golden on both sides, turning once. Serve with salsa. Makes about 4 servings.

Brennan's Red Hot Baby Lobster Tails

These spicy, saucy, succulent lobster tails are flashy, both to prepare and to serve. Guests can adjust the heat by drizzling more or less of the peppery-hot butter sauce atop the tails, but even tender-mouthed diners always seem to enjoy the layer of sauce spooned into the shell beneath each tail. Serve as a light entree, as the fish course for a larger meal or even as an appetizer.

8 (4- to 6-inch-long) rock lobster tails
1/2 cup unsalted butter
1/4 cup minced green onions (including some green tops)
2 large cloves garlic, finely minced
1 small red radish, finely minced
Juice of 1 lime
2 teaspoons pequin quebrado
1 fresh jalapeño chile, seeded, de-ribbed, very thinly slivered;
   or 1 pickled jalapeño chile, minced
1 tablespoon freshly grated Parmesan cheese
1 tablespoon freshly grated Romano cheese
2 teaspoons ground pure California mild red chile
4 large sprigs watercress or other greens
1 lime, cut lengthwise in quarters
Additional pequin quebrado, if desired

Preheat broiler. Cut each tail in half lengthwise, using a very sharp knife (leave tails unsplit at back end). Peel meat back off shells. Place tails in a broiler pan and set aside. Melt butter in a skillet. Add green onions, garlic, radish, lime juice and 2 teaspoons pequin. Cook, stirring, until garlic is light golden and onions are soft but not browned. Divide 1/4 of butter sauce equally among lobster shells; replace meat in shells. Then evenly divide another 1/4 of butter sauce among tails, drizzling it over top of each. Sprinkle each tail with jalapeño slivers, cheeses and some of ground chile. Broil 4 to 5 inches below heat source about 5 minutes or until meat is just turning white in center (cut to test). To serve, place 2 tails on each of 4 warmed plates; garnish each serving with a watercress sprig and a wedge of lime, lightly rubbing cut edge of lime wedges with ground chile. Offer remaining butter sauce and a small dish of pequin, if desired, for guests to add to their servings as they please. Makes 4 servings.

Pastel de Pescado

Straight from Old Mexico comes this pastry overflowing with the sea's bounty. The quiche-like filling—shrimp, scallops and lobster in a rich Swiss-cheese custard—nestles in a curved golden crust that's easily made from browned flour tortillas. If you like, you can substitute the catch of the day or any favorite seafood for the choices in the recipe. Serve with a tossed salad and perhaps a vegetable for a wonderful lunch or light supper.

> 1/4 cup unsalted butter
> 3 (9- to 10-inch) flour tortillas
> 18 medium shrimp, shelled, deveined, tails removed
> 36 bay scallops (about 1/2 lb. total)
> 1/2 pound lobster or crab meat, drained, all bits of shell
>   removed
> 2 cloves garlic, minced
> 1 cup fresh peas or 1 cup frozen green peas, thawed, undrained
> 4 eggs
> 1 cup whipping cream
> 1/4 cup dry sherry
> 1/4 teaspoon salt (or to taste)
> 1/4 teaspoon freshly ground white pepper (or to taste)
> 1/2 cup slivered Swiss cheese
> 1 tomato, cut in thin wedges
> 1 or more fresh jalapeño chiles, thinly sliced, seeded
> 2 tablespoons minced chives
> Freshly grated nutmeg to taste

Lightly butter a 9-inch pie plate, using about 1/2 tablespoon butter. Using a sharp knife, cut 3 equal "scallops" off rounded edges of each of 2 tortillas. Melt remaining butter in a medium skillet; quickly brown remaining whole tortilla, then the 6 "scallops." Place whole tortilla in bottom of buttered pie plate and surround with "scallops," forming sides of crust. Preheat oven to 375F (190C). Then evenly distribute seafood across bottom of tortilla shell. I like to place shrimp interlocking each other all around outside edge, then fill center with scallops and lightly scatter lobster or crab over all. Top with garlic and peas. Beat together eggs, cream, sherry, salt and white pepper; pour evenly over all. Scatter cheese on top. Then attractively decorate top of pie: arrange tomato wedges overlapping each other around outside edge, jalapeño slices over tomatoes and chives in a circle in center. Grate nutmeg over all. Bake 30 to 40 minutes or until a knife inserted in center comes out clean. Serve warm. Makes 6 to 8 servings.

Cioppino Caliente

Super hot and so much fun! Served with a warmed loaf of French or Italian bread and a tossed green salad, this robust seafood stew is guaranteed to "wow" your guests. Cioppino is one of my longtime favorite entrees for entertaining. It's best served at intimate, informal dinner parties—preferably only four diners (or even just two!)—since it's frankly messy to eat.

1/4 cup virgin olive oil
1 large onion, chopped
4 cloves garlic, minced
1/4 cup caribe (crushed Northern New Mexico red chile)
4 large red-ripe tomatoes, peeled, coarsely chopped
1 (6-oz.) can tomato paste
1/2 cup burgundy or other good-quality dry red wine (or to taste)
2 teaspoons minced fresh rosemary or 1 teaspoon dried leaf rosemary
1 tablespoon minced fresh thyme
2 bay leaves
2 tablespoons minced fresh basil
1 tablespoon minced fresh oregano
1 teaspoon salt (or to taste)
1 pound medium shrimp, shelled, deveined, tails left on
1/2 pound king or other crab legs
1 (1-1/2-lb.) lobster
18 bay scallops (about 1/4 lb. total)
1/2 pound firm-fleshed white fish such as cod, cut in 1-inch cubes
12 cherrystone or other small clams, scrubbed
1/4 cup dry brandy, if desired

Heat oil in a large skillet, paella pan or wok. Add onion and garlic and cook until garlic just starts to turn golden. Then add caribe, tomatoes, tomato paste, wine, herbs and salt. Cover and simmer about 30 minutes or until flavors are well blended and sauce is somewhat reduced; add a little water if sauce starts getting too thick. Taste and adjust seasonings. Place all seafood on top of sauce, arranging it in a pretty pattern. Cover and cook 10 to 15 minutes or until shrimp turn pink, lobster turns red, scallops and fish are opaque and clams pop open. If desired, quickly heat brandy; carefully flame and pour over cioppino just before serving. To serve, divide seafood equally among large, shallow bowls (you'll need to cut lobster apart). Be sure to provide bibs and plenty of napkins! Makes 4 servings.

San Francisco Sassy Scallops

A student in one of my Santa Fe Cooking Schools shared this special recipe with me. A former Harvard and Stanford professor who now lives in Woodside, California, he generously told us all how to create one of his favorite appetizer specialties. I'm sure you'll agree it's wonderful!

> **1 pound bay scallops**
> **1/2 cup fresh lemon juice or enough to cover scallops**
> **4 red bell peppers, parched (see page 9), peeled, seeded**
> **2 tablespoons raspberry vinegar**
> **2 tablespoons extra-virgin olive oil**
> **1/2 teaspoon pequin quebrado (or to taste)**
> **Salt to taste, if desired**
> **1 medium Hass avocado**

Place scallops in a glass or porcelain bowl and cover with lemon juice; stir. Cover and refrigerate, stirring frequently, about 2 hours or until scallops "cook" in lemon juice and turn opaque. Meanwhile, prepare sauce: in a blender or food processor, process bell peppers, vinegar, oil, pequin and salt, if desired, until pureed. Taste and adjust seasonings. To serve, pit and peel avocado, then cut lengthwise in slivers. Divide bell-pepper sauce equally among 4 to 6 clear glass plates. Drain scallops; center scallops on sauce and garnish edge of each plate with avocado slivers. Makes 4 to 6 appetizer servings.

Scallops with
Sherried Green Peppercorn Sauce

This fabulously rich, flavorfully sauced dish is surprisingly easy to make and oh, so delicious. It's especially good as a brunch entree or a late-night dinner; smaller portions make an elegant first course.

> **1/4 cup unsalted butter**
> **1-1/2 pounds bay scallops**
> **1/4 cup dry sherry**
> **1/2 cup whipping cream**
> **1 (1-oz.) jar pickled green peppercorns, drained**
> **Salt to taste**
> **1 teaspoon caribe (crushed Northern New Mexico red chile)**
> **4 patty shells or croissants, heated**

Melt 2 tablespoons butter in a large, heavy skillet over medium-high heat. Add scallops and quickly cook, stirring, until edges are light golden and almost all liquid has evaporated, leaving skillet almost dry. Remove scallops to a platter and keep warm. Add sherry to skillet; deglaze skillet, then add cream and cook, stirring, until mixture is reduced by about 1/3. Stir in scallops, peppercorns, salt and caribe. Cook a few minutes; taste and adjust seasonings. Serve in patty shells or over split croissants on warmed plates. Makes 4 servings.

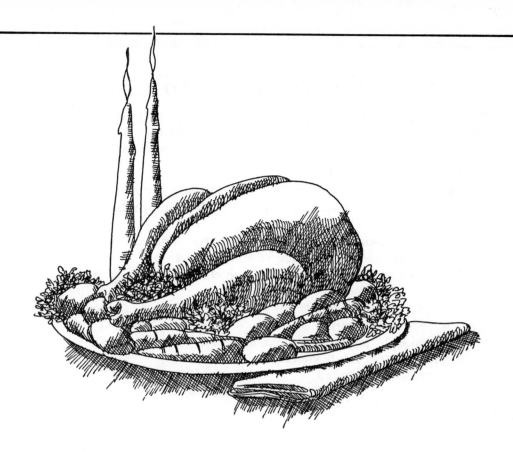

Poultry

Chicken is a chameleon, flavor-wise—absorbing, reflecting and enhancing the seasonings it captures. One of the very best buys, it's also a nutritional star. And you can prepare it in an almost infinite number of ways, from simple to complex, mild to fiery. The recipes in this chapter will delight you with their diversity, and all can be altered to suit even the most timid palate. Coq au Vin, Caliente starts with a great classic dish and adds a spicy twist to make a memorable meal. Thai-inspired Secret Siamese Chicken is as simple and quick to prepare as it is delicious; Phenomenal Pollo offers a wonderful palette of colors and spicy flavors. Hotter than Hell Buffet Barbecued Chicken, made with our world-famous barbecue sauce, is sure to be a crowd-pleaser every time.

Turkey, like chicken, is low in cost, high in nutrition and compatible with myriad seasonings—including chiles and hot spices, of course. I've included a pair of turkey recipes in this chapter: Roast Turkey with Garbanzo-Chorizo Stuffing and flavor-rich Turkey Mole. Both are perfect for holiday and other special-occasion meals.

Tia's Favorite Mexican Chicken

Select a very young spring fryer, not over 2-1/2 pounds, layer it in a pot with fresh vegetables ... then set it over low heat and let dinner cook itself. This easy-to-make entree is straight from the Western ranges; similar dishes were originally prepared over an open fire in heavy cast-iron pots.

1/4 cup unsalted butter
1 (2- to 2-1/2-lb.) young broiler-fryer chicken, cut for frying
1 zucchini, about 6 inches long and 1-1/2 inches in diameter, sliced
1 yellow crookneck squash, about 6 inches long and 1-1/2 inches in diameter at thickest point, sliced
1 large green bell pepper or poblano chile, cut in long, thin strips
4 ears fresh corn, kernels cut off the cob, or 2 cups frozen whole-kernel corn
1 pound red-ripe tomatoes, peeled, cut in wedges
2 small onions, thinly sliced
4 cloves garlic, minced
2 or 3 fresh jalapeño chiles, very thinly sliced crosswise
Water or chicken broth, if needed
Chopped fresh jalapeño chiles, if desired

Melt butter in a large, heavy pot. Add chicken, skin side down; cook until browned. Then layer on zucchini, crookneck squash, bell pepper or poblano chile, corn, tomatoes and onions. Sprinkle with garlic and sliced jalapeños. Cover and cook over low heat 30 minutes. Check; if more liquid is needed, add water or broth. Cover; cook 15 minutes longer or until chicken and vegetables are tender. Do not overcook. Serve on a warmed platter with vegetables encircling chicken. If desired, offer a dish of chopped jalapeños for the fire-eaters in your crowd. Makes 4 servings.

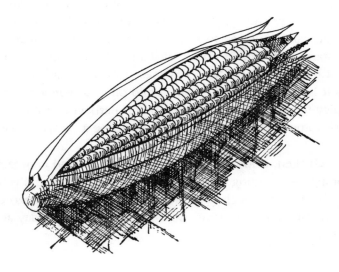

Winter Chicken-Chile Stew

Though it's delightful any time, this stew is perfect for cozy, chilly winter evenings. It's great "comfort food," combining the soothing qualities of chicken soup with the hearty surprise of a rosy, chile-sparked sauce laced with dry white wine. If you like, offer spicy caribe at the table for the daring to add at will.

1/4 cup vegetable oil
2 large cloves garlic, coarsely chopped
1 (about 3-1/2-lb.) broiler-fryer chicken, cut for frying
6 large carrots, peeled, cut in 3-inch lengths
6 medium-small onions, peeled, quartered
6 medium-small turnips, peeled, quartered
6 medium potatoes, peeled, quartered
2 large stalks celery, cut in 2-inch lengths
7 cups water
1 teaspoon salt (or to taste)
3 sprigs fresh oregano or 1/2 teaspoon dried leaf oregano
1 fresh bay leaf
6 leaves fresh purple sage or 1 teaspoon dried leaf sage
2 tablespoons ground pure New Mexico hot red chile
1 cup dry white wine
Caribe (crushed Northern New Mexico red chile), if desired

Heat oil in a large, heavy pot, then add garlic and cook just until heated. Add chicken pieces and cook until browned on all sides, turning as needed. Remove from pot. Add carrots, onions, turnips, potatoes and celery; cook, stirring, until slightly browned on edges. Return chicken pieces to pot, placing them on top of vegetables. Add water, salt, herbs, ground chile and 3/4 cup wine. Bring to a boil, then reduce heat, cover and simmer 45 minutes to 1 hour or until chicken and vegetables are tender. Taste and adjust seasonings. Serve hot, laced with remaining 1/4 cup wine. If desired, offer a small bowl of caribe on the side for those who wish to add extra heat. Makes 6 to 8 servings.

Coq au Vin, Caliente

My all-time favorite *coq* recipe, developed during my early New Mexico years. Fired with caribe and flamed with cognac, it's a fabulous dish with a perfect marriage of flavors, certain to be a hit with family and guests—though you may want to hoard it all for yourself! Since this stew is so robust, accompany it with a soothing side dish. And never, never waste a drop of the savory sauce; if you have any leftover, freeze it for later use. It's wonderful in stews, even beef stews.

**1/2 cup all-purpose flour
2 tablespoons caribe (crushed Northern New Mexico red chile)
1 teaspoon salt
1 (3-1/2- to 4-lb.) broiler-fryer chicken, cut for frying
1/2 cup unsalted butter
6 tablespoons cognac
1 clove garlic, crushed
1 fresh bay leaf
4 sprigs fresh thyme or 1/2 teaspoon dried leaf thyme
1/4 cup minced flat-leaf parsley
6 small white boiling onions, peeled
1/2 pound fresh mushrooms, thinly sliced
6 thick slices lean, heavily smoked country bacon, cut in
   1/2-inch pieces, partially cooked and drained
Freshly ground black pepper to taste
1 cup burgundy or other good-quality dry red wine
1/2 cup Fried Croutons, see below, if desired**

Fried Croutons:
**1-inch French bread cubes
Olive oil
Unsalted butter**

In a paper bag or large, shallow bowl, mix flour, caribe and salt. Dredge chicken in flour mixture. Meanwhile, melt butter in a large, deep, heavy skillet (or in a chicken fryer) over medium-high heat. Add chicken pieces and cook until browned on all sides, turning as needed; adjust heat as necessary to prevent overbrowning. Then add cognac to hot skillet and flame carefully, keeping a lid nearby to extinguish flames should they rise too high. When flames die, stir in garlic, bay leaf, thyme, 3 tablespoons parsley, onions, mushrooms, bacon and a generous grinding of black pepper. Pour wine over all. Bring to a boil, then reduce heat, cover and simmer about 45 minutes or until chicken is tender and sauce is thickened. Meanwhile, prepare Fried Croutons, if desired. To serve, place chicken on a large warmed platter and cover with sauce, arranging onions decoratively around chicken. Sprinkle croutons (if used) over top, then sprinkle with remaining 1 tablespoon parsley. Makes 6 servings.

Fried Croutons:
In a skillet, toast French bread cubes in a mixture of half oil, half melted butter until light golden on all sides, stirring as needed. Cool.

Phenomenal Pollo (Mexican Almond Chicken in Green Sauce)

Subtle and complex in flavor, this chicken is elegant enough to serve company. Don't be daunted by the long list of ingredients; the dish can be made in only about an hour. It's absolutely wonderful in warmed fresh corn tortillas with a topping of guacamole and sour cream; you might also serve it over rice or with a side dish of stewed beans.

> **1 (3-lb.) broiler-fryer chicken, cut for frying**
> **About 2 cups chicken broth**
> **2 tablespoons juice from pickled jalapeño chiles**
> **1 large onion, quartered**
> **6 to 8 leaves dark green lettuce (romaine, leaf lettuce or outer**
> **   leaves of iceberg lettuce)**
> **1/2 cup fresh cilantro leaves**
> **1 cup flat-leaf parsley sprigs**
> **1 large clove garlic**
> **6 fresh or pickled jalapeño chiles, stemmed**
> **2 tablespoons virgin olive oil**
> **1 cup ground almonds**
> **Salt to taste, if desired**
> **12 corn tortillas, warmed, or 3 to 4 cups hot cooked rice**
> **Guacamole, page 20, if desired**
> **2 cups sour cream, if desired**

Place chicken in a single layer in a large pot. Pour in broth and jalapeño juice. Bring to a boil, then reduce heat, cover and simmer 35 to 45 minutes or just until tender. Cool in cooking broth. Lift chicken from broth (reserve broth); discard skin and bones and tear meat in bite-size pieces. To prepare sauce, in a food processor or blender, process onion, lettuce, cilantro, parsley, garlic and jalapeños until quite smooth. Add about 1 cup chicken cooking broth, a few tablespoons at a time, until mixture has the consistency of whipping cream. Set aside. Heat oil in a medium, heavy saucepan, then add almonds. Lightly cook and stir over medium-low heat 3 to 5 minutes—just long enough to slightly toast almonds and heighten their flavor. Add green sauce and cooled chicken and simmer together 10 to 15 minutes or until flavors are blended and sauce is hot. Taste and adjust seasonings; add salt, if desired. Serve in warmed tortillas or over rice, topped with Guacamole and sour cream, if desired. Makes 6 servings.

Chicken Cutlets with Five Peppers

So mouthwatering for the ease of preparation! You can make these tender, juicy chicken breasts as fiery or tame as you wish by adjusting the quantity of chiles and pepper you use. Serve with a simple vegetable dish and a crisp salad of your choice.

> 2 whole (1-1/4-lb.) chicken breasts, skinned, boned, split,
>   pounded very thin
> 1/4 cup olive oil
> 1 large or 2 medium cloves garlic, crushed
> 2 teaspoons minced fresh rosemary or 1 teaspoon dried leaf
>   rosemary, crushed
> 3 tablespoons finely minced fresh or pickled jalapeño chiles
> 3 tablespoons caribe (crushed Northern New Mexico red chile)
> 1 tablespoon pickled green peppercorns, crushed
> 1/4 cup unsalted butter
> 1 medium or 1/2 large green bell pepper, cut in long, thin
>   strips
> 1 medium or 1/2 large red bell pepper, cut in long, thin strips

Brush chicken breasts generously with oil (reserve remaining oil), then sprinkle with garlic, rosemary, jalapeños, caribe and green peppercorns; press seasonings into meat. Melt butter in a large, heavy skillet; add reserved oil not used for brushing chicken. When fat is very hot, add green and red bell pepper and cook until limp. Add chicken; cook until golden on bottom, then turn and cook until second side is golden and meat is no longer pink in center. Serve on warmed plates. Makes 4 servings.

Double-Mustard-Coated Baked Chicken

With its crunchy, tingly-tart coating of mustard, mustard seeds, pepper and herbs, this baked chicken is especially great for warm weather. Serve with a pasta salad or a vegetable and thick slices of warm, crisp-crusted bread slathered with butter.

> 3 tablespoons unsalted butter, melted
> 1/3 cup olive oil
> 3 tablespoons mustard seeds
> 3 tablespoons Dijon-style mustard
> 2 teaspoons freshly ground white pepper
> 1 tablespoon dried leaf tarragon
> 2 teaspoons dried dill weed
> 1 (3-lb.) broiler-fryer chicken, cut for frying

In a blender or food processor, process melted butter, oil, mustard seeds, mustard, white pepper, tarragon and dill until blended. (Or beat together with a wire whisk.) Pour marinade into a large, shallow roasting pan; roll each piece of chicken in marinade. Let stand at least 30 minutes at room temperature. Preheat oven to 350F (175C). Bake chicken in marinade, uncovered, 1 hour or until coating is crisp and meat is tender; baste once after 30 minutes. Makes 4 servings.

Hotter than Hell
Buffet Barbecued Chicken

The superb spicy sauce that tops this chicken can do wonders for most any meat—and it's party perfect, since its flavor only improves with age. You can just keep reheating the chicken if your guests don't all come to the table at once, as often happens at a swim party, after tennis, and so forth. For a real treat, serve with Red Hot Warm Potato Salad, page 41.

> **1/4 cup bacon drippings from maple-syrup-glazed bacon; or 1/4 cup drippings from regular bacon plus 1 tablespoon maple syrup**
> **1 cup chopped onion**
> **4 large cloves garlic, minced**
> **1 (44-oz.) bottle ketchup**
> **1/4 cup cider vinegar**
> **1/4 cup dark molasses**
> **1/4 cup Worcestershire sauce**
> **1/2 cup flat beer**
> **2 tablespoons coarse-grained Dijon-style mustard**
> **1 tablespoon liquid smoke**
> **1 teaspoon pequin quebrado (up to 1 tablespoon for really hot sauce)**
> **1 teaspoon freshly ground black pepper**
> **1 tablespoon finely minced pickled jalapeño chiles (3 or more tablespoons for really hot sauce)**
> **2 (3-lb.) broiler-fryer chickens, cut for frying**

To make barbecue sauce, melt bacon drippings in a heavy 3-quart or larger pot. Then add onion and garlic and cook about 3 minutes. Add ketchup, vinegar, molasses, Worcestershire sauce, beer, mustard, liquid smoke, pequin, pepper and jalapeños. Stir well, then cover and simmer 30 minutes to combine flavors. Meanwhile, preheat oven to 400F (205C). Place chicken pieces, skin side up, in 2 large, shallow roasting pans. Bake 30 to 40 minutes or until skin is parched, then turn pieces over and reduce oven temperature to 350F (175C). Generously baste each piece with sauce, using 3 cups of the sauce; bake 15 minutes longer. Turn; baste skin side with pan drippings and 1 cup more sauce. Bake 20 to 30 minutes longer or until sauce is glazed and tips of chicken pieces are lightly browned. Makes 8 to 12 servings, depending on the rest of the menu.

Secret Siamese Chicken

Chiles, fresh ginger and garlic pack a powerful punch in this dish—yet the blend of flavors is suprisingly subtle. If possible, get the tiny, thin, fresh green chiles sold in Asian markets; otherwise, substitute caribe or any other crushed very hot chile. And do be sure to use fresh basil if you can get it.

> **1 tablespoon chopped fresh ginger**
> **2 cloves garlic, finely minced**
> **2 tablespoons dark soy sauce**
> **1/4 cup dry sherry**
> **1/4 cup vegetable oil**
> **1 whole (1-1/4-lb.) chicken breast, skinned, boned (or about 14 oz. skinned, boned chicken breast), cut in 1-inch cubes**
> **2 tablespoons vegetable oil**
> **1/4 pound fresh snow peas, cut diagonally in thirds**
> **1/4 pound pearl onions, each cut in 3 or 4 thin slices**
> **1/4 cup minced fresh basil or 2 tablespoons dried leaf basil, crushed**
> **2 to 4 teaspoons finely minced fresh Oriental hot green chile, caribe (crushed Northern New Mexico red chile) or other hot chile**
> **Hot cooked rice**
> **Hot Hot Oil, page 141, if desired**

Combine ginger, garlic, soy sauce, sherry and 1/4 cup vegetable oil in a shallow glass or stainless steel bowl, then add chicken cubes and stir well. Cover and let stand 2 hours at room temperature (or refrigerate at least 8 hours), stirring at least twice. About 10 minutes before serving, heat a wok or very large, heavy skillet until medium-hot, then add 2 tablespoons vegetable oil. When oil is hot, but not smoking, drain chicken cubes, reserving marinade; add to pan and stir-fry about 3 minutes or until meat has almost lost its pink color. Remove chicken to a warmed platter. Add snow peas, onions and reserved marinade to pan; stir-fry about 2 minutes. Turn off heat, then evenly mix in chicken, basil and chile. Pour onto platter. Serve over rice; offer Hot Hot Oil to add to individual servings, if desired. Makes 3 or 4 servings.

Spicy Summer Chicken Stir-Fry

As summery as a day in June, this medley of light greens and yellows is as flavorful as it's pretty. Serve with the salad of your choice—I like orange or grapefruit slices and red onion rings with a honey and poppy seed dressing.

> 3 whole (1-1/4-lbs. each) chicken breasts, skinned, boned (or about 2-1/2-lbs. boned, skinned chicken breasts), cut in 1- to 2-inch-long strips about 1/2 inch wide
> 3/4 teaspoon salt (or to taste)
> 3 tablespoons unsalted butter
> 1 small onion, sliced, separated into rings
> 2 or 3 cloves garlic, minced
> 2 zucchini, each about 6 inches long and 1-1/2 inches in diameter, thinly sliced
> 2 yellow crookneck squash, each about 6 inches long and 1-1/2 inches in diameter at thickest point, thinly sliced
> 6 fresh New Mexico hot green chiles, parched (see page 9), peeled, seeded, chopped
> 1/4 cup chopped fresh cilantro

Sprinkle chicken with salt and stir together. Melt butter in a large wok or very large, heavy skillet over a medium-high heat. Add chicken strips and stir-fry until meat begins to lose its pink color. Then push chicken to 1 side, away from hot center of pan. Add onion and stir-fry until it barely begins to get limp; then add garlic, zucchini and crookneck squash. Stir-fry 2 to 3 minutes or just until color of squash heightens. Add chiles and cilantro; stir chicken back into center of pan. Stir-fry until chicken is done and squash is still slightly crisp. Makes 6 to 8 servings.

Hot Drunken Thighs

So wonderfully flavored, the Devil himself could not have played a better hand in the seasonings! This dish is my improved version of basic deviled chicken, good hot or cold. Serve it with favorite vegetables or salads; Red Hot Warm Potato Salad, page 41, is a perfect partner. The chicken is great for picnics, too (transport it in a rigid container).

2 eggs or 4 egg yolks
1/2 cup vodka
10 dashes liquid hot-pepper sauce
1-1/2 teaspoons freshly ground white pepper
1 teaspoon dry mustard
12 chicken thighs
2 quarts vegetable oil for deep-frying
1 cup all-purpose flour
1/4 teaspoon freshly ground white pepper
1 teaspoon salt
1 cup seasoned fine dry bread crumbs (or 1 cup plain fine dry
bread crumbs mixed with 1/4 teaspoon each onion salt, garlic
powder and ground oregano)
Liquid hot-pepper sauce, sherry pepper sauce or other hot
sauce to taste

Beat eggs or egg yolks in a large, shallow bowl. Gradually stir in vodka. Stir in 10 dashes hot-pepper sauce, 1-1/2 teaspoons white pepper and mustard. Then add chicken thighs, rolling each several times to coat evenly. Let stand at least 30 minutes or up to 2 hours at room temperature, frequently spooning marinade over each thigh. In a deep-fat fryer, heat oil to 350F (175C). Meanwhile, mix flour, 1/4 teaspoon white pepper and salt. To fry, coat each thigh in flour mixture, then dip back into marinade, then coat in crumbs. Add thighs to hot oil, 2 to 4 at a time; be careful not to add so many that the oil temperature drops. Cook 10 to 12 minutes or until meat near bone is no longer pink. Drain on paper towels. Serve with liquid hot-pepper sauce, sherry pepper sauce or other hot sauce of your choice. Makes 6 servings.

Spaghetti Diablo

The Devil's own choice! Sprightly and subtly spicy—with the potential for real heat, if that's how you like it (just add more pequin). I was given this recipe by Amy White, a Californian whom I met in Albuquerque.

> 1/2 to 1 tablespoon unsalted butter, room temperature
> 8 ounces dried capellini
> 2 tablespoons unsalted butter
> 1 onion, finely chopped
> 1 clove garlic, minced
> 1 cup fresh mushrooms, sliced
> 2-1/2 cups peeled, cooked fresh tomatoes
> 1/2 teaspoon salt (or to taste)
> Freshly ground black pepper to taste
> 1 tablespoon sugar
> 1 teaspoon pequin quebrado (or to taste)
> 1 cup diced cooked chicken
> 1/4 cup freshly grated Parmesan cheese
> 1/4 cup freshly grated Romano cheese

Butter a 2- to 3-quart casserole, using 1/2 to 1 tablespoon butter. Preheat oven to 350F (175C). Following package directions, cook capellini in boiling water just until tender to bite. Then drain and pour into buttered casserole. Melt 2 tablespoons butter in a medium skillet. Add onion, garlic and mushrooms and cook until onion is limp and slightly golden. Stir tomatoes, salt, pepper, sugar and pequin into onion-mushroom mixture; simmer, stirring, a few minutes. Taste and adjust seasonings. Add sauce and chicken to spaghetti; toss to mix well. Mix cheeses and sprinkle over top. Bake, uncovered, 20 to 30 minutes or until cheese is melted and slightly golden. Makes 4 to 6 servings.

Roast Turkey
With Garbanzo-Chorizo Stuffing

The flavors of chorizo, garbanzos and *salsa verde* complement mild-tasting turkey deliciously. You can cook the garbanzos a day or two in advance; be sure to make the cilantro-laced salsa about an hour before serving.

Garbanzo-Chorizo Stuffing, see below
1 (15- to 17-lb.) turkey
1 tablespoon salt
1/2 cup unsalted butter (or more, as needed), melted
Salsa Verde, see below

Garbanzo-Chorizo Stuffing:
1-1/2 pounds chorizo, casings removed, thinly sliced
1 recipe Garbanzos, page 155, or 2 (15-oz.) cans garbanzos,
    drained
1/2 cup unsalted butter
2 onions, chopped
2 large or 3 medium cloves garlic, minced
1 pound chicken livers, trimmed, quartered
1 pound turkey livers, trimmed, quartered
2 tablespoons minced parsley
2 teaspoons salt (or to taste)

Salsa Verde:
1 pound fresh tomatillos, husks and stems removed, steamed
    over boiling water until soft (about 5 minutes); or 1 (13-oz.)
    can tomatillos, undrained
1 clove garlic
4 fresh mild green chiles, parched (see page 9), peeled, seeded;
    or 1 (7-oz.) can whole green chiles
1 cup fresh cilantro sprigs
1/2 onion, chopped

Prepare stuffing; set aside. Preheat oven to 400F (205C). Rub turkey inside and out with salt. Stuff neck and body cavities of turkey; truss with skewers and cotton thread. Set turkey, breast up, on a rack in a roasting pan. Roast 3-1/2 to 4 hours or until skin is golden brown and a meat thermometer inserted in thickest part of thigh (not touching bone) registers 185F, 85C. (Temperature of stuffing should be 170F, 80C.) During roasting, brush turkey with melted butter every 15 minutes until drippings collect, then baste with drippings. About 30 minutes before turkey is done, prepare Salsa Verde. When turkey is done, let rest about 25 minutes to let juices settle; then carve. Serve sliced turkey with stuffing and salsa. Makes about 15 servings.

Garbanzo-Chorizo Stuffing:
Cook chorizo in a large skillet over medium-high heat until lightly browned. Drain off all but 2 tablespoons fat; add garbanzos and cook about 15 minutes or until browned. Remove from heat. In another skillet, melt butter. Add onions and garlic and cook until onions are soft. Add livers; cook, stirring, until livers are crisp and brown on the outside. Mash livers coarsely with a fork or potato masher; combine liver mixture with garbanzo mixture. Stir in parsley; season with salt.

Salsa Verde:
Combine all ingredients in a food processor or blender; process until smooth. Let stand about 1 hour at room temperature to blend flavors before serving.

Turkey Mole

A traditional holiday dish in Mexico, often served at Christmas and on other red-letter days, turkey mole is a good choice any time you want a special entree. My uncle, who lived in Mexico, perfected this mole sauce; I'm pleased to share his very favorite dinner dish with you.

2 tablespoons vegetable oil (or more, as needed)
1-1/2 pounds turkey thighs or breast
Chicken broth
2 dried poblano or New Mexico chiles, stemmed, or 1/4 cup
　　ground pure New Mexico hot red chile
1 red-ripe tomato, peeled, seeded, quartered
8 whole blanched almonds
1/2 corn tortilla or 3 tortilla chips
1/2 small onion, cut in chunks
1 tablespoon raisins
4 teaspoons sesame seeds, toasted
1 teaspoon pequin quebrado
1/4 teaspoon anise seeds
1/4 teaspoon ground cinnamon
1/4 teaspoon ground cloves
1/2 ounce unsweetened chocolate
1/2 to 1 tablespoon unsalted butter, room temperature
1 lime, cut lengthwise in 6 wedges

Heat oil in a large, heavy skillet; add turkey and cook until browned on all sides, turning as needed. Set skillet aside without washing. Place browned turkey in a saucepan; add just enough broth to cover turkey. Bring to a boil; then reduce heat, cover and simmer about 1 hour or until turkey is tender. Cool in cooking broth. Lift turkey from broth (reserve broth); discard skin and bones and tear meat (do not cut) into large chunks. Set aside. Soak chiles in boiling water to cover until softened. Place chiles and soaking liquid (or ground chile) in a blender or food processor. Add tomato, almonds, tortilla or tortilla chips, onion, raisins, 1 teaspoon sesame seeds, pequin, anise seeds, cinnamon and cloves. Process until smoothly pureed (if using ground chile, add a little hot water as needed). Pour mixture into reserved skillet; cook over low heat about 5 minutes, stirring constantly. If mixture seems dry, add a bit of oil. Stir in chocolate and 1 cup turkey cooking broth. Stir until chocolate is melted. Taste and adjust seasonings. Preheat oven to 350F (175C). Butter a 2-quart baking dish and place turkey in it. Pour mole sauce evenly over turkey, cover and bake at least 1 hour or until turkey has absorbed most of sauce; stir well after 30 minutes. To serve, sprinkle with remaining 3 teaspoons sesame seeds and encircle with lime wedges. Makes 4 to 6 servings.

Meats

The assertive flavors of red meats—pork, lamb, veal and beef—stand up deliciously to spicy-hot seasoning. From Perky Porky Pigtails to Red, White & Blue Lamb Chops to Tres y Tres Carne, this chapter captures some of my all-time favorite flavor combinations.

Innovation has run high here; almost every recipe was created just for this book. The remaining few are old family favorites and recipes from friends, revised and sparked with plenty of extra heat. Flames will dance from your tongue when you sample them!

Fiery Mediterranean Roast Pork

The seasonings are so strong, you might be afraid to try this—but don't be! The rich, flavorful blend encrusting the roast is savory and magnificent. Serve with a simple side dish of *al dente* capellini (thin spaghetti), tossed with sweet butter, olive oil, minced parsley and Parmesan, then drizzled with the pork pan juices. For buffet service or a formal presentation, encircle the pork with the capellini.

2 heads garlic (20 to 24 cloves), separated into cloves, peeled
1/4 cup chopped fresh rosemary or 2-1/2 tablespoons dried leaf
    rosemary
2 teaspoons salt
2 tablespoons freshly ground black pepper
1-1/2 teaspoons caribe (crushed Northern New Mexico red
    chile)
1/4 cup extra-virgin olive oil
1 (5-lb.) bone-in pork loin roast

In a blender or food processor, process garlic, rosemary, salt, pepper and caribe until pureed. With motor running, slowly pour in oil; process until a paste forms. Place pork in a roasting pan, bone down; then coat with rosemary mixture. Let stand at least 2 hours at room temperature to allow flavors to penetrate. Preheat oven to 400F (205C); roast pork 15 minutes, then reduce oven temperature to 325F (165C) and continue to roast 1-1/2 hours longer or until a meat thermometer inserted in thickest part of pork (not touching bone) registers 170F (75C). Remove from oven and let stand 20 to 30 minutes to let juices settle. To serve, cut in medium-thick slices, cutting straight into bone so each serving will have some of the crust. Makes 8 servings.

Double Cilantro Roast Pork

This is a grand company dish with a most delightful flavor. Crushed cilantro (coriander) seeds make a crunchy, exotic-tasting coating for the pork; minced fresh cilantro leaves blend with honey, caribe and lime juice for a marvelous sauce. And because the roast is so easy to prepare, you'll have plenty of time free for hosting your party. For an attractive presentation, surround the pork with capellini; drizzle some of the sauce over the pasta, reserving the rest to spoon over the meat at the table. A tartly dressed salad and perhaps a vegetable side dish nicely complete the meal.

1/3 cup coriander seeds, crushed
1-1/4 cups fine dry bread crumbs
3/4 cup extra-virgin olive oil
1 teaspoon freshly cracked black pepper
3/4 teaspoon salt (or to taste)
1 (3-lb.) boneless pork loin roast
1 red bell pepper, cut in small squares
1/2 cup caribe (crushed Northern New Mexico red chile)
1 cup honey
1/2 cup fresh lime juice
1/4 cup minced fresh cilantro

Combine coriander seeds, crumbs, oil, black pepper and salt. Mix well. Then preheat oven to 400F (205C). Lay pork roast out flat, inside (cut side) up. Place about 1/3 of crumb mixture on pork, evenly distributing it across surface, then roll up meat and tie securely in 2 or 3 places with kitchen cord. Place roast, seam side down, on a rack in a shallow roasting pan; coat with remaining crumb mixture. Roast 15 minutes; then reduce oven temperature to 325F (165C) and roast 1 hour longer or until a meat thermometer inserted in center of meat registers 170F (75C). Remove from oven; let stand about 20 minutes to let juices settle. Meanwhile, prepare sauce: in a small saucepan, combine bell pepper, caribe, honey and lime juice. Cook, stirring often, about 15 minutes or until sauce is slightly thickened and looks somewhat glazed. Remove from heat and mix in cilantro. Serve sauce in a separate bowl to spoon over meat. Makes about 8 servings.

Hot as a Pistol Pulled Pork

Straight from South Carolina, this typical regional barbecue is especially fiery. A slowly grilled pork butt that's pulled into strands for serving in sandwiches, it's vastly different from traditional barbecued ribs basted with a tomato-based sauce—in fact, local feuds have even erupted over which is better! You might enjoy this authentic barbecue served Carolina-style: mix some of the searing-hot pork baste into a bowl of coleslaw, then tuck the shredded pork into warm, soft, freshly baked buns and top with spoonfuls of the "heated" slaw.

> **3 cups cider vinegar**
> **2 tablespoons Worcestershire sauce**
> **3 tablespoons finely ground black pepper**
> **2 tablespoons liquid hot-pepper sauce**
> **3/4 teaspoon salt (or to taste)**
> **1 (3-lb.) pork butt or shoulder roast**

Combine vinegar, Worcestershire sauce, pepper, hot-pepper sauce and salt. Mix well. Let stand at least 1 hour at room temperature before using. (Never use this sauce as a marinade—it's too hot!) Meanwhile, prepare grill; it's best to use a covered smoker type. If none is available, you may use any charcoal-type grill, but be sure to cover the pork with heavy foil to equalize the temperature. Since the roast grills for a long time at a low temperature, prepare a large bed of coals. When coals are covered with white ash, spread them out to make a bed. Position grill 5 inches above coals. Let grill heat about 2 minutes, scouring it with a metal brush, if necessary; when grill is hot, set roast in place. Sear 2 to 5 minutes on each side or until uniformly browned, then brush generously with baste. Close hood and cook 1 to 1-1/2 hours or until meat is tender enough to fall from bone; turn roast over and baste every 15 minutes. Transfer to a large cutting board. When slightly cooled, use 2 large forks or your hands to pull meat into shreds (this is why it's called "pulled pork"). Serve as desired or as suggested in recipe introduction, above. Makes 6 to 8 servings.

Carne Adobada with a Halo of Blue Cornbread

So luscious and unusual! Pretty as a picture, too, with tender pork strips in bright red chile sauce both filling and encircling a ring of blue cornbread layered with two cheeses. Get the pork in the oven first, then mix up the cornbread and bake it alongside the meat; pork and cornbread should be done at about the same time.

> 1/2 cup caribe (crushed Northern New Mexico red chile)
> 2 cups water
> 1 teaspoon salt
> 2 cloves garlic
> 1 tablespoon ground oregano, preferably Mexican
> 1 tablespoon ground cumin
> 2-1/2 pounds pork loin chops, cut about 1/2 inch thick, trimmed of excess fat
> About 1 tablespoon unsalted butter, room temperature
> 1 cup blue cornmeal
> 1-1/2 teaspoons baking powder
> 3/4 teaspoon salt
> 2 eggs
> 2/3 cup unsalted butter, melted
> 1-1/2 cups dairy sour cream
> 1 (1-lb.) can whole-kernel corn, drained
> 4 ounces Monterey Jack cheese, cut in 1/4-inch-thick slices
> 4 ounces Cheddar cheese, cut in 1/4-inch-thick slices
> 1/2 cup chopped onion

Preheat oven to 350F (175C). Combine caribe, water, salt, garlic, oregano and cumin in a food processor or blender and process until well blended. Pour a little of the chile puree into a 9" x 13" or other large baking pan, then add a layer of pork chops. Add more puree, then remaining chops, then remaining puree. Cover and bake 30 minutes; uncover and bake 30 minutes longer or until sauce is thickened and meat is fork-tender. Meanwhile, prepare cornbread. First, generously butter a 9-inch ring mold; line bottom only of mold with waxed paper. Butter paper. In a large bowl, stir together cornmeal, baking powder and salt. In another bowl, beat eggs to blend, then beat in 2/3 cup melted butter and 1 cup sour cream. Combine egg mixture with dry ingredients and stir just until blended. Gently fold in corn. Pour 1/3 of batter into prepared ring mold, then alternate slices of jack and Cheddar cheese on top of batter. Pour on remaining 2/3 of batter and bake about 45 minutes or until bread is golden brown on top and a wooden pick inserted in center (not down through cheese) comes out clean. Cool in mold on a cooling rack 10 minutes. When pork is tender, remove from oven. Remove and discard bones from chops and cut meat into 1/2-inch-thick strips. Return meat strips to sauce in baking pan. To serve, gently run a dull knife around edges of partially cooled cornbread; then invert onto a platter. Lift off mold and peel off paper. Spoon 2/3 of pork mixture into center of ring; spoon remaining 1/3 around ring. Garnish pork mixture with chopped onion and 1/2 cup sour cream. Serve hot. Makes 6 to 8 servings.

Perky Porky Pigtails

A distant (and very feisty) cousin of fettuccine Alfredo, this full-flavored dish is one you can never serve often enough—if my family is any indication! They tasted it for the first time when I created it for this book; now it's one of their favorites. Serve with side dishes of Parmesan cheese and caribe and a crisp green salad with a tart dressing.

> **2 tablespoons unsalted butter**
> **2 large cloves garlic, minced**
> **1/2 pound boneless pork steak (cut 1 inch thick), cut in strips 2**
>   **to 3 inches long and 1/4 inch wide**
> **1 tablespoon caribe (crushed Northern New Mexico red chile),**
>   **or to taste**
> **1 pound dried fusilli (corkscrew spaghetti)**
> **1/2 cup unsalted butter**
> **1/2 cup whipping cream**
> **1 cup freshly grated Parmesan cheese**
> **1 tablespoon ground pure California mild red chile**
> **1/2 cup Italian-style pimento-pepper piccalilli**

Melt 2 tablespoons butter in a heavy skillet; add garlic and cook until just beginning to turn golden. Then add pork strips and cook quickly, turning often, about 5 minutes or until pork begins to brown. Sprinkle with caribe and continue to cook until meat is quite browned and crisp. Remove from skillet; keep warm in a 250F (120C) oven along with 4 to 8 serving plates. Following package directions, cook pasta in boiling water just until tender to bite. Drain well, return to cooking pan and cover. In skillet used to cook pork, melt 1/2 cup butter; add cream and 1/2 cup cheese. Cook until bubbly, stirring to free browned bits from bottom of skillet. Stir in ground chile, taste and adjust seasonings. Drizzle sauce over pasta, add pork strips and piccalilli and toss gently, sprinkling with remaining 1/2 cup cheese. Continue to stir carefully until well blended. Serve hot, on warmed plates. Makes about 8 appetizer servings, 4 to 6 main-dish servings.

Puerco con Chile

The robust flavors of chiles and pork marry beautifully in this quick-to-fix dish. You really can use any type of chile you like; I prefer to use a green chile in the sauce and serve a hotter red chile—as hot as my guests can handle!—alongside the pork strips. Serve *puerco con chile* as a hearty snack, tucked inside a burrito, soft taco, omelet or crepe; or serve over rice as a main course.

> **2 pounds boneless pork shoulder, cut in 2" x 1/2" strips about 3/4 inch thick**
>
> **1 tablespoon ground pure New Mexico hot red chile, caribe (crushed Northern New Mexico red chile) or pequin quebrado**
>
> **1/4 cup unsalted butter**
>
> **3 cloves garlic, minced**
>
> **3 green onions, thinly sliced**
>
> **6 fresh New Mexico hot green chiles, parched, (see page 9), peeled, seeded, cut in strips**
>
> **1-1/2 pounds red-ripe tomatoes, peeled, cut in 1/2-inch-thick wedges**
>
> **Additional caribe (crushed Northern New Mexico red chile) or pequin quebrado, if desired**

Dredge pork strips in ground chile, caribe, or pequin. Melt butter in a heavy skillet; add garlic and green onions and cook until lightly browned. Push to 1 side; add chile-dredged pork strips and cook until crisp and brown. Add green-chile strips; cook, stirring, a few minutes longer or until chiles are warm. Then add tomatoes; cook 5 to 10 minutes or until tomato juice begins to cook down. Serve immediately; accompany with additional caribe or pequin, if desired. Makes about 4 servings.

Lasagne à la Baroque

After thoroughly enjoying this lasagne in the Baroque Restaurant in New York City ages ago (September, 1967, to be exact), I chased after the chef to get the recipe, then spiced it up—and here it is!

2/3 pound hot Italian sausages, casings removed, thinly sliced
2 tablespoons Italian crushed hot red pepper
1 teaspoon anise seeds
2 tablespoons unsalted butter
1 cup fresh mushrooms, sliced
2 medium red-ripe tomatoes, peeled, thinly sliced
1 (12-oz.) package wide green lasagne noodles
1/3 cup unsalted butter
1/3 cup all-purpose flour
2-1/4 cups light cream
Salt to taste
1/4 teaspoon liquid hot-pepper sauce or cayenne pepper (or to taste)
1/4 teaspoon freshly ground white pepper (or to taste)
Freshly grated nutmeg to taste
About 1 tablespoon unsalted butter, room temperature
8 ounces mozzarella cheese, thinly sliced
1/2 cup freshly grated Parmesan cheese

Place sausage slices in a heavy skillet and sprinkle with 1-1/2 tablespoons crushed red pepper. Cook until sausages are lightly browned; drain off fat and sprinkle sausages with anise seeds, then take out of skillet and set aside. Wipe out skillet. Melt 2 tablespoons butter in skillet; add mushrooms and cook until mushrooms are lightly browned and all liquid has evaporated. Add tomatoes; cook just until tomatoes soften and begin to release juice. Set tomato mixture aside. Following package directions, cook lasagne in boiling water just until tender to bite. Meanwhile, prepare cream sauce: heat 1/3 cup butter in a skillet until light golden, then stir in flour until well blended. Using a whisk, stir in cream; whisk until sauce is slightly thickened. Season with salt, hot-pepper sauce or cayenne, white pepper and nutmeg. Remove from heat. Drain cooked lasagne well. Preheat oven to 375F (190C); generously butter a large, shallow casserole, at least 9" x 13". Layer ingredients in casserole as follows: drained noodles, sausage slices, mushroom-tomato mixture, more noodles, mozzarella cheese and cream sauce. Repeat layers until all ingredients are used, finishing with cream sauce. Sprinkle with Parmesan cheese and dust with remaining 1/2 tablespoon crushed red pepper. Bake, uncovered, 30 minutes or until bubbly. Makes 6 generous servings.

Lively Leg of Spring Lamb

Spruce up leg of lamb with a mustard-herb coating and serve with a trio of accompaniments: homemade Jalapeño Jelly, mint jelly and gravy made from the pan juices.

1 (7- to 8-lb.) leg of spring lamb, trimmed of excess fat
2 large cloves garlic, slivered
4 teaspoons Dijon-style mustard
1 teaspoon minced fresh rosemary or 1/2 teaspoon dried leaf
    rosemary, crushed
1 teaspoon freshly ground black pepper or caribe (crushed
    Northern New Mexico red chile), or to taste
1/4 cup all-purpose flour
Salt
Jalapeño Jelly, page 149, or purchased jalapeño jelly
Mint jelly

Using a very sharp knife with a pointed tip, pierce lamb evenly all over; insert slivers of garlic in slits. Set lamb on a rack in a roasting pan; coat with mustard and sprinkle with rosemary and pepper or caribe. Preheat oven to 425F (230C) 5 minutes; then roast lamb 20 minutes. Reduce oven temperature to 325F (165C) and roast 2 hours longer or until a meat thermometer inserted in thickest part of lamb (not touching bone) registers 150F (65C) for medium. To serve, remove lamb to a large platter; let stand about 20 minutes to let juices settle. Meanwhile, sprinkle flour over pan drippings and stir to mix well. Place over medium heat and stir until bubbly; then add enough water to make a smooth, medium-thick gravy. Season gravy with salt and additional pepper or caribe, if desired. Serve lamb with side dishes of jellies and gravy. Makes 10 to 12 servings.

Cajun Lamb Chops

Inspired by the "blackened dishes" so popular in Cajun cooking, these are spitefully hot and really best grilled out of doors. If the weather won't permit outdoor cooking, wait for a sunnier day unless you have a really powerful fan above your range to pull the smoke off.

2 teaspoons onion powder
2 teaspoons pequin quebrado or cayenne pepper
1-1/2 teaspoons garlic juice or powder
1 teaspoon ground thyme
1 teaspoon dry mustard
Freshly ground black pepper to taste
8 lamb loin chops, cut at least 1-1/4 inches thick
1/2 cup unsalted butter (or more, as needed)

Prepare a bed of very hot coals. Heat a very large, heavy skillet over hot coals or high heat of range until at the smoking point. Meanwhile, combine onion powder, pequin or cayenne, garlic juice or powder, thyme, mustard and several grinds of black pepper. Set lamb chops on a large baking sheet and trim off any excess fat or membrane. Melt butter in a small saucepan and brush 1 side of each chop; then evenly divide half the spice mixture among chops, gently rubbing mixture into each. Turn chops over and brush again with butter; rub with remaining spice mixture. Add remaining melted butter to smoking-hot skillet. Immediately add coated lamb chops, making certain that skillet stays incredibly hot. If skillet begins to cool as you continue adding chops, then cook chops a portion at a time (keep cooked chops warm in a low oven). Grill very quickly, allowing only 1 to 2 minutes per side; turn each chop only once and add more butter as needed. Chops should be charred on the outside and still rare on the inside. Serve hot, on warmed plates. Makes 4 servings.

Red, White & Blue Lamb Chops

Surprisingly flavorful, these patriotic chops are also quite easy to make. Do be sure to include the whole new potatoes—they're so delicious with the rich sauce.

4 (8-oz.) lamb shoulder chops
2 tablespoons caribe (crushed Northern New Mexico red chile)
4 ounces blue cheese, crumbled
Freshly ground black pepper to taste
1 cup double-strength beef broth
12 very small thin-skinned potatoes, peeled

Preheat oven to 350F (175C). Trim excess fat from chops, then arrange chops in a single layer in a shallow baking pan. Evenly divide caribe among chops, crushing it into both sides of each one. Sprinkle chops with cheese and several grinds of pepper, then pour broth over all. Bake, uncovered, 1-3/4 hours, basting generously every 30 minutes. Then cook potatoes in boiling water about 20 minutes or until tender; drain and arrange around chops. Spoon lots of pan juices over potatoes; continue to bake 15 minutes longer or until chops are fork-tender. Serve sauce separately to spoon over chops and potatoes. Makes 4 servings.

My Favorite Lamb Curry with Condiments

I have worked to perfect this recipe for almost longer than I'd like to admit. I find this particular blend of flavors especially appealing, and it seems to suit everyone else very well, too. Do be sure to use only the very freshest of curry powders, preferably an imported powder (purchased at a specialty shop) or even one that you've made yourself. The grocery-store brands are often terribly stale and contain far too much turmeric.

3 pounds boneless lamb shoulder, cut in 1- to 1-1/2-inch chunks
1/2 cup all-purpose flour
2 cloves garlic, minced
2 large onions, chopped medium-fine
3/4 cup unsalted butter
2 large apples, unpeeled, cored, cut in 1/2-inch cubes
3 tablespoons curry powder (or to taste)
1/4 cup packed dark brown sugar
1/3 cup raisins
2 tablespoons Worcestershire sauce
2 lemons, unpeeled, thinly sliced, seeds removed
1/4 cup sweetened shredded coconut
3/4 cup chopped black walnuts
1/2 teaspoon grated lime peel
2 teaspoons salt (or to taste)
2 cups water
Hot cooked rice
Condiments: Sieved hard-cooked eggs, chutney, peanuts, sweetened flaked or shredded coconut, raisins, grated lemon or lime peel, pineapple chunks, sliced bananas

Dredge lamb in flour; set aside. Combine garlic, onions and butter in a very large skillet; stir over medium heat until onions are lightly browned. Add floured lamb and cook until lightly browned all over, stirring as needed to brown evenly. Add apples, curry powder, brown sugar, raisins, Worcestershire sauce, lemon slices, coconut, black walnuts, lime peel, salt and water. Bring to a boil; then reduce heat to low, cover and simmer about 1 hour or until meat is fork-tender. Serve curry with rice and your choice of condiments. Makes 6 servings.

Hotter than Hell Veal Roast

This luscious oven pot roast requires very little advance preparation. Mild, tender veal, heartily spiced with garlic, herbs and caribe, slowly roasts to tenderness with baby potatoes, onions and miniature carrots. It's a delicious dish that's certain to be popular with you and yours.

**1 (4-lb.) boneless veal shoulder roast, trimmed of excess fat and
    tissue**
4 cloves garlic, minced
**1 tablespoon caribe (crushed Northern New Mexico red chile),
    or to taste**
2 teaspoons dried leaf sage, crushed
1-1/2 teaspoons dried leaf tarragon, crushed
2 teaspoons dried leaf rosemary, crushed
**3 or 4 fresh or pickled jalapeño chiles, cut in long, thin strips,
    if desired**
12 very small red thin-skinned potatoes, scrubbed
12 very small carrots, scrubbed
12 small whole onions, peeled
1/2 cup unsalted butter
Freshly ground black pepper to taste

Preheat oven to 400F (205C). Lay veal roast inside (cut side) up and rub with half each of the garlic, caribe and herbs; then turn over and rub with remaining garlic, caribe and herbs. Turn cut side up again; sprinkle with jalapeño strips, if desired. Roll up meat and tie securely with kitchen cord at 2-inch intervals. Place meat, seam side down, in a roasting pan. Roast 15 minutes, then remove from oven and surround with potatoes, carrots and onions. Dot vegetables with butter; sprinkle generously with pepper. Reduce oven temperature to 325F (165C). Return roast to oven. Roast 2 hours longer, turning vegetables over and basting with pan juices frequently. After 2 hours, vegetables should be fork-tender. Veal should be crisp and brown on the outside, just barely pink in center (cut to test); a meat thermometer inserted in center of veal should register about 165F (75C). Remove roast from oven and let stand about 20 minutes to let juices settle; remove cord, set roast on a platter and surround with vegetables. Skim fat from pan juices; offer juices separately to spoon over meat and vegetables. Makes 6 to 8 servings.

Vicious Veal Chops

"Naughty but nice" describes these cleverly spiced, sinfully hot chops. Serve them simply, with any seasonal vegetable and a salad of endive, watercress and radishes dressed with a tart vinaigrette.

> **6 veal chops, cut about 1-1/2 inches thick**
> **1 lime**
> **2 cloves garlic**
> **1 teaspoon ground oregano, preferably Mexican**
> **1 large onion**
> **1/2 cup unsalted butter**
> **4 fresh New Mexico hot green chiles, parched (see page 9),**
>   **peeled, seeded, chopped**
> **1 large Hass avocado**
> **Watercress sprigs**
> **12 cherry tomatoes**

Arrange veal chops in a single layer on a baking sheet. Cut lime in half; squeeze juice evenly over both sides of each chop. Press garlic and evenly distribute among chops, rubbing it into both sides of each; then sprinkle oregano evenly over chops. Set aside. Cut onion in thin slices; separate slices into rings. Melt butter in a large, heavy skillet or 2 medium, heavy skillets. When butter is almost at the smoking point, add onion rings; cook quickly until lightly browned, then push evenly around sides of skillet. Add chops to skillet and cook until browned on bottom. Turn; evenly spread chiles in skillet around chops and cook quickly just to brown second side. Then reduce heat to low, cover and cook about 10 minutes or until flavors are blended and meat is done to your liking (cut to test). Meanwhile, halve, pit and peel avocado; cut each half lengthwise in 6 slices. Serve chops on warmed plates, spooning pan juices evenly over them. Top each chop with 2 avocado slices and arrange watercress and 2 cherry tomatoes along 1 side. Serve chile-onion mixture from skillet along other side of each chop. Makes 6 servings.

Golden Crispy Veal Birds

This dish is another of Brennan's divine creations. Each thin veal slice is seasoned with herbs and spices and rolled around Swiss cheese, fiery jalapeños and a sharp-flavored green onion, then cuddled in a crumb coating and fried until crisp and golden. You can successfully freeze the veal birds at several steps along the way: after rolling the goodies inside, after coating and before frying, or after frying.

4 green onions
1/2 pound veal for scaloppine, cut in 4 thin slices
1/4 teaspoon dried dill weed
4 ounces Swiss cheese, cut in 4 thin slices
4 medium pickled jalapeño chiles, cut in very thin strips
1/4 teaspoon dried leaf thyme, crushed
2 teaspoons finely minced fresh ginger
1 teaspoon light soy sauce
2 quarts vegetable oil for deep-frying
1 egg
1-1/2 teaspoons all-purpose flour
1-1/2 teaspoons cornstarch
Pinch of salt
Pinch of baking powder
2 teaspoons caribe (crushed Northern New Mexico red chile)
2/3 cup seasoned fine dry bread crumbs

About 1 hour before serving, trim roots and any wilted tops from green onions; "butterfly" both ends by shredding lengthwise with a sharp knife. Set aside. Pound each veal slice as thin as possible, being careful not to tear meat. Sprinkle veal with dill, then place a slice of Swiss cheese on each veal slice. Place jalapeño strips, then a butterflied green onion, on each slice. Evenly sprinkle with thyme, ginger and soy sauce. Tightly roll slices and secure with wooden picks. Cover loosely and set aside at least 30 minutes at room temperature. About 15 minutes before serving, in a deep, heavy pan, heat about 4 inches of oil to 375F (190C). Then prepare batter: beat egg well, then whisk in flour, cornstarch, salt and baking powder. Dip each veal roll in batter; evenly sprinkle each with 1/2 teaspoon caribe and roll in crumbs to coat completely. Cook rolls in hot oil 4 to 5 minutes or until golden. Drain on paper towels and serve hot. Makes 4 servings.

Grilled Veal Chops with Spicy Onions

Easy and elegant. The flavor of the grilled onions is such a terrific complement to the veal chops! If possible, add some soaked hardwood or mesquite chips or chunks to the coals for extra flavor.

> **4 large onions**
> **1/3 cup unsalted butter, melted**
> **1/4 cup packed dark brown sugar**
> **1 teaspoon freshly ground white pepper**
> **Freshly grated nutmeg to taste**
> **4 large veal chops, cut 2 inches thick**
> **3 cloves garlic, crushed**
> **Freshly ground black pepper to taste**

Peel onions and cut in half crosswise. Brush onion halves evenly with half the melted butter, reserving remaining butter for chops. Place each onion half, cut side up, on a square of foil large enough to enclose it. Sprinkle each cut side with 1/2 tablespoon brown sugar. Sprinkle evenly with white pepper and nutmeg. Fold foil around onions; seal edges of foil securely. Set aside. Brush both sides of each chop with remaining melted butter. Evenly divide garlic among chops, rubbing it into both sides of each chop. Sprinkle chops with black pepper. Prepare a bed of hot coals; sprinkle soaked wood chips (if used) on hot coals. Adjust grill to about 4 inches above coals; grease grill lightly. Place onions on grill and cook about 10 minutes, then start chops. Grill to desired doneness, turning once; allow 7 to 8 minutes per side for medium-rare. When meat is done, onions should be tender throughout and golden on the outside (open foil packets to check). Serve veal and onions very hot, placing 2 onion halves alongside each veal chop. Makes 4 servings.

Voluptuous Veal with Rigatoni

Rich, fine, overflowing with goodness! Melt-in-your-mouth veal scallops are cloaked in a mustard cream sauce and served over chewy, substantial rigatoni.

6 tablespoons unsalted butter
1 medium onion, chopped
1/4 cup minced shallots
1/2 cup dry white wine
2 cups whipping cream
1 tablespoon freshly cracked black pepper
2 tablespoons chopped fresh basil or 1 tablespoon dried leaf
    basil
1-1/4 pounds veal for scaloppine, cut in 4 slices, each pounded
    1/4 inch thick
8 ounces dried rigatoni
2 tablespoons olive oil
1/2 pound lean, heavily smoked country bacon, cut in 1/2-inch
    pieces, crisply cooked, drained
1/4 cup Dijon-style mustard
Liquid hot-pepper sauce to taste, if desired
2 tablespoons finely chopped parsley

Melt 2 tablespoons butter in a heavy skillet. Add onion and shallots and cook until lightly browned. Stir in wine; simmer until mixture is reduced by about 1/3. Add cream, bring to a simmer and cook until slightly thickened. Set aside. Pound pepper and basil into veal slices. In another heavy skillet, melt remaining 1/4 cup butter; add veal and cook, turning once, until lightly browned on both sides. Lift out, reserving pan juices; keep warm on a large platter in a 250F (120C) oven. Following package directions, cook pasta in boiling water (with oil added) just until tender to bite. Drain; return to cooking pan. Add bacon and cover pan. Reheat cream sauce, adding mustard, reserved pan juices from veal and hot-pepper sauce, if desired. Taste and adjust seasonings. Add sauce to pasta and toss until well coated. Remove platter from oven; transfer veal to another dish temporarily. Place pasta mixture in center of platter, then encircle with veal. Sprinkle parsley over center of pasta. Serve with additional hot-pepper sauce, if desired. Makes 4 servings.

Peppered Pan-Broiled Beef

Hot, tangy green peppercorns in a rich brandy cream sauce make this a perfect company dish, especially when you don't want to work. You can plan to serve it just 20 minutes after starting to cook (unless, of course, you or your guests prefer well-done beef).

Freshly ground white pepper to taste
2 pounds beef fillet (tenderloin)
2 tablespoons walnut oil
1 teaspoon dried leaf rosemary, crushed
1/4 cup unsalted butter
2 tablespoons chopped shallots
1/2 cup double-strength beef broth
1 tablespoon Dijon-style mustard
1/2 cup whipping cream
1/4 cup drained, crushed pickled green peppercorns
1/3 cup dry brandy

Preheat oven to hottest temperature—500F to 550F (260C to 285C). Grind white pepper generously over entire surface of beef, then rub beef with oil and press in rosemary. Melt butter in a large, heavy skillet until smoking hot, then add beef and cook quickly, turning as needed, until uniformly dark brown all over. Transfer beef to a baking pan and roast 12 to 15 minutes or until flesh yields readily when pressed (for rare) or yields slightly when pressed (for medium-rare). If in doubt, pierce meat to center with a sharp knife—if juice is very red, meat is rare. While meat roasts, make sauce: add shallots to butter and meat drippings remaining in skillet and cook until lightly browned, then add broth, mustard, cream and green peppercorns. Bring to a boil; boil until slightly reduced. Add brandy and ignite, keeping skillet lid handy to cover flames, if necessary. Continue to reduce sauce, stirring constantly. When beef is done, sauce should have desired consistency. To serve, cut beef in slices; drizzle sauce over center of slices. Makes 4 to 6 servings.

"Far-Out" Filled Flank Steak

Contagiously spicy—each peppery bite of this South American-inspired steak demands another! If some of the cornbread stuffing falls out as you're rolling up the meat, don't despair—just pat it back in with your fingers.

Peppered Cornbread, opposite
1 (2-lb.) flank steak
1/2 teaspoon salt (or to taste)
Freshly ground black pepper to
  taste
1/2 cup unsalted butter
2 large onions, chopped
4 cloves garlic, minced
2 eggs, slightly beaten
Milk, if necessary
1 recipe Ranchero Sauce, page 144,
  or Margarita Jalapeño Salsa, page
  143

Peppered Cornbread:
1/2 cup unsalted butter
1 cup canned creamed corn
1 cup yellow cornmeal
1/4 cup finely chopped pickled
  jalapeño chiles (or to taste)
3 eggs
1/2 teaspoon salt
1/2 teaspoon baking soda
1/4 teaspoon baking powder
1 cup grated Monterey Jack cheese

The day before serving or early in the morning, prepare cornbread. When ready to prepare filled flank steak, crumble cornbread into a 3-quart bowl and set aside. Trim excess fat and connective tissue from steak; if steak is wider than 6 inches across the shortest side, cut in half to make 2 long, slender pieces. Firmly and evenly pound steak as thin as possible; season with salt and pepper. Set aside. Melt butter in a very large, flat-bottomed skillet with an ovenproof handle. Add onions and garlic and cook until onions are clear. Using a slotted spoon, lift out half the onion mixture and add to crumbled cornbread. Mix eggs into cornbread mixture, combining well. If mixture seems too dry, mix in a little milk. Spoon cornbread mixture in a long strip down center of steak (or spoon half the mixture down center of each steak half). Roll carefully, picking up any loose pieces of stuffing and patting them back into steak. Secure rolled steak closed with sharp skewers. Add rolled steak to skillet; brown rapidly, spooning remaining onion mixture over sides of steak and being sure onions don't overbrown. Meanwhile, preheat oven to 350F (175C). When steak is uniformly browned, spoon Ranchero Sauce or Margarita Jalapeño Salsa over top. Bake in skillet, uncovered, spooning sauce over meat occasionally, 1 to 1-1/2 hours or until meat is easily pierced to center with a sharp knife and is no longer pink. Cut crosswise in slices to serve. Makes 8 to 10 servings.

Peppered Cornbread:
Preheat oven to 400F (205C). Place butter in a 9- to 10-inch cast-iron skillet or baking pan; set in oven just until melted, but not browned. In a bowl, combine creamed corn, cornmeal, jalapeños, eggs, salt, baking soda and baking powder. Stir in melted butter, then cheese. Pour into skillet or baking pan and bake 30 to 45 minutes or until golden brown. Makes 8 servings or 4 cups, crumbled.

Hula Steak

A winner at an outdoor barbecue contest! My family and friends really raved about this Polynesian dish. It goes perfectly with Hawaiian drinks, banana or coconut chips or macadamia nuts. For a dramatic presentation, garnish the steak with a lei of flowers such as petunias or roses.

> **1 (2- to 3-inch) piece fresh ginger, peeled, finely chopped; or 1 teaspoon ground ginger (or to taste)**
> **2 cloves garlic, minced, or 1/2 teaspoon garlic powder**
> **2 cups soy sauce**
> **1/4 cup packed brown sugar**
> **1/4 cup brandy or bourbon**
> **4 pounds well-aged beef sirloin or other lean, tender boneless beef steak, cut 1 inch thick**
> **Garnish, if desired: a lei of flowers or 1 large green bell pepper, cut in 1-inch squares, and 1/2 fresh pineapple, peeled, cored, cubed**

Mix ginger, garlic, soy sauce, brown sugar and brandy or bourbon in a shallow dish just large enough to hold meat. Place meat in marinade and turn to coat; let stand 1 hour at room temperature, turning frequently. Prepare a bed of hot coals or preheat broiler. Adjust barbecue grill 4 to 6 inches above coals; position oven rack so meat will be 4 to 6 inches below heat source. Brush barbecue rack or broiler pan with a piece of meat fat. Lift meat from marinade; rub a thin layer of ground ginger on both sides of meat for a spicier, more pungent flavor, if desired. Grill or broil to desired doneness, turning once; allow 6 to 8 minutes per side for medium-rare. Remove steak to a warmed platter and garnish with a lei or with squares of bell pepper and cubes of pineapple, if desired. Makes 6 to 8 servings.

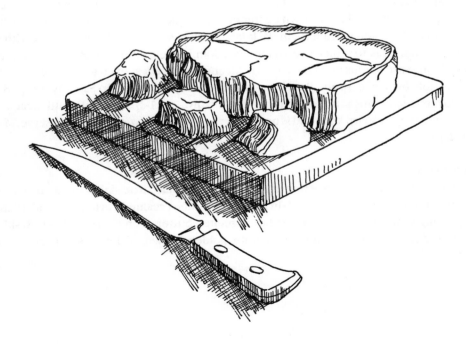

Double-Hot Chile Steaks

One of the heirs to a New Mexico mercantile fortune developed this Albuquerque special. These fiery-hot steaks sort of go with the territory—in New Mexico, they say you can tell the natives by how hot they can handle their chiles! Though it's virtually steaming, the steak sauce is a super complement for the strong flavor of beef.

1/2 cup ground pure New Mexico hot red chile
2 cups canned whole tomatoes or 4 large red-ripe tomatoes,
    peeled, quartered
1 cup parched (see page 9), peeled, seeded, chopped fresh New
    Mexico hot green chiles or 1 (7-oz.) can diced green chiles
1 hot red onion, cut in cubes
4 large cloves garlic
1/2 teaspoon salt
1/2 teaspoon ground oregano, preferably Mexican
1/4 teaspoon ground cumin
4 pounds well-aged beef sirloin, cut 1-1/2 to 2 inches thick

In a blender or food processor, combine ground chile, tomatoes, chiles, onion, garlic, salt, oregano and cumin. Process until pureed. If made ahead, refrigerate until ready to use. To prepare steak, let both steak and sauce come to room temperature. Then place steak in a shallow dish, coat generously on both sides with sauce and let stand 2 hours at room temperature, spooning more sauce over steak occasionally. Preheat broiler or prepare a bed of hot coals. Adjust oven rack so meat will be 4 to 6 inches below heat source; adjust barbecue grill 4 to 6 inches above coals. Lightly grease rack in broiler pan or barbecue grill. Broil or grill steak (with sauce that clings to it) to desired doneness, turning once; allow 10 to 15 minutes per side for medium-rare. Serve with additional sauce, warmed over low heat. Makes 8 servings.

Rosalea's Steak Duncan

This wonderful steak for two comes from the famed Pink Adobe Restaurant in Santa Fe, New Mexico. Rosalea, owner and chef, gave me the recipe to pass on to a Texas couple who attended my Santa Fe Cooking School. They'd tasted the dish at her restaurant and enjoyed it so much, they insisted on learning how to prepare it at home! The recipe calls for 6- to 8-ounce steaks, but for bigger appetites, you can use bigger steaks—up to 15 ounces each.

> **2 (6- to 8-oz.) New York cut prime steaks**
> **Hickory-smoked salt**
> **Green Chile Sauce, see below**
> **4 large fresh mushrooms**
> **1/4 cup unsalted butter**
>
> *Green Chile Sauce:*
> **2 tablespoons olive oil**
> **1 medium onion, finely chopped**
> **6 to 8 fresh New Mexico hot green chiles, parched (see page 9),**
> **   peeled, seeded, chopped**
> **1/4 teaspoon ground oregano, preferably Mexican**
> **1/4 teaspoon ground coriander or 1 tablespoon chopped fresh**
> **   cilantro**
> **1/4 teaspoon salt**
> **1 teaspoon finely chopped fresh jalapeño chile or liquid**
> **   hot-pepper sauce to taste**

Trim any excess fat or connective tissue from steaks, then sprinkle both sides of each steak with hickory-smoked salt. Set aside. Preheat broiler or prepare a bed of hot coals. Meanwhile, prepare Green Chile Sauce; set aside. Thinly slice mushrooms. Melt butter in a skillet, add mushrooms and cook until soft. Keep warm. To prepare steaks, position oven rack so meat will be 4 to 6 inches below heat source; adjust barbecue grill 4 to 6 inches above coals. Lightly grease rack in broiler pan or barbecue grill. Broil or grill steaks to desired doneness, turning once. Allow 5 to 8 minutes per side for rare, 7 to 10 minutes per side for medium. Remove steaks to hot platters; top with mushrooms, then with Green Chile Sauce. Makes 2 servings.

Green Chile Sauce:
Heat oil in a skillet; add onion and cook until clear. Stir in green chiles, oregano, coriander or cilantro, salt and jalapeño or hot-pepper sauce; cook together about 5 minutes or until flavors are blended. Remove from heat.

VARIATION
Serve the Green Chile Sauce over burgers, chops, chicken or almost any other meat, poultry or fish for a great-tasting, peppy change from the usual. It's a great omelet topping, too!

Hot Shot Steaks

My husband, Brennan, creates these steaks for a quickie lunch, late-night snack, or even an early-morning breakfast before an active day. They're terrific with a salad and a heap of cottage fries, or with eggs for breakfast.

1/2 pound beef sirloin
Freshly ground black pepper to taste
2 tablespoons chopped onion
2 cloves garlic, finely minced
Generous pinch of pequin quebrado
1/4 cup diced red bell pepper
6 or more jalapeño chile slices
1 small loaf French bread or 2 large French rolls, split in half

Very carefully, cut steak in half horizontally to make 2 thin steaks. Trim excess fat from meat; add fat trimmings to a large heavy skillet and render over high heat. Grind pepper generously over steaks; then press onion and garlic into steaks. When fat is smoking, add pequin to skillet, sprinkling it very evenly across the surface. Add steaks and sprinkle bell pepper around edges of skillet. Brown steaks quickly on bottom, turn over and sprinkle with jalapeño slices. Then add bread or roll halves, cut side down, to skillet. Continue to cook until bread is toasted and meat is done to your liking; meat takes only a very short time to cook rare, so watch closely. Serve steaks very hot, on grilled bread on warmed plates; spoon bell pepper alongside. Makes 2 servings.

Peppered Beef Fondue

Wonderful—and surprisingly easy to make. Simply pounding freshly ground pepper into the beef cubes really sets this fondue apart, especially for the "pepper bellies" among us! Buy the best beef you can find and serve with an assortment of your favorite dipping sauces, such as anchovy butter, mustard mayonnaise and béarnaise, barbecue or dilled horseradish-sour cream sauce.

1-1/2 pounds beef sirloin or other lean, tender boneless beef
steak
1/4 cup freshly ground black pepper
Parsley sprigs
2 quarts peanut oil for deep-frying
Dipping sauces, see suggestions in recipe introduction, above

Trim any excess fat and gristle from beef, then cut meat in 1-inch cubes. Crush each side of each cube into pepper, then place beef cubes in a serving bowl and garnish with parsley. Refrigerate until ready to cook. To serve, heat oil to 375F (190C) in a fondue pot, chafing dish or any electric pan (such as a wok or frying pan). Let guests spear meat on fondue forks and cook in hot oil until as done as desired, then dunk into dipping sauces. Makes 6 servings.

Flaming Fajitas

One of the most popular Tex-Mex foods is fajitas—thinly sliced skirt steak that's pounded and seasoned with lime and garlic, then quickly grilled and wrapped in warm flour tortillas. Credit for inventing the dish goes to Mexican workers in the citrus orchards along the Texas border, who grilled skirt steaks (a less tender, "throwaway" cut of beef) this way over open mesquite fires.

Fajitas are traditionally served with *pico de gallo*, an intensely hot salsa, but I prefer to use my own homemade Margarita Jalapeño Salsa. It's an exciting alternative that makes the dish that much more special. For another twist on tradition, my fajitas are quickly flamed with brandy before serving.

If you can't find skirt steak (belly steak) in your area, just use bottom round instead.

**1-1/2 pounds very lean skirt or bottom round steak, cut 1/4 inch
  thick
1 lime
4 large cloves garlic, pressed
1 to 2 teaspoons pequin quebrado
4 to 6 (12-inch) flour tortillas
1/4 cup dry brandy
4 to 6 leaves romaine lettuce, cut crosswise in 1-inch strips
Guacamole, page 20
Margarita Jalapeño Salsa, page 143, or your favorite pico de gallo
  or other hot salsa
1/4 cup chopped onion
1 tomato, chopped
1/3 cup chopped fresh cilantro
2 cups sour cream**

Trim steaks of all excess fat and sinew, then cut in 4 to 6 equal rectangles. Pound steak pieces as thin as possible. Cut lime in half; squeeze juice over both sides of each piece of steak, then evenly sprinkle steak with garlic and press in pequin. (Pequin quebrado is intensely hot: 2 teaspoons will give a fiery-hot flavor, 1 teaspoon will get your attention. Use the amount that best suits you and your guests.) Stack steaks on a plate and let rest about 30 minutes at room temperature. Meanwhile, prepare a bed of hot coals, using regular briquets or mesquite charcoal. Or, if no barbecue is available, heat a large, heavy, well-seasoned cast-iron skillet over high heat about 20 minutes or until very hot. Also stack tortillas, wrap in foil and place in a 250F (120C) oven; warm 4 to 6 dinner plates in the same oven. Quickly grill or pan-grill steaks, turning to sear both sides. Heat brandy in a small saucepan; carefully ignite. Spoon over steaks. (Keep a large piece of foil or skillet lid at hand; if flames rise too high, just cover them until they subside.) When flames die, place each steak piece in a warm tortilla. Then add toppings of lettuce, Guacamole, salsa, onion, tomato, cilantro and sour cream (or let guests add toppings themselves). Roll as for a blintz, folding sides of tortilla to center to cover all fillings. Makes 4 to 6 servings.

"Bitchy" Beef Bourguignonne

Hearty and ornery, this deep-colored, rich-flavored stew is wonderful to make and eat on foggy, rainy days at any time of year. But if you live in a sunny climate, don't wait for bad weather—go ahead and try it. Everybody will love it! Serve on a bed of thick, flavorful egg noodles or with warm, crusty, fresh French bread oozing with sweet butter.

> 1 onion, coarsely chopped
> 2 tablespoons chopped fresh parsley or 1 tablespoon dried
>   parsley flakes
> 1 teaspoon dried leaf thyme, crushed
> 2 bay leaves
> 2 tablespoons coarsely ground black pepper
> 2 tablespoons pickled green peppercorns, crushed
> 2 tablespoons extra-virgin olive oil
> 3 cups burgundy or other good-quality dry red wine
> 3 pounds beef sirloin, bottom round or London broil, cut in
>   1-inch cubes
> 2 tablespoons lard
> 1/4 cup unsalted butter
> 1/4 cup dry brandy
> 2 cups double-strength beef broth
> 36 small white boiling onions
> 2 large cloves garlic, minced
> Salt to taste, if desired

Combine chopped onion, parsley, thyme, bay leaves, black pepper, green peppercorns, oil and wine in a 2-quart glass or stainless steel bowl. Stir to blend well. Add beef, stir well and let stand at least 2 hours at room temperature, stirring occasionally. Melt lard and 2 tablespoons butter together in a large, heavy saucepan. Drain beef cubes, reserving marinade. Add beef to pan; cook until browned, stirring as needed. Add brandy and flame carefully, stirring it so it ignites well. Add reserved marinade and broth. Bring to a boil; reduce heat, cover and simmer 2 to 3 hours or until beef is fork-tender. Meanwhile, prepare onions. Cut stem and root ends off each; cook trimmed onions in boiling water 10 minutes, then pop onions out of their skins. Melt remaining 2 tablespoons butter in a heavy skillet; add onions and garlic. Cook until onions are golden brown, then add to stew and simmer at least 30 minutes longer. Taste and add salt, more wine or other seasonings as desired. Makes 6 to 8 servings.

Tres y Tres Carne

Three kinds of beans and three colors of bell peppers join up with tender beef in this rich, robust, flavorful dish. Though it does require time to make, it doesn't demand much attention. The stew is truly best if you start with dried beans; you can cook them while the beef chunks cozy into the wine-herb marinade, then just simmer beef and beans together slowly to build a rich sauce. Serve over wide-cut egg noodles; complete the meal with a salad.

2-1/2 cups red wine, preferably burgundy or Zinfandel
3 tablespoons olive oil
1 bay leaf
2 sprigs fresh oregano or 1 teaspoon dried leaf oregano
4 leaves fresh sage or 1 teaspoon dried leaf sage
2 or more fresh jalapeño chiles, finely minced
2-1/2 pounds beef sirloin or bottom round, cut in 1-inch cubes
1/2 cup dried baby lima beans or 1 (1-lb.) can lima beans
1/2 cup dried pink or pinto beans or 1 (1-lb.) can pinto beans
1/2 cup white navy or pea beans or 1 (1-lb.) can white navy
  beans
1 teaspoon salt (omit if using canned beans)
4 cups water (omit if using canned beans)
3/4 cup unsalted butter
3 large Italian frying peppers or fresh poblano chiles, cut in
  1-inch strips
2 cups beef broth
1 cup 1/2-inch squares green bell pepper
1 cup 1/2-inch squares red bell pepper
1 cup 1/2-inch squares yellow bell pepper
8 to 12 ounces dried wide egg noodles

In a glass or stainless steel bowl, stir together wine, oil, herbs and jalapeños. Add beef cubes, stir well and let stand at least 2 hours at room temperature, stirring occasionally. Meanwhile, sort and rinse dried beans, then place in a heavy 4- to 5-quart saucepan. Add salt and 4 cups water; bring to a boil, then cover, turn off heat and let stand 1 hour. Return to a boil; reduce heat, cover and simmer about 1-1/2 hours or until almost tender, adding more water as necessary. Melt 1/4 cup butter in a skillet; add frying peppers or poblano chiles and cook until browned. Set aside. Drain beef, reserving marinade. Melt remaining 1/2 cup butter in another skillet over medium heat. Add beef and cook until well browned, stirring as needed. Add browned beef, reserved marinade, browned frying peppers or poblano chiles and broth to beans. (If using canned beans, drain and rinse; then combine with beef, marinade, frying peppers and broth in saucepan. Add a little water, if necessary.) Cover and simmer 1 to 1-1/2 hours or until beans are very tender and meat is almost tender. Then add bell peppers and simmer 15 to 30 minutes longer or until peppers and beef are tender. Following package directions, cook noodles in boiling water just until tender to bite. Drain well; mound on a platter and nestle beef stew in the middle for a very pretty entree. Makes 6 to 8 servings.

Sassy Stroganoff

A tried-and-true favorite, spiced up to make a very new and different dish. The beef gets a generous coating of freshly ground black pepper; fresh horseradish, dry mustard and the subtle heat of ground pure chile spruce up the sauce. Serve with an optional garnish of chopped jalapeño and caribe for a great family or party entree.

> 2 tablespoons freshly ground black pepper
> 1-1/4 pounds beef sirloin or fillet (tenderloin), cut in strips 2 to
>   3 inches long and 1/4 inch wide
> 1/2 cup unsalted butter
> 1 large onion, thinly sliced, separated into rings
> 2 cloves garlic, finely minced
> 8 ounces dried egg noodles
> 1 cup double-strength beef broth
> 2 tablespoons tomato paste
> 1 tablespoon ground pure New Mexico hot red chile
> 2 tablespoons freshly grated horseradish
> 2 teaspoons dry mustard
> 1-1/2 cups dairy sour cream
> 1 or 2 fresh jalapeño chiles, seeded, finely minced, if desired
> 2 tablespoons caribe (crushed Northern New Mexico red chile),
>   if desired

Pound pepper into steak strips; set aside. Melt butter in a large, heavy skillet. Add onion and garlic and cook until onion is lightly browned on edges; remove from skillet and place in a bowl. Increase heat to high. When skillet is very hot, add steak strips; cook quickly until browned on outside but still rare on inside. Place on top of onion in bowl; keep warm. Following package directions, cook noodles in boiling water just until tender to bite. While noodles are cooking, prepare sauce: add broth, tomato paste, ground chile, horseradish and mustard to meat drippings in skillet. Cook over medium-low heat, stirring until well blended. Reduce heat, taste and adjust seasonings. Drain noodles and divide among 4 to 6 warmed plates. Then immediately stir sour cream and meat-onion mixture into sauce; heat through and spoon over noodles. Garnish with jalapeños and caribe, if desired. Makes 4 to 6 servings.

Five-Pepper Stir-Fried Beef

This pretty, flavorful dish is extremely quick to cook, but do be sure to allow ample preparation time for slicing and dicing the vegetables and marinating the meat. Once you start to stir-fry, don't budge from the range—if overcooked, the vegetables will lose their beautiful bright colors. Serve over sushi rice or steamed rice; start the rice cooking before you begin to stir-fry. (You can make sushi rice with a simple mix imported from Japan.)

1/2 cup dark soy sauce
1 (1- to 2-inch) piece fresh ginger, peeled, grated
2 tablespoons packed dark brown sugar
1/4 cup dry sherry
2 cloves garlic, finely minced
1-1/4 pounds beef sirloin or London broil, cut 1/2 inch thick,
    partially frozen, very thinly sliced
2 tablespoons unsalted butter
1/4 cup vegetable oil
1 red bell pepper, cut lengthwise in thin strips
1 green bell pepper, cut lengthwise in thin strips
1 yellow bell pepper, cut lengthwise in thin strips
4 green onions, thinly sliced
1 large leek, rinsed well, cut crosswise in 1/4-inch slices
    (including about 3 inches of green leaves)
1 teaspoon caribe (crushed Northern New Mexico red chile)
1 pound fresh spinach, rinsed well, stemmed
1/4 cup sliced pickled red cherry peppers
2 slices capicola (see note), finely chopped
Hot cooked rice

Combine soy sauce, ginger, brown sugar, sherry and garlic in a shallow glass or stainless steel bowl. Add beef strips and stir well, then let stand 2 hours at room temperature. To cook, melt butter in oil in a wok or very large, heavy skillet. When fat is very hot (so that a drop of water quickly sizzles and dances on pan), add bell peppers, green onions and leek. Sprinkle with caribe; stir-fry 5 minutes. Lift beef from marinade; add to pan and stir well, then add spinach and stir-fry 5 minutes longer. Stir in cherry peppers and capicola and cook until heated through. Serve over rice. Makes 4 or 5 servings.

NOTE: Capicola is an Italian sausage similar to salami, though not as spicy. It's available in delicatessens.

Liver alla Romana

The Italians have a way of creating romance and excitement where others seem to lack the knack. Their skill is evident in this recipe—it's spicy, delicious, quick to prepare and economical, too.

2 green onions
1 tablespoon unsalted butter (or more, as needed)
2 tablespoons olive oil (or more, as needed)
1 pound liver, very thinly sliced
1/2 cup all-purpose flour (or more, as needed)
2 medium onions, diced
1 clove garlic, minced
1/2 teaspoon salt
Freshly ground black pepper to taste
1 teaspoon Italian crushed hot red pepper (or to taste)
1/2 teaspoon dried leaf oregano
1/2 teaspoon dried leaf basil
1/2 teaspoon dried leaf marjoram
1 (8-oz.) can tomato sauce
1/4 cup dry red wine
1-1/2 tablespoons wine vinegar
Juice of 1/2 lemon
Buttered spaghetti with Parmesan cheese, if desired
1/4 cup finely minced parsley

Trim roots and any wilted tops from green onions. Cut each onion in half lengthwise, then in quarters crosswise; very thinly slice each piece. Set aside. In a large, heavy skillet, melt butter in oil. Meanwhile, dredge liver slices in flour. When butter is melted and hot, add liver slices. Then add diced onions, green onions and garlic; cook until liver and onions are lightly browned. Turn liver and season with salt, black pepper, crushed red pepper and herbs. Cook until browned on second side, adding more butter and oil as needed to prevent sticking. Mix tomato sauce, wine, vinegar and lemon juice; pour over liver and reduce heat so sauce simmers. Cook a few minutes or until flavors are blended. Taste and adjust seasonings. Place liver slices on warmed plates or arrange around a mound of spaghetti on a platter, if desired. Top liver with sauce, sprinkle with parsley and serve. Makes 4 servings.

TIP

To prepare spaghetti, cook enough dried spaghetti for 4 servings according to package directions. Drain and toss with 1/4 cup extra-virgin olive oil and 1/4 cup melted unsalted butter. Then toss with 1/2 cup or more freshly grated Parmesan cheese.

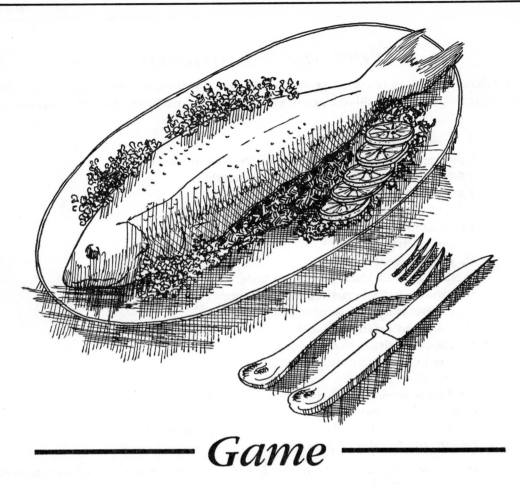

Game

Hot seasonings and careful preparation make these game dishes incomparably delicious. Because venison, antelope, hare and other game meats can be quite tough, a number of my recipes rely on tenderizing marinades, acidic ingredients or long, slow cooking—as in Jugged Hare and Ranch-Hand Chili, for example.

In addition to the red-meat recipes in this chapter, you'll find a handful of poultry and fish dishes. Try Roast Pheasant in Horseradish-Brandy Cream for your next holiday or special-occasion feast; celebrate a successful fishing trip with Spicy Stuffed Trout, a specialty straight from New Mexico.

Oven-Barbecued Venison

Plenty of barbecue sauce and long, slow baking make this venison especially tender and flavorful, sure to be lapped up even by those who profess to dislike gamy flavors. The fiery sauce is so special that you'll want to use it on other meats—try it with pork or beef ribs, or even chicken.

1/3 cup granulated sugar
1/4 cup packed dark brown sugar
1/3 cup double-strength beef broth
2 cups hot water
1/3 cup prepared yellow mustard
3 tablespoons cider vinegar
2 tablespoons liquid smoke
3/4 cup tomato paste
3 tablespoons ground pure New Mexico hot red chile (or to taste)
3 medium pickled jalapeño chiles, finely minced
1/2 teaspoon pequin quebrado (or to taste)
1 clove garlic, minced
Salt to taste
1/3 cup all-purpose flour
1 teaspoon salt
1/4 cup bacon drippings or vegetable oil
2 pounds venison round steak
1 medium onion, thinly sliced, separated into rings

To prepare barbecue sauce, combine sugars, broth and hot water in a saucepan. Simmer until sugars are dissolved; then add mustard, vinegar, liquid smoke, tomato paste, ground chile, jalapeños, pequin and garlic. (If tender-mouthed guests will eat this sauce, go easy on the ground chile and pequin; offer more at the table for fire-eaters.) Bring to a boil; reduce heat and simmer, uncovered, at least 30 minutes. Taste and adjust seasonings, adding salt to taste. Combine flour and 1 teaspoon salt. Heat bacon drippings or oil in a large, deep pot (such as a Dutch oven) over high heat. Dredge venison in flour mixture; add to hot oil and cook until browned on both sides, turning as needed. Spoon off excess fat. Preheat oven to 325F (165C). Drizzle about 1/4 of sauce over meat; arrange half the onion rings on top. Cover and bake 30 minutes; then turn, drizzle with some of the remaining sauce and top with remaining onion rings. Cover and continue to bake 1-1/2 hours longer or until meat is very tender when pierced. Keep remaining sauce simmering while venison is baking; pass at the table to serve over meat. Makes 4 to 6 servings.

TIP
If you want to make this barbecue sauce alone, to use as a sauce for cooked meats or a baste for barbecued meats, simmer about 2 hours or until slightly thickened. Then adjust seasoning as directed.

Antelope or Venison Ranch-Hand Chili

Patterned after the original "bowl of red" chili, this version is heartier and more robustly seasoned, designed to satisfy appetites sharpened by long days of work outdoors. Since antelope and venison are drier than beef, the chili includes some extra fat—salt pork, lard or bacon drippings—to keep the meat moist. Burgundy wine, beer and tequila help balance the game's strong flavor; the tequila also smooths and softens the heat of the ground chile (what I've often called the "housebreaking" of chili).

> 1/2 cup diced salt pork, lard or bacon drippings
> 1 cup chopped onion
> 3 pounds antelope or venison, cut in 1/2-inch cubes
> 4 large cloves garlic, minced
> 2 tablespoons ground pure California mild red chile
> 1/4 cup ground pure New Mexico hot red chile
> 2 tablespoons caribe (crushed Northern New Mexico red chile),
>   or to taste
> 1 tablespoon ground cumin
> 1 (12-oz.) can or bottle beer
> 1 cup beef broth
> Salt to taste
> 1/2 cup burgundy or other good-quality dry red wine
> 6 shots tequila
> "Fixin's 'n' mixin's": Chopped onion, sliced jalapeño chiles,
>   pequin quebrado, half-and-half mixture of grated Monterey
>   Jack and Cheddar cheeses, sour cream with fresh lime wedges
> 6 to 12 warm, buttered flour tortillas

Melt fat in a large, flat-bottomed pot. Add onion and cook until limp; then add meat, garlic, mild and hot ground chile, caribe, cumin, beer and broth. Bring to a boil, then reduce heat to medium and simmer, uncovered and stirring frequently, 3 to 4 hours or until meat is so tender it's starting to shred apart and sauce is thick, red and rich. Add water during cooking as needed to prevent scorching. Taste and adjust seasonings, adding salt to taste. Then stir in wine. (If you're holding the chili for an hour or more before serving, wait to add the wine until about 30 minutes before serving.) To serve, ladle into bowls and serve with a shot of tequila on the side. Place "fixin's 'n' mixin's" in separate bowls. Let guests douse their chili with tequila, then top with the fixin's 'n' mixin's of their choice. Accompany with tortillas. Makes 6 servings.

Jalapeño-Glazed Saddle of Venison

Marinated in wine and caribe and wrapped in bacon before roasting, this venison is as moist and tender as game can be. A glaze of homemade Jalapeño Jelly adds a sweet-hot finish that truly sets the dish apart. If you're a game lover, this is almost certain to become a regular in your repertoire.

>
> **1-1/2 cups burgundy wine**
> **1-1/2 teaspoons ground ginger**
> **2 tablespoons caribe (crushed Northern New Mexico red chile)**
> **1 (3- to 4-lb.) venison saddle (or use elk or antelope)**
> **3 cloves garlic, slivered**
> **1/4 cup minced onion**
> **1/2 cup Jalapeño Jelly, page 149, or purchased jalapeño jelly (or**
>   **to taste)**
> **6 thick slices lean, heavily smoked country bacon**

Combine wine, ginger and caribe. Set aside. With a sharp knife, carefully pierce roast about 1 inch deep all over. Insert a sliver of garlic in each gash. Set roast in an ovenproof glass roasting dish or casserole and top with onion. Drizzle marinade all over roast. Let stand at room temperature at least 2 hours (6 to 8 hours if time allows), basting frequently. Preheat oven to 450F (230C). Drain off marinade and reserve for basting. Then glaze roast with jelly, spooning and smoothing it uniformly all over surface of meat. Wrap bacon slices around roast, laying them adjacent to each other. Fasten bacon with skewers or tie with heavy cooking twine to keep in place. Roast 15 minutes or until bacon starts to crisp. Then reduce oven temperature to 325F (165C) and continue to roast to desired doneness, basting every 15 minutes with reserved marinade. Allow about 12 minutes per pound for rare, then check for doneness by piercing with a sharp knife (make cut in bottom of roast to avoid marring its appearance). Remember that game meats are inherently dry, so they are most tender when roasted rare or medium-rare. Cooking beyond the medium stage makes for very dry meat. When venison is done to your liking, let rest at least 30 minutes to let juices set. Then cut into slices across the grain, cutting through bacon so each slice is encircled with bacon. Cut slices 1/4 to 1/2 inch thick, depending on the tenderness of the venison; as a general rule, the tougher the meat, the thinner the slices should be. Makes 6 servings.

Peppered Venison Steaks with Rosemary Butter

Just the thought of these steaks brings back fond memories of my native New Mexico, where I savored many a venison steak prepared just this way. Depending on your guests' ability to handle hot flavors, rub the steaks with the hot or mild chile of your choice—or even black pepper, though I consider this a cop-out! These are good for any meal from brunch through dinner; I like to accompany them with broiled tomatoes topped with cheese, crumbs and herbs.

> **8 (6- to 8-oz.) venison steaks or chops**
> **2 tablespoons caribe (crushed Northern New Mexico red chile),**
>   **or to taste**
> **1/2 cup unsalted butter, room temperature**
> **2 teaspoons minced fresh rosemary or 1 teaspoon dried leaf**
>   **rosemary, crushed (or to taste)**

Two hours before serving, set venison chops out at room temperature; trim off any membrane and excess fat. Spread caribe on a piece of waxed paper; press chops into caribe to coat both sides. (Remember that caribe is a fairly hot chile; a full teaspoon per chop will really get most people's attention.) Set chops aside. Then prepare rosemary butter: in a bowl, blend butter and rosemary with a spoon. Set aside at room temperature. To cook, prepare a bed of hot coals; or, if cooking inside, preheat broiler. Position barbecue grill 4 to 6 inches above coals; adjust oven rack so meat will be 4 to 6 inches below heat source. Lightly grease grill or rack in broiler pan. Grill or broil meat until browned on bottom; turn and cook on second side to desired doneness. Place a spoonful of rosemary butter on each chop before serving. Makes about 8 servings.

Jerky

Perhaps America's first convenience food, nutritious meat jerky sustained many a hungry traveler, trail driver, prospector and even bandito in years past. The dried meat strips are traditionally seasoned with red chile—one of the first uses of chiles, as far as I know. In addition to flavoring the meat, the fiery flakes act as a preservative: as the Indians discovered long ago, chiles contain an anti-oxidant that prevents meat (especially the fatty parts) from turning rancid as it dries in the hot sun. The peppery coating also discourages birds, insects and other marauders.

Making jerky is a simple process, still common among the Pueblo Indians of the Rio Grande area. In late September, when hunting season begins and red chile pods are harvested, you'll see chile-coated strips of venison, antelope and occasionally elk hanging from clotheslines and drying racks made of sinew. You can sun-dry jerky at home in your own back yard, or simply dry it for 8 hours or so in a low oven.

Enjoy homemade jerky "as is" for a snack, or serve it in a sauce, as you would dried beef. Or stew it in water to make a very simple chile—the original "bowl of red," I've often thought! For added flavor, season your jerky chile with chopped onion, garlic, cumin and perhaps more ground pure hot chile.

> **Round steak of venison, elk or antelope**
> **Ground pure New Mexico hot red chile**
> **Salt**

For tender jerky, cut meat in 1/8-inch-thick strips across the grain. (Authentic jerky is made by tearing the meat in strips *with* the grain—hence the name "jerky"—but tearing makes for tougher jerky.) Sprinkle meat strips generously with ground chile and salt; the more salt you use, the faster the meat will dry. Place strips of seasoned meat on rack of a broiler pan or on a cooling rack set on a rimmed baking sheet; or use any rack-and-pan combination that will allow air circulation and let juices drain away. Set oven at 150F (65C), set panful of meat in oven and prop oven door open by about 2 inches to let juices evaporate. Dry in oven 8 hours or until of desired dryness. Store jerky in the freezer, or in a cool, dry place in a container that allows air circulation. Airtight storage often causes jerky to mold, since it's very hard to get the meat completely dried. One pound fresh meat yields just under 1 pound jerky.

NOTE: To sun-dry jerky, hang the seasoned strips of meat over a line and cover with cheesecloth to keep insects away. Let dry to desired dryness.

Jugged Hare (Hasenpfeffer)

Though hare or rabbit is becoming increasingly available as a domestic eating animal, wild rabbit can still be very good, as this recipe shows. A German classic, *hasenpfeffer* offers a perfect way to tenderize and richly flavor potentially tough meat; this version of the dish came from the Queen Elizabeth Hotel in Montreal, where it appeared on the menu as "jugged hare." Barley or bulgur pilaf makes an excellent side dish.

In general, rabbit may be substituted in any recipe calling for chicken; you'll note some similarities between this recipe and *coq au vin*, for example. For best results, cook rabbit according to age: young animals can be roasted, broiled or fried, while older ones should be stewed or braised.

> 1 (6-lb.) hare or rabbit
> 3-1/4 cups burgundy or other good-quality dry red wine
> 1 teaspoon dried leaf thyme
> 1 medium onion, finely chopped
> 2 cloves garlic, minced
> 2 stalks celery, finely chopped
> 2 carrots, peeled, finely chopped
> 2 bay leaves
> 12 whole black peppercorns
> 12 whole white peppercorns
> 12 pickled green peppercorns
> 1/2 cup bacon drippings or vegetable oil
> 1 cup sliced fresh mushrooms
> 3 cups beef broth
> 12 pearl onions
> 3 tablespoons unsalted butter
> 18 small whole fresh mushrooms, stems trimmed flush with
>   caps
> 1-1/4 cups cubed salt pork (in 1/2-inch cubes)
> Salt to taste
> 1/2 cup unsalted butter, if needed
> 1/3 cup all-purpose flour, if needed

Cut hare or rabbit into serving-size pieces, reserving liver and any blood to thicken the sauce. Combine 2 cups wine, 1/2 teaspoon thyme, chopped onion, garlic, celery, carrots, bay leaves and all peppercorns in a glass, stainless steel or porcelain bowl. Place cut-up hare in marinade, turn to coat, cover and refrigerate 24 hours, turning frequently. Preheat oven to 350F (175C). Remove hare from marinade and pat dry. Strain marinade; reserve vegetables and strained marinade separately. Heat bacon drippings or oil in a large skillet until very hot. Add hare and brown lightly on all sides, turning as needed. Add remaining 1/2 teaspoon thyme and reserved vegetables. Turn into a casserole presentable for the table; bake, uncovered, 30 minutes or until hare is well browned on outside, checking frequently. Then stir in remaining 1-1/4 cups wine, reserved marinade, sliced mushrooms and broth. Cover and continue to bake 2 to 3 hours longer or until nearly tender (time depends on age of hare). Meanwhile, steam pearl onions until almost fork-tender. Set aside. Melt 3 tablespoons butter in a small skillet, add mushroom caps and cook until light golden on edges. Also simmer salt pork cubes in a small amount of water (just enough to cover the bottom of a skillet) until softened; drain, if necessary, then sauté until browned. When hare is nearly tender, stir in salt pork. Finely chop reserved liver; stir liver and reserved blood into hare mixture. Arrange pearl onions and mushroom caps in a ring around pieces of hare; cover and return to oven. Continue to bake until all vegetables are tender and meat is very tender. Taste and adjust seasonings, adding salt to taste. If sauce is thin, remove most of it with a ladle and reserve it on the side. Then melt 1/3 cup butter in a skillet; stir in flour to make a roux. When roux is golden, stir in reserved sauce, a little at a time, cooking until smooth and thickened. To serve, spoon sauce over hare and under onions and mushrooms, lifting them to spoon it in. Makes 6 servings.

NOTE: For a hotter version, increase the amount of peppercorns.

Peppy Roasted Rabbit

Red-hot and powerful, this dish is definitely not mild-mannered. For genuine game flavor, use jack rabbit; it's much darker and richer-tasting than domestic rabbit.

2 sprigs rosemary, chopped
1 shallot, minced
2 cloves garlic, minced
1/2 cup vegetable oil
1 medium onion, chopped
1 (3-lb.) jack rabbit, cut for frying
1/2 cup unsalted butter
1/2 cup dry brandy
1/2 cup dry red wine
2 teaspoons beef stock base (or to taste)
1 cup beer or water
2 teaspoons pequin quebrado
Salt to taste, if desired

Combine rosemary, shallot, garlic, oil and onion in a large glass or stainless steel bowl. Add rabbit pieces and turn to coat; then let stand 2 hours at room temperature, stirring and turning frequently. Lift rabbit from marinade; reserve marinade. Preheat oven to 375F (190C). Melt butter in a large, heavy roasting pan or ovenproof skillet over high heat; add rabbit pieces and cook until browned on all sides, turning as needed. Add brandy and flame carefully. Then spoon reserved marinade evenly over rabbit, stirring brandy into marinade and basting rabbit. Add wine, stock base and beer or water; sprinkle pequin evenly over all. Stir well and spoon once more over rabbit. Cover and bake about 1 hour or until meat is very tender, basting frequently. Taste and adjust seasonings, adding salt, if desired. Makes 4 servings.

Testy Trout Amandine

Hot green chile provides a delightfully spicy contrast to mild, mellow trout and buttery almonds.

**1 (3-lb.) filleted trout, cut in half lengthwise, or 2 (1-1/2-lb.)
    filleted trout**
1/2 cup unsalted butter
1/4 cup sliced almonds
1/4 cup dry white wine
Juice of 1/2 lemon
**1 small fresh hot green chile such as jalapeño or serrano, thinly
    sliced crosswise**

Rinse trout and pat dry. Melt butter in a large, heavy skillet. Add trout, flesh side down; cook until golden brown on bottom, then turn. Add almonds and stir until browned. Pour wine over all, then sprinkle with lemon juice and chile slices. Cover and cook over medium-low heat about 5 minutes or until fish flakes readily when prodded in thickest part. Serve hot. Makes 2 servings.

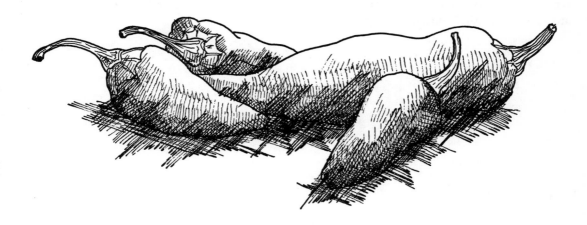

Spicy Stuffed Trout

In New Mexico, I was often fortunate enough to catch dozens of trout, so many that I constantly tried out new stuffings and spices to vary the flavor. This combination of cheeses, herbs and chiles has become a family favorite; perhaps your family and friends will enjoy it, too.

> **4 (10- to 12-inch-long) fresh brook trout (such as rainbow or**
> **German brown trout), cleaned**
> **1/2 cup unsalted butter, melted**
> **4 fresh New Mexico hot green chiles, parched (see page 9),**
> **peeled, seeded, de-ribbed**
> **1 cup grated Monterey Jack cheese**
> **1/2 teaspoon ground oregano, preferably Mexican**
> **1/4 cup finely chopped onion**
> **1 clove garlic, finely minced**
> **1 lime, cut lengthwise in quarters**
> **1 teaspoon ground pure New Mexico hot red chile**
> **4 cherry tomatoes**
> **4 leaves green or red leaf lettuce**

Prepare a bed of hot coals or preheat broiler. Rinse trout; remove scales but leave on heads and tails. Brush cavity of each trout with some of the melted butter. Split each green chile lengthwise; open out. Line each trout cavity with an opened-out chile. Spoon 1/4 cup cheese into each; then sprinkle cheese with oregano, onion and garlic. Brush outside of each trout with remaining melted butter. Adjust barbecue grill about 4 inches above coals or position oven rack so fish will be 4 inches below heat source. Lightly grease grill or rack in broiler pan. Grill or broil fish just until flesh is opaque in center but still juicy. Serve on warmed plates. Dust center edge of each lime wedge with ground chile; garnish each serving with a lime wedge and a cherry tomato set atop a lettuce leaf. Makes 4 servings.

Sassy Southern Crumb-Coated Bass

Any large lake fish can be prepared this way; the cornmeal coating holds in the moisture and adds tons of flavor. For a real down-South meal, serve with coleslaw and potato salad.

> **2 (2-lb.) bass or similar lake fish, cleaned**
> **1 cup milk**
> **1/2 cup all-purpose flour**
> **1/2 cup white, yellow or blue cornmeal**
> **1/4 cup finely minced green onions (including some green tops)**
> **1/2 teaspoon kosher or sea salt**
> **1/2 teaspoon pequin quebrado or cayenne pepper (or add liquid hot-pepper sauce to the milk)**
> **1 lemon, cut lengthwise in 4 to 6 wedges**
> **1 tablespoon minced parsley**
> **1 cup unsalted butter**
> **4 to 6 sprigs parsley**

Cut fish in chunks or fillets; rinse well, then soak in salted water 30 minutes. Drain and rinse. Pour milk into a large, shallow bowl and add fish. In another large, shallow bowl, combine flour, cornmeal, green onions, salt and pequin or cayenne. Dust center edge of each lemon wedge with minced parsley; set lemon wedges aside and combine any remaining minced parsley with coating mixture. Melt butter in a large, deep, heavy skillet. Then dip each piece of fish into coating mixture, being sure to crush coating into fish for maximum flavor. Cook fish until golden on all sides, turning as needed; drain on paper towels. Serve hot; garnish each serving with a parsley-edged lemon wedge and a parsley sprig. Makes 4 to 6 servings.

Brandied Duck with Green Peppercorns

Making wild ducks flavorful can be quite a challenge, depending on the age of the birds and the environment where they developed. This terrific recipe beautifully answers the challenge. A mixture of wine and brandy sparked with green peppercorns doubles as a tenderizing marinade and a flavorful sauce.

> **2 (3-lb.) ducks**
> **2 large onions, coarsely chopped**
> **1/4 cup minced parsley**
> **1 bay leaf**
> **2 teaspoons minced fresh thyme or 1 teaspoon dried leaf thyme**
> **3 cloves garlic, minced**
> **1/4 cup drained pickled green peppercorns (or to taste)**
> **1/3 cup cognac**
> **About 1-3/4 cups (1/2 750-ml. bottle) dry red wine**
> **1/4 cup olive oil**
> **1/2 pound fresh mushrooms, sliced**
> **Salt to taste**

Cut duck in serving-size pieces and place in a porcelain, stainless steel or glass baking dish. Add onions, parsley, bay leaf, thyme, garlic, green peppercorns, cognac and wine; stir to coat duck well. Let stand 4 hours at room temperature, turning duck pieces frequently. Then lift out and pat dry, reserving marinade. Heat oil in a heavy skillet over high heat. Add drained duck and cook until evenly browned on all sides, turning as needed; this usually takes 10 to 15 minutes. Add reserved marinade and mushrooms. Reduce heat to low, cover and simmer 1 hour or until duck is tender and leg joints wiggle easily. Season with salt. Makes 4 to 6 servings.

Crumb & Caribe-Coated Roast Doves

Wild game birds—particularly the smaller ones, such as dove and quail—often have to work very hard just to get food, making them lean and very tough. Long, slow cooking is the best way to tenderize them. For a great palate-pleaser, serve these roast doves with Wild Rice Baked with Almonds & Mushrooms, page 165.

> **1/2 cup fine dry bread crumbs**
> **1/2 teaspoon dried leaf oregano (preferably Mexican oregano), crushed**
> **2 tablespoons caribe (crushed Northern New Mexico red chile)**
> **2 cloves garlic, crushed**
> **4 sprigs flat-leaf parsley, finely minced**
> **6 (8-oz.) doves**
> **1/3 cup olive oil**
> **1/2 cup dry white wine (or more, as needed)**

Preheat oven to 350F (175C). Combine crumbs, oregano, caribe, garlic and parsley. Then thoroughly clean doves, rinse and pat dry. Brush each with oil, then roll each in crumb mixture, patting in crumbs and covering each bird as completely as possible. Place a rack in a roasting pan that's large enough to hold birds with room for air circulation around each. Pour wine into bottom of pan, then place birds on rack. Cover and roast 2 hours, basting frequently, or until doves are tender; wiggle thigh joint to test (it should move easily). Watch level of wine; if wine evaporates, add more as needed during roasting. Serve whole. Makes 6 servings.

Roast Pheasant in Horseradish-Brandy Cream

Horseradish is the hot one this time! Though not as searing as hot chile, it's still extremely stimulating to the palate. Here, a sauce of freshly grated horseradish, cream and brandy tops roast pheasants in a great dish for entertaining and holiday meals (it was a Thanksgiving favorite at our house). Try the Popped Wild Rice as a different garnish—you'll like the taste and appearance.

A note of caution: Fresh horseradish is truly wonderful, but purchased varieties can be as dull as sawdust; they're often stale and sometimes extended with turnips. To taste this dish at its best, grate the horseradish yourself or select a very fresh, pure, locally produced brand.

1/4 cup unsalted butter
8 green onions, thinly sliced
3 (2- to 3-lb.) pheasants
1/2 cup dry brandy
2 cups double-strength chicken broth
Freshly ground black pepper to taste
1 teaspoon dried leaf thyme, crushed
6 thick slices lean, heavily smoked country bacon
2 cups whipping cream
1/4 cup freshly grated horseradish (or to taste)
Popped Wild Rice, see below
Salt to taste

Popped Wild Rice:
About 1/2 cup uncooked wild rice
Vegetable oil

Melt butter in a heavy roasting pan large enough to hold the 3 pheasants. Add green onions and cook until slightly browned. Push onions to side of pan; add pheasants and cook until well browned on all sides, turning as needed. If onions start to overbrown, remove them. Meanwhile, preheat oven to 375F (190C). When birds are browned, add brandy, splashing it over pheasants; at once, flame carefully. When flames die, add broth, pepper and thyme. Return onions to pan, if removed. Place 2 slices of bacon on breast of each pheasant. Stir pan juices well, then baste birds. Roast, uncovered, 45 minutes, basting frequently. Stir cream and horseradish into pan juices; taste and add more horseradish, if desired. Then roast 15 minutes longer or until thigh joints of birds wiggle easily, basting frequently. Meanwhile, prepare Popped Wild Rice. Season sauce to taste with salt; serve pheasants drizzled with sauce and encircled with Popped Wild Rice. Make 6 servings.

Popped Wild Rice:
In a heavy pot or popcorn popper, pop rice like popcorn, using a little oil (enough to coat bottom of pot lightly).

Light Meals

Satisfying meals don't have to be multicourse feasts! The recipes in this chapter are meals in themselves, requiring only your favorite beverage and perhaps a crisp salad as accompaniments. The secret is *flavor*—and lots of it. What better way to tantalize the tastebuds than to "spice it up"? Hot seasonings such as chiles, pepper, mustard, ginger and horseradish really help appease the most hearty appetites, even if serving sizes are modest.

These light meals are versatile and varied. Serve Hot French Eggs for breakfast, Jon's Veggie Crepe Cake for brunch; try Nacho-Sauced Cartwheels for dinner, Beautiful Bagel Sandwiches for a late-night snack. Many of the recipes are quick to whip up, too—keep them in mind for days when you're short on time.

Spanish Tortilla, Ensenada Style

A Mexican tortilla is a flat, unleavened bread—but not so this Spanish tortilla! It's a delicious potato omelet, here spiced Mexican-style with pequin chiles. This Castilian delight should always be cooked in the best olive oil you can find, preferably extra-virgin Spanish olive oil.

> **1 cup extra-virgin Spanish olive oil**
> **4 medium potatoes, peeled and finely diced or grated**
> **1 medium onion, finely chopped**
> **8 eggs**
> **1 teaspoon pequin quebrado (or to taste)**
> **1 teaspoon salt**
> **1 recipe Ranchero Sauce, page 144, if desired**

Heat 1/4 cup oil to smoking in each of 2 heavy skillets (at least 12 inches in diameter). Add half the potatoes to each pan and cook, stirring often, until golden and crisp. Add half the onion to each skillet and continue to cook, stirring often, until potatoes are well browned and tender but have no blackened edges. Remove from heat and cool about 5 minutes. Meanwhile, in each of 2 bowls, beat together 4 eggs, 1/2 teaspoon pequin and 1/2 teaspoon salt. Add 1 panful of cooled potato-onion mixture to each bowl of eggs; stir well. Add 1/4 cup more oil to each skillet and heat until smoking. Then add 1 bowl of egg mixture to each skillet. Cook, shaking skillet often, until bottom of omelet is slightly golden; lift edges often with a spatula to check, running spatula around edge of omelet to free it. When omelets are almost firm, turn them: place a plate the same size as skillet over each skillet; invert omelet onto plate. Then slip omelet back into skillet, browned side up. Cook, shaking skillet, until second side is golden; then slide out of pan and serve at once. These omelets are generally served cut in quarters; serve 1 quarter as a light course of a meal, 2 quarters as a breakfast, lunch or brunch main dish. If desired, serve omelet with Ranchero Sauce. Makes 4 to 8 servings.

Zucchini Julienne Tossed with Pesto

Julienned zucchini is a light substitute for pasta—and a very flavorful one, especially when sauced with this spicy, chile-flavored pesto. You'll only need about half the pesto for this much zucchini; I've deliberately given you a large-quantity pesto recipe, since the sauce keeps several months in the freezer or refrigerator. (If you don't want leftovers, just cut the pesto recipe in half.)

> **3 large cloves garlic**
> **3 cups lightly packed stemmed fresh basil leaves**
> **1/3 cup piñon nuts (pine nuts)**
> **3/4 cup parched (see page 9), peeled, seeded fresh New Mexico**
> **   hot green chiles; or 3/4 cup canned whole green chiles**
> **3/4 cup extra-virgin olive oil**
> **3/4 cup freshly grated Parmesan cheese**
> **1/3 cup freshly grated Romano cheese**
> **1/3 cup unsalted butter, room temperature**
> **2 large or 3 medium zucchini, ends trimmed**
> **Additional freshly grated Parmesan or Romano cheese**

In food processor, combine garlic, basil leaves, piñon nuts, chiles and oil. Process just until pureed; do not overprocess. Pour mixture into a 3-quart bowl and add 3/4 cup Parmesan cheese, 1/3 cup Romano cheese and butter. Mix with a spoon, sprinkling in very hot tap water a little at a time, until mixture has the consistency of whipping cream. Using a food processer, julienne zucchini lengthwise into matchstick-size strips. Or use a mandolin adjusted to make thin julienne; when each zucchini is reduced to a piece that is too thin to slice safely, cut it in strips by hand. Into a steamer or large saucepan, pour water to a depth of about 2 inches and bring to a boil. Scatter zucchini strips in steamer basket and set basket in pan; basket should not touch water. Cover pan and steam zucchini about 2 minutes or until strands droop slightly when lifted. Immediately transfer zucchini to a warmed serving dish. Spoon a generous amount of pesto onto zucchini. Using 2 wooden spoons to keep the tender strands from breaking, lightly toss zucchini with sauce; serve immediately, with additional cheese, if desired. Makes about 12 first-course servings, about 6 light main-dish servings.

Chili Combo

A fluffy soufflé topping mellows the bite of hot chile in this simple, elegant-looking dish. It's a great way to use up leftover tortilla chips and chili.

About 1 tablespoon unsalted butter, room temperature
Topping, see below
3 cups chili
1 cup tortilla chips

Topping:
2 cups milk
1 tablespoon unsalted butter
3 eggs, separated
1/4 cup all-purpose flour
1/4 teaspoon salt
3/4 cup grated Monterey Jack cheese
4 teaspoons ground pure New Mexico hot red chile
2/3 cup canned creamed corn

Preheat oven to 350F (175C). Butter a 9-inch-square baking pan. Prepare Topping and set aside. In buttered baking pan, layer chili and tortilla chips, ending with a layer of chili. Cover evenly with Topping. Bake, uncovered, 45 minutes or until a wooden pick inserted in center of Topping comes out clean. Makes about 6 servings.

Topping:
In a saucepan, scald 1-1/2 cups milk with butter. Cool. In another saucepan, beat egg yolks until blended; beat in remaining 1/2 cup milk, flour and salt. Cook over low heat, stirring, until thickened. Remove from heat. Slowly add cooled scalded milk, whisking well; gently stir in cheese, ground chile and corn. Beat egg whites until they hold stiff peaks; fold in.

Sombrero Jalapa

Eggs to "put your hat on and get you going!" That's one way to translate *sombrero jalapa,* the Southwestern version of eggs Benedict. This dish is superb for brunch; make it with leftover or freshly made Chile con Queso.

> **1 cup Chile con Queso, page 20**
> **8 eggs**
> **4 corn tortillas**
> **1/4 cup vegetable oil**
> **1 tablespoon caribe (crushed Northern New Mexico red chile)**
> **1 cup or more shredded mixed lettuce, such as romaine and iceberg**
> **4 cherry tomatoes, cut in "roses"**

Warm 4 plates. Heat Chile con Queso just until warm. Poach or soft-fry eggs; soft-fry tortillas in oil. (Or, for a lower-calorie version, poach eggs; heat tortillas, 1 at a time, over a gas or electric burner until just hot and barely crisped.) To assemble, place a tortilla on each plate; top each with 2 eggs, then with 1/4 cup Chile con Queso. Sprinkle servings evenly with caribe; garnish with lettuce and tomatoes. Makes 4 servings.

Tasty Tomato Taglierini

A totally sunny experience! The blissful flavor of sun-dried tomatoes is even more tempting when spiced.

> **1 cup sun-dried tomatoes in oil (to measure, spoon tomatoes into a 1-cup measuring cup, then fill cup to brim with oil from tomatoes)**
> **2 eggs**
> **1/4 cup mixed freshly grated Romano and Parmesan cheeses**
> **2 tablespoons chopped parsley**
> **1 tablespoon caribe (crushed Northern New Mexico red chile) or Italian crushed hot red pepper**
> **2 cloves garlic, minced or pressed**
> **1 tablespoon fresh lemon juice**
> **8 ounces dried taglierini**
> **Salt and freshly ground black pepper to taste**

Lift tomatoes from cup; cut in 1/8-inch-wide slivers. In a serving bowl, whisk together eggs, slivered tomatoes and their oil, cheeses, parsley, caribe or crushed red pepper, garlic and lemon juice until blended. Following package directions, cook taglierini in boiling water just until tender to bite; drain well. Add drained pasta to egg mixture; lift with 2 forks to mix. Season with salt and pepper. Makes 2 to 4 servings.

Nacho-Sauced Cartwheels

Cheery pasta cartwheels in a creamy, vegetable-laden sauce make a delightful dish. Though Italian-inspired, it's not Italiano all the way—nacho-sliced pickled jalapeño chiles add a snappy Mexican accent.

2 medium leeks
1/4 cup unsalted butter
1 medium zucchini
1/2 pound fresh mushrooms
6 to 8 cherry tomatoes
1 tablespoon chopped fresh basil or 1 teaspoon dried leaf basil
1 to 1-1/2 cups light cream
1/2 cup nacho-sliced pickled jalapeño chiles (or to taste)
1/2 cup freshly grated Parmesan cheese
1/2 cup freshly grated Romano cheese
Freshly grated nutmeg to taste
Freshly ground black pepper to taste
1 pound dried cartwheel-shaped pasta

Thoroughly rinse leeks, then thinly slice leeks crosswise. Melt butter in a large skillet, add leeks and cook over medium heat about 10 minutes, stirring several times. Meanwhile, thinly slice zucchini. Thinly slice mushrooms lengthwise so all will have some stem attached to cap, if possible. Chop tomatoes. Add zucchini, mushrooms, tomatoes and basil to leeks and stir-fry over medium-high heat until zucchini is barely tender; it should remain bright green. Stir in 1 cup cream, jalapeños, 1/4 cup each of the Parmesan and Romano cheeses, nutmeg and pepper. Taste and adjust seasonings. Just before mixture comes to a boil, turn off heat. Following package directions, cook pasta in boiling water just until tender to bite. When pasta is just tender, drain well and return to cooking pot. Pour sauce over pasta and stir well. Heat briefly over high heat, stirring constantly. If pasta has absorbed too much sauce, gently stir in 1/2 cup more cream. Combine remaining 1/4 cup each Parmesan and Romano cheeses and pass at the table. Serve immediately. Makes 4 to 6 servings.

Pristine Penne

A zippy, mushroom-laced red sauce dresses sharp-ended penne beautifully.

> 1/4 cup olive oil
> 1 pound fresh mushrooms, thinly sliced
> 2 cloves garlic, minced
> 1 (32-oz.) can Italian plum tomatoes, mashed with a fork
> 1/2 cup finely chopped onion
> 1/2 teaspoon salt (or to taste)
> 2 tablespoons chopped fresh oregano or 1 tablespoon dried leaf
>   oregano
> 1 teaspoon chopped fresh rosemary or 1/2 teaspoon dried leaf
>   rosemary
> 1 tablespoon chopped fresh marjoram or 1 teaspoon dried leaf
>   marjoram
> 2 tablespoons chopped fresh basil or 1 tablespoon dried leaf
>   basil
> 2 teaspoons Italian crushed hot red pepper (or to taste)
> 12 ounces dried penne
> 4 ounces Romano cheese (or more), grated
> 4 ounces Parmesan cheese (or more), grated
> Additional Italian crushed hot red pepper, if desired

Heat oil in a large, deep pot. Add mushrooms and cook until mushrooms are lightly browned and all liquid has evaporated; then add garlic, tomatoes, onion, salt, herbs and 2 teaspoons crushed red pepper. Bring to a boil; reduce heat, cover and simmer about 1 hour or until flavors are blended. Taste and adjust seasonings. Following package directions, cook pasta in boiling water just until tender to bite. Drain pasta well and toss with sauce. Serve with cheeses on the side and additional crushed red pepper, if desired. Makes 4 servings.

Hot French Eggs

Zippy and rich-tasting, right from the villages of France! The spice is American, though. Serve as a brunch, light lunch or supper entree with a nice bottle of red wine, warm, crusty French bread and perhaps a salad.

3/4 cup unsalted butter
1/2 cup coarsely chopped chicken livers
1/2 cup chopped shallots or green onions
3/4 cup sliced fresh mushrooms
1/4 cup all-purpose flour
3/4 cup double-strength beef broth
Salt to taste
1/2 teaspoon freshly ground white pepper (or to taste)
1/2 cup dry red wine
About 1 tablespoon unsalted butter, room temperature
8 eggs
Chopped chives or parsley

Melt 3/4 cup butter in a medium, heavy skillet, then add chicken livers. Cook until livers start to brown; add shallots or green onions and mushrooms and cook until browned. Reduce heat and sprinkle flour over livers and vegetables, stirring constantly. When flour starts to brown, stir in broth, salt, white pepper and wine. Simmer, uncovered, stirring often, 15 to 20 minutes. Preheat oven to 350F (175C). Butter 4 small French cassoulet dishes or ovenproof bowls. Place 2 tablespoons of the chicken liver sauce in each (keep remaining sauce warm), then carefully break 2 eggs on top of each. Bake, uncovered, 15 to 20 minutes or until eggs are firm. When eggs are done, top equally with remaining sauce; sprinkle with chives or parsley. Makes 4 servings.

Chile-Crusted Chorizo Quiche

Quiche is usually quite mild in flavor—but never say no to this sassy version. Good for brunch, lunch or supper, it's easy to put together, especially if you already have parched green chiles on hand in the freezer. If you'd like to turn down the heat a bit, just substitute fried tortillas for the green-chile "crust" (see Pastel de Pescado, page 62, for instructions).

> **1 tablespoon unsalted butter, room temperature**
> **6 to 8 large fresh New Mexico hot green chiles, parched (see page 9), peeled, seeded, de-ribbed; or 6 to 8 canned whole green chiles**
> **1/2 pound chorizo or hot Italian sausage, casings removed, meat crumbled, browned and drained**
> **4 eggs**
> **1 tablespoon chopped fresh cilantro**
> **1 cup light cream**
> **1 cup grated Monterey Jack cheese**
> **1 small onion, thinly sliced, separated into rings**
> **1 tablespoon caribe (crushed Northern New Mexico red chile) or 1 teaspoon pequin quebrado (or to taste)**
> **1/2 cup hot salsa, if desired**

Preheat oven to 375F (190C). Butter a 9-inch pie plate, preferably ovenproof glass or pottery. Line pie plate with chiles, opening each one out completely and arranging with points at center of plate. Arrange chorizo in an even layer across bottom of chile "crust." Beat together eggs, cilantro and cream; very carefully pour into pie plate, being sure not to disturb distribution of sausage. Evenly sprinkle cheese over egg mixture, then place onion rings in a circle just inside edge of pie plate. Sprinkle caribe or pequin evenly over all and bake 30 minutes or until a knife inserted in center comes out clean. Serve with salsa, if desired. Makes 6 servings.

VARIATION
To vary the filling, substitute almost any kind of meat—or crab, shrimp, fish or chicken—for the sausage; use Cheddar or other cheese in place of the jack.

Touchdown Chile Puff

This make-ahead dish is terrific for brunch on Super Bowl Sunday—or for brunch, lunch or supper on any other weekend or weekday. It's great plain, but you may want to add chorizo, ham or a favorite breakfast meat. Cornbread or hot flour tortillas plus perhaps a salad or some fresh fruit nicely complement the puff.

> 1 tablespoon unsalted butter, room temperature
> 1 pound Monterey Jack cheese, coarsely grated
> 1 pound sharp Cheddar cheese, coarsely grated
> 1 cup parched (see page 9), peeled, seeded, chopped fresh New
>   Mexico hot green chiles; or 1 (7-oz.) can diced green chiles
> 1/2 cup all-purpose flour
> 6 eggs, separated
> 2/3 cup light cream
> 1/2 teaspoon salt
> 1/2 teaspoon ground oregano, preferably Mexican
> 1/4 teaspoon ground cumin
> 1/4 teaspoon baking powder

Preheat oven to 325F (165C). Butter a 9" x 13" baking dish or other 3-quart casserole. Combine cheeses, chiles and 2 tablespoons flour. Mix well, then distribute evenly in buttered casserole. Beat egg yolks well with a whisk or an electric mixer; beat in remaining 6 tablespoons flour, cream, salt, oregano and cumin. Then beat egg whites with baking powder until they hold stiff, moist peaks. Fold whites into egg yolk mixture. Spoon over cheese mixture in casserole. (At this point, you may cover and refrigerate 1 to 2 hours.) Bake, uncovered, about 1 hour or until top is golden brown and a knife inserted in center comes out clean. Cool about 10 minutes before cutting and serving. Makes 10 to 12 servings.

Southern California Omelet

This omelet is especially popular just north of the California-Mexico border, yet it's very easy to make and enjoy anywhere! Serve it for a nice light meal or snack.

2 tablespoons unsalted butter
1 (10- to 12-inch) flour tortilla
2 green onions, finely minced
1/2 Hass avocado, pitted, peeled, cut in 1/2-inch cubes
1/2 medium tomato, cut in 1/4-inch cubes
3 eggs
1 tablespoon tequila or water
1/4 cup Margarita Jalapeño Salsa, page 143
1/4 cup dairy sour cream
2 tablespoons chopped fresh cilantro

Melt butter in a large skillet or on a griddle. Place tortilla in skillet and lightly cook both sides; do not crisp. Set aside on a serving plate. Add green onions, avocado and tomato to skillet; stir 1 to 2 minutes or until heated through. Beat together eggs and tequila or water; pour over vegetables in skillet. Cook until set on bottom; carefully turn over as directed for Spanish Tortilla, Ensenada Style, page 124, and cook on other side until as done as desired. (Or cook without turning: as edges set, constantly lift them with a spatula and allow uncooked egg to flow underneath. Cook until omelet is as firm as desired.) Slide omelet out of pan on top of tortilla. Top with salsa, spoon sour cream in center and garnish with cilantro. Makes 1 serving.

Italian Omelet Roll

This impressive rolled omelet offers a kaleidoscope of colors and flavors: hot sausage, pickled peppers and fiery pequin tempered with mild mozzarella cheese and the delicate omelet base. Not as difficult to make as it looks, the omelet is quick to put together. Once baked and assembled, it must be served immediately.

1 tablespoon unsalted butter, room temperature
12 eggs, separated
3/4 teaspoon salt (or to taste)
Pinch of pequin quebrado
1 pound hot Italian sausage
1 teaspoon Italian crushed hot red pepper (or to taste)
1 medium onion, thinly sliced, separated into rings
12 or more pickled Tuscan peppers
8 ounces mozzarella cheese, cut in 1/8-inch-thick slices

Butter a 10" x 15" jelly-roll pan. Cover bottom of pan with a piece of waxed paper, cut to size; butter paper. Preheat oven to 350F (175C). Beat egg whites until stiff; set aside. Combine salt, pequin and egg yolks; beat with a whisk until blended. Fold whites and yolks together. Turn egg mixture into prepared pan, carefully smoothing with a spatula. Bake 15 to 20 minutes or until a knife inserted in center comes out clean. Meanwhile, remove casings from sausage. Crumble meat into a large skillet and cook briefly; then add crushed red pepper and onion. Cook, stirring often, 10 to 12 minutes or until sausage is cooked through. Drain off fat. As soon as omelet is done, place it on a cooling rack; then loosen edges all around pan. Grasp edge of paper and pull omelet out onto a cloth towel; invert omelet onto another towel and peel off paper. Sprinkle with cooked sausage and onion, then scatter Tuscan peppers over top. Evenly arrange cheese slices over all. Quickly roll, starting with a long side; set on an ovenproof platter and place in oven briefly to melt cheese. Then slice and serve. Makes 6 servings.

Beautiful Bagel Sandwiches

Lavishly layered open-face sandwiches, featuring some unexpected but entirely delicious flavor combinations, make a satisfying lunch or snack.

Horseradish Sauce, see below
4 bagels, sliced in half
1 cup alfalfa sprouts
4 ounces Monterey Jack cheese, sliced
6 ounces smoked salmon, thinly sliced
2 kiwifruit, peeled, thinly sliced

Horseradish Sauce:
1/4 cup dairy sour cream
1/4 cup mayonnaise
1/4 cup freshly grated horseradish

Prepare Horseradish Sauce; spread a layer of sauce on each bagel half. Sprinkle sprouts on each half, then layer with cheese and salmon. Top each half with kiwifruit slices, arranged in an overlapping ring. (If desired, heat the sandwiches to melt cheese before adding kiwifruit.) Makes 4 to 8 servings.

Horseradish Sauce:
Thoroughly mix all ingredients.

Quick Tricks

Brennan makes these quick, Mexican-influenced open-face sandwiches when short on time or ingredients.

8 slices Cheddar cheese
8 slices whole-grain whole-wheat bread, toasted
16 slices bacon, crisply cooked, drained
1/4 cup Margarita Jalapeño Salsa, page 143, or other hot salsa
4 green onions, thinly sliced
8 slices Swiss cheese
4 slices Monterey Jack cheese
2 tablespoons caribe (crushed Northern New Mexico red chile)
4 pickled Tuscan peppers or jalapeño chiles, thinly sliced

Preheat broiler. Place a slice of Cheddar on each piece of bread, then place bread in a broiler pan. Top each sandwich with 2 bacon slices, then top evenly with salsa and green onions. Cut remaining cheeses in 1/2-inch-wide strips. Place Swiss strips diagonally across each sandwich, leaving a space between strips; crisscross jack strips at right angles over Swiss strips. Sprinkle caribe and peppers or chiles over sandwiches. Broil until cheeses are melted; serve hot. Makes 4 servings.

Pride of Guaymas
Shrimp-Avocado Delights

Beautiful to behold! Butterflied green onions create a perfect accent for rosy shrimp framed with curving avocado slices and served on toast. Fun and easy to make—and fiesta perfect, combining Mexico's national colors of red, white and green.

1 ripe avocado, preferably Hass or Fuerte variety

1 lime

8 green onions

1/2 cup mayonnaise

2 tablespoons parched (see page 9), peeled, seeded, diced fresh
New Mexico hot green chiles (or to taste)

4 slices firm-textured white bread

1 pound cooked, shelled, deveined medium shrimp, sliced in
half lengthwise

1/2 cup Margarita Jalapeño Salsa, page 143, made without
tequila; or 1/2 cup other hot red salsa

4 large sprigs fresh cilantro or watercress

Halve and pit avocado, then peel each half. Cut lime in half; squeeze 1 half evenly all over avocado halves. Set avocado halves aside. Trim roots and any wilted tops from green onions; then, using a sharp knife, shred top of each onion lengthwise for 2/3 of its length. Cut each of these "butterflied" onions in half lengthwise and set aside. Squeeze remaining lime half; blend juice (you need only about a teaspoon) with mayonnaise and chiles. Taste; add more chiles, if desired. Toast bread. Generously spread each slice with mayonnaise mixture. Cut avocado halves lengthwise in 1/2-inch-thick slices. On each toast slice, place 2 avocado slices facing each other with tips at opposite corners of toast, positioning slices to make an oval. Combine shrimp with remaining mayonnaise mixture and evenly divide among sandwiches, spooning shrimp mixture within avocado slices. Arrange butterflied green onion halves atop shrimp mixture, with white part of onion overlapping avocado and green top extending to corners of toast. Top each sandwich with 2 tablespoons salsa and a cilantro or watercress sprig. Then enjoy! Makes 4 servings.

Chic Crab Crepes

These are a very special reward for a hard day spent doing anything tedious—or any time you'd like a nice, light, easy-on-the palate treat. At breakfast, serve with luscious drinks; at lunch or late at night, serve with a salad.

> 2 eggs
> 2 cups milk
> 1-1/2 cups all-purpose flour
> 1 teaspoon baking powder
> Dash of salt
> 1/2 cup unsalted butter, melted
> 1/3 cup all-purpose flour
> 1 cup double-strength chicken broth
> 1 cup light cream
> 1/2 cup thinly slivered Swiss cheese
> 2 tablespoons freshly grated Parmesan cheese
> 2 tablespoon freshly grated Romano cheese
> 2 tablespoons dry sherry
> Freshly grated nutmeg to taste
> 1/2 pound crab meat, drained, all bits of shell removed
> 1/2 cup finely diced green bell pepper
> 1/2 cup finely diced celery
> 1 fresh or pickled green jalapeño chile, finely diced
> 1 fresh or pickled red jalapeño chile or pickled red cherry
>   pepper, finely diced

In a bowl, beat eggs with a whisk or an electric mixer until fluffy. Beat in milk, 1-1/2 cups flour, baking powder and salt until well blended. (Or process ingredients in a blender until well mixed.) Add 2 tablespoons melted butter and mix well. Brush a little melted butter in a well-seasoned 6- to 8-inch crepe pan set over medium heat. When butter is hot, add just enough batter to cover pan bottom, rotating pan to spread batter evenly. When crepe is set on bottom, flip it over and quickly cook other side. Remove from pan. Repeat to cook remaining batter; you should have about 12 crepes. Stack crepes as made; wrap in foil and keep warm in a 350F (175C) oven. Then prepare sauce: combine remaining melted butter and 1/3 cup flour in a saucepan and cook, stirring, until lightly browned. Add broth and cream; cook, stirring, until thick and smooth. Stir in cheeses. When cheeses are melted, stir in sherry and a little nutmeg. Keep warm. Thoroughly mix crab, bell pepper, celery and about 1/2 cup sauce—just enough to make mixture hold together. To fill each crepe, spread a ribbon of crab mixture down center and sprinkle with a little green jalapeño chile. Fold to enclose. Place crepes on ovenproof individual plates or a platter and drizzle with remaining sauce. Sprinkle with red jalapeño or cherry pepper and bake, uncovered, in a 350F (175C) oven about 10 minutes or until bubbly. Makes 4 servings.

Jon's Veggie Crepe Cake

One of Jon Eben's very favorite brunch dishes is this glorious-looking, French-inspired crepe cake. You can vary the recipe as much as you wish; in fact, Jon says this dish is a wonderfully practical way to use up leftover vegetables, cheeses, sauces—and even meats, if you like. Just be sure to select foods with compatible flavors, colors and textures. We particularly like this combination.

> 3 eggs
> 1-3/4 cups milk
> 1-1/2 cups all-purpose flour
> 1 teaspoon baking powder
> Pinch of salt
> 1/2 teaspoon freshly ground white pepper
> 1 teaspoon dry mustard
> 1 teaspoon mustard seeds
> 1 tablespoon unsalted butter, melted
> Vegetable oil
> 2 cups chopped onions
> 2 cups coarsely grated Cheddar cheese
> 2 cups well-rinsed, stemmed, lightly packed fresh spinach
>   leaves
> 2 cups chopped fresh tomatoes
> 1/3 cup freshly grated Parmesan cheese
> 1/4 cup minced fresh parsley or 2 tablespoons dried parsley
>   flakes

In a bowl, beat eggs with a whisk or electric mixer until fluffy. Beat in milk, flour, baking powder, salt, white pepper, dry mustard, mustard seeds and melted butter until well blended. In a well-seasoned 6- to 8-inch crepe pan, heat just enough oil to coat pan bottom (only enough to prevent crepes from sticking). Add a scant 1/4 cup batter or just enough to cover pan bottom, rotating pan to spread batter evenly. When crepe is set on the bottom, flip it over and quickly cook other side. Remove from pan. Repeat to cook remaining batter. If made ahead, stack crepes, separating with plastic wrap; cover and refrigerate as long as a day. About 30 minutes before serving time, preheat oven to 350F (175C). Then assemble crepe cake. Lay 1 crepe in a soufflé dish or ovenproof casserole or on a round ovenproof platter. Sprinkle with onions; top with another crepe, then a layer of Cheddar cheese. Add another crepe, a layer of spinach, a fourth crepe and a layer of tomatoes. Repeat layers, using remaining crepes, vegetables and Cheddar. Sprinkle with Parmesan cheese and parsley and bake, uncovered, 20 minutes or until hot and bubbly. Makes 4 to 6 servings.

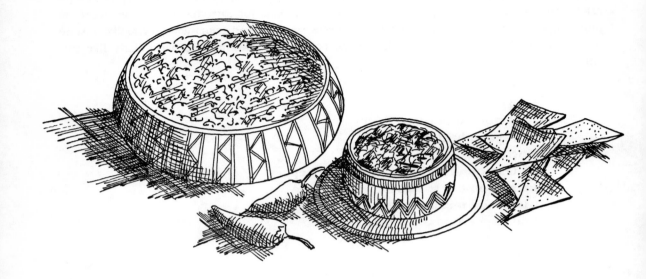

Condiments
& Sauces

Change the predictable to the pleasurable with spicy, imaginative sauces, relishes, oils and seasonings. Their origins ranging from the Far East to the Southwest, the favorites presented in this chapter add exciting flavor to a variety of dishes. Hot Salt, Chile Mayonnaise, Hot Hot Oil and more—all are easy to prepare and well worth the small effort involved. And many make wonderful presents from your pantry. Ribbon-tied glasses of Jalapeño Jelly, for example, will delight your friends at holiday time—and even if you've never attempted jelly-making before, you'll find it so simple and so much fun to do!

Hot Salt

This easy-to-prepare condiment offers a great alternative to hot mustard or oil when you want to add some fire to Chinese foods. Sprinkle it over meats and combination dishes, or use it as a dipping salt. The tiny, reddish-brown Szechwan peppers, encased in flowerlike star-shaped husks, are sold in Asian markets and some spice shops.

1 tablespoon dried Szechwan peppers
1/4 cup kosher or sea salt

Preheat oven to 325F (165C). Crush peppers slightly by processing briefly in a blender, then spread on a baking sheet and toast 5 to 10 minutes or until color deepens and aroma heightens. Combine with salt. Store in the refrigerator. Makes 1/4 cup.

Hot Hot Oil

Ouch! If you make this oil hot enough, it really can cause long-lasting pain. When dried chiles are mixed with vegetable oil, their own volatile oils—the source of chile heat—are quickly drawn out and dispersed throughout the oil, ready to cling to the tastebuds of the unwary. Nonetheless, Hot Hot Oil is a terrific table condiment for those who take hot foods seriously, as well as a great appetizer dip for bland vegetables and seafood (such as jicama and scallops). You can make the oil just plain hot to painfully hot, depending on the chiles you use.

2 cups soybean or other vegetable oil
1-1/2 cups caribe, crushed Northern New Mexico red chile (for
    hot oil); pequin quebrado (for very hot oil); or tiny dried
    Chinese hot red chiles (for painfully hot oil)

Mix oil and caribe, pequin or chiles in a small, heavy saucepan. Warm until oil almost begins to bubble, then reduce heat; caribe or chiles should not turn black. (If you do not have a good source of low, controlled heat and a heavy saucepan, heat oil first, then add 1 bit of caribe or chile. If it floats and keeps its redness, add the rest; cover and watch carefully, stirring occasionally.) Cook over low heat until chiles darken but do not turn black. Cool overnight at room temperature, then strain oil through cheesecloth. Stored tightly covered in the refrigerator, this orange-red oil will keep indefinitely. Let warm to room temperature to serve. Makes 1-1/2 cups.

NOTE: Asian cooks typically allow the chiles to blacken in the oil. I feel that this results in stronger, less fresh-tasting oil, so I recommend removing the oil from the heat *before* the chiles blacken.

Hot Pepper Butter

A very convenient condiment to keep at the ready in the freezer, this spread heightens the flavor of meat, seafood, poultry and vegetables. For extra-hot butter, use caribe rather than ground chile.

> **2 tablespoons ground pure New Mexico hot red chile or caribe**
> **(crushed Northern New Mexico red chile)**
> **1 cup unsalted butter, room temperature**
> **1/4 teaspoon fresh lime juice**
> **1 tablespoon dry white wine (or more, as needed)**

In a food processor, process all ingredients until well blended, adding enough wine to give mixture a soft consistency. (Or beat together with an electric mixer.) Use immediately; or shape into a log on a double layer of waxed paper and freeze until firm, then seal in a plastic bag. To use, just cut off a slice of butter and place atop food. (These round pats of butter make a very attractive topping; you might also sprinkle the butter with minced parsley.) Makes 1 cup.

Hot Tempura Sauce

Zesty on almost any batter-fried seafood, poultry or vegetable. If you like, let your guests temper the sauce's heat: serve the wasabi (green Japanese horseradish paste) on the side, to be blended to taste into individual servings of dipping sauce.

> **1/2 cup mirin (sweet sake) or dry sherry**
> **1/2 cup soy sauce**
> **1 (1-inch) piece fresh ginger, peeled, finely grated**
> **1/4 pound daikon, peeled, finely grated**
> **2 green onions, thinly sliced**
> **Wasabi to taste**

Combine all ingredients; add wasabi to taste or serve it on the side. Makes about 1-1/2 cups (enough for 6 servings).

NOTE: I often add only 2 ounces daikon to the sauce, then coarsely grate the remainder and batter-fry it (in spoonfuls) along with the other tempura vegetables.

Very Hot Shrimp Cocktail Sauce

Super-hot and passionate, this sauce is great over any seafood. Make it as painful as you wish by adding more hot pepper sauce or pequin.

3/4 cup ketchup
1/2 cup freshly grated horseradish
Juice of 1/2 lime
Liquid hot-pepper sauce to taste
1/2 teaspoon pequin quebrado (or to taste)

Combine all ingredients; taste and adjust seasonings. Makes 1 cup.

Margarita Jalapeño Salsa

A splash of tequila makes all the difference in this robust salsa; it has a way of mellowing the searing nature of terrifically hot foods. I like this sauce on seafood, chicken and any kind of chops—pork, veal or lamb.

1/2 cup cubed tomato (1/2-inch cubes)
1/2 cup medium-fine-chopped white or red onion
4 or more fresh jalapeño chiles, very finely minced (remove
seeds and ribs from chiles for a milder salsa)
1 clove garlic, minced
1/2 teaspoon salt (or to taste)
1/4 cup gold or white tequila

Combine all ingredients and let stand at least 30 minutes at room temperature. Taste and adjust seasonings. Makes about 1-1/2 cups.

Ranchero Sauce

This sauce is traditionally served over poached eggs atop softly fried corn tortillas, but as a change of pace, I like to perch the eggs on avocado halves or beds of crab or chicken in a casserole. Try the sauce on hamburgers and omelets, too. You can make it hours or even a day ahead of time.

1 tablespoon olive oil
1/2 cup chopped onion
3/4 cup tomato juice
1 medium tomato, chopped
1 large clove garlic, chopped
1/2 cup parched (see page 9), peeled, seeded, chopped green
chiles, as hot as you like
3/4 teaspoon ground cumin
1/4 teaspoon ground oregano, preferably Mexican
1/2 teaspoon salt (or to taste)

Heat oil in a medium saucepan or small skillet. Add onion and cook until limp. Add tomato juice, tomato, garlic, chiles, cumin, oregano and salt; simmer at least 10 minutes or until flavors are blended. Taste and adjust seasonings. Makes 2 cups (about 4 servings).

Great Green Sauce

The perfect dunk for any green vegetable—florets of broccoli, zucchini slices, blanched green beans, snow peas, you name it. Serve at room temperature.

> **1 cup unsalted butter**
> **1 cup well-rinsed, stemmed, firmly packed fresh spinach leaves, steamed over boiling water until limp, drained**
> **1/4 cup parsley sprigs**
> **2 green onions, chopped**
> **1 tablespoon chopped fresh dill or 1 teaspoon dried dill weed**
> **1 tablespoon chopped fresh tarragon or 1 teaspoon dried leaf tarragon**
> **1 tablespoon chopped fresh basil or 1 teaspoon dried leaf basil**
> **2 fresh New Mexico hot green chiles, parched (see page 9), peeled, seeded, chopped (or to taste)**
> **Salt to taste, if desired**

Melt butter in a saucepan; keep warm. In a food processor or blender, combine spinach, parsley, green onions, herbs and chiles. Process until pureed. Taste; adjust seasonings, adding salt, if desired. Add to butter and cook, stirring, until mixture is heated through and flavors are well blended. If made ahead, refrigerate in a tightly covered jar; warm by holding jar under hot running water before serving. Makes 1-3/4 cups.

Beer Garden Spread

From the *Bierstuben* of Bavaria—but enhanced with horseradish, mustard and pequin. Serve any favorite seasonal vegetables alongside.

8 ounces small-curd cottage cheese (1 cup)
1/2 cup unsalted butter, room temperature
1 tablespoon caraway seeds
1 tablespoon freshly grated horseradish (or to taste)
1 tablespoon dry mustard (or to taste)
1 teaspoon pequin quebrado or cayenne pepper (or to taste)
1 tablespoon capers
1/4 cup chopped onion
1 (2-oz.) can anchovy fillets, undrained, mashed
Fresh vegetables of your choice, sliced or cut in sticks or
wedges as appropriate

In a food processor, process all ingredients (except vegetables) until smooth. (Or beat together in a bowl.) Place in a crock or pottery bowl and refrigerate at least 2 hours or until firm. To serve, place on a platter; attractively arrange vegetables around crock of dip. Dunk vegetables in dip or spread dip on vegetables with a knife. Makes about 2 cups.

Jalapeño Hollandaise

The snappy sharpness of jalapeños and the tang of fresh lime juice give this popular sauce a heated edge. Spoon it over poached eggs, as in eggs Benedict; or serve it with asparagus, broccoli, artichokes or other favorite green vegetables.

For best results, use the yolks of large, very fresh eggs. To add extra flavor, stir in chopped fresh basil leaves.

3 egg yolks
1 to 2 tablespoons fresh lime juice
1/2 cup unsalted butter, melted
1/4 teaspoon salt (or to taste)
2 or 3 fresh jalapeño chiles, parched (see page 9), peeled,
**   seeded, finely chopped; or 2 or 3 pickled jalapeño chiles,**
**   finely chopped**
Generous pinch of caribe (crushed Northern New Mexico red
**   chile)**

In the top of a double boiler, beat together egg yolks and 1 tablespoon lime juice. Drizzle in about 1/3 of melted butter in a thin stream, then set over boiling water. Add remaining melted butter in a thin stream, beating constantly. Continue to beat until thickened, adding salt and jalapeños. Taste; if desired, add 1 tablespoon more lime juice. Spoon sauce over foods of your choice; garnish with caribe. Makes 2/3 cup.

Chile Mayonnaise

The simple addition of extra-hot crushed pequin chiles can lift mayonnaise from the ordinary to the very special. Use as a dunk for fresh vegetables or as a sauce for sliced meats or broiled or boiled seafood.

1-1/4 cups olive oil or salad oil
1 egg
2 tablespoons white wine vinegar
1 teaspoon sugar
1 teaspoon pequin quebrado (or to taste)
1/2 teaspoon salt

In a blender or food processor, combine 1/4 cup oil, egg, vinegar, sugar, pequin and salt. Process briefly just to blend. Then, with motor running, add remaining 1 cup oil in a very thin stream, processing until mayonnaise has the desired thick, creamy consistency. Makes 1-1/4 cups.

Jalapeño Jelly

Serve this all kinds of ways! It's especially good with cream cheese and crackers as an hors d'oeuvre, as a sauce for roasted meats (see Lively Leg of Spring Lamb, page 87) and even as an ingredient in meat and vegetable dishes. And homemade jelly is always well received as a gift from your kitchen. For gift-giving, pour the jelly into decorative glasses or goblets and tie a ribbon around each jar; you might even make fabric coverings to fit over the tops.

3 large, very ripe red bell peppers, cored, seeded
6 to 8 fresh jalapeño chiles, seeded (for a milder flavor, remove
ribs too)
1-1/2 cups cider vinegar (5% acidity)
6-1/2 cups sugar
6 ounces bottled liquid pectin

Using a food processor or food chopper, finely chop bell peppers and jalapeños. Turn chopped peppers and chiles into a large saucepan, stir in vinegar and sugar and bring to a boil. Boil, uncovered, about 30 minutes or until mixture is slightly thickened and peppers are clear. Remove thickened pepper mixture from heat; cool about 10 minutes. Stir in pectin, return to heat, bring to a boil and boil about 2 minutes longer (at sea level) or until jelly sheets off the edge of a large metal spoon held at right angles above pan. Remove from heat, skim off and discard foam and immediately pour jelly equally into 5 or 6 hot, sterilized 1/2-pint jelly glasses. Cool, then seal with paraffin and cover with lids. Makes 2-1/2 to 3 pints.

Pickled Jalapeños

Home-pickled peppers are much prettier and more flavorful than the commercial variety, and really worth the effort. Use them for flavoring sauces, soups, stews and main dishes—or, if you're very brave, just eat them as is! To speed preparation, you can use a food processor to slice the onions and carrots.

> **15 pounds whole, blemish-free, small to medium fresh jalapeño chiles**
> **2 cups extra-virgin olive oil**
> **10 small white onions, sliced, separated into rings**
> **5 large cloves garlic, chopped**
> **5 medium carrots, peeled, thinly sliced crosswise**
> **2 teaspoons ground oregano, preferably Mexican**
> **3 fresh bay leaves**
> **2 tablespoons salt**
> **3 cups distilled white vinegar (5% acidity)**
> **2-1/2 cups distilled water**

Scrub jalapeños, trimming off stems. Set aside. Into a large, deep, heavy pot, pour 1/2 cup oil (enough to coat pot bottom). Heat oil until almost at the smoking point, then turn off or reduce heat. Add onions, garlic and carrots; stir only until onions are clear, making sure not to brown any of the vegetables. Add oregano, bay leaves and salt and stir to mix; then add vinegar and water and bring to a boil, stirring often. Continue to boil and stir until salt is dissolved, then add remaining 1-1/2 cups oil and return to a boil. Stir in jalapeños and remove from heat. Fill 16 to 20 hot, sterilized 1-pint canning jars (or eight to ten 1-quart jars), leaving 1-1/2 inches head space. Wipe rims clean with boiling water, then seal jars tightly with canning lids and rings. Cool filled jars at room temperature, out of drafts. Store in a cool, dry place until ready to use. Makes 16 to 20 pints (8 to 10 quarts).

New Mexico Piccalilli Relish

Perhaps looking for ways to use the zucchini squash cultivated by local Pueblo Indians, the Spanish, English and German settlers of the Southwest all concocted hot relishes like this one. It's a favorite of several old Spanish families in New Mexico.

> **8 cups chopped zucchini**
> **1/2 cup parched (see page 9), peeled, seeded, chopped fresh**
> **New Mexico hot green chiles**
> **4 cups chopped hot onions**
> **1/3 cup pickling salt**
> **2-1/4 cups cider vinegar (5% acidity)**
> **4 cups sugar**
> **1 tablespoon dry mustard**
> **1 tablespoon celery seeds**
> **1 tablespoon caribe (crushed Northern New Mexico red chile)**

Stir together zucchini, chiles, onions and salt in a large bowl. Let stand 2 hours at room temperature, stirring occasionally. Then cover and refrigerate overnight. Drain; rinse with cold water until water runs clear. Turn into a large saucepan and stir in vinegar, sugar, mustard, celery seeds and caribe. Bring to a boil; boil, uncovered, 30 minutes. Pour relish into 6 hot, sterilized 1-pint canning jars, leaving 1-1/2 inches head space; wipe rims clean with boiling water, then seal jars tightly with canning lids and rings. Cool filled jars at room temperature, out of drafts. Store in a cool, dry place until ready to use. Makes 6 pints.

—Vegetable Dishes —

Spicy, sassy main dishes call for mild-mannered accompaniments—like those in this chapter. From fluffy whipped Sweet Potatoes Teased with Tequila to Luscious Leeks to crunchy Zucchini Fritters, these side dishes are welcome alongside any extra-hot entree. I've included some spicy selections, too, sure to be favored by dedicated fire-eaters as well as those looking for snappy accompaniments to milder main courses. Try Hot Green Beans Vinaigrette or Chile-Cheese Onions—or, for a special treat, sweet-hot Cavolfiore alla Medusa, a wonderful Italian creation.

Luscious Leeks

A soothing dish that goes very well with punishingly hot entrees. The sweet caramel coating on the leeks quickly cools down overheated palates.

4 leeks
1/4 cup unsalted butter
2 tablespoons packed dark brown sugar
Freshly grated nutmeg to taste
Freshly ground black pepper to taste

Rinse leeks very thoroughly, then cut in half lengthwise. Rinse leek halves, separating layers to wash out dirt; then cut crosswise in 1-inch-thick slices. Melt butter in a large, heavy skillet over medium heat; add leeks and sprinkle with brown sugar, several grates of nutmeg and generous grindings of pepper. Cook, stirring, until leeks are caramelized on the outside. When edges are as brown as desired, serve. Makes 6 servings.

Sweet Potatoes Teased with Tequila

My daughter Amy has always been able to eat her weight in sweet potatoes. Just for a change, I once added tequila to a favorite recipe instead of the usual orange juice, rum or brandy. It gave the potatoes a different, interesting taste—and we've been "into" tequila'd sweet potatoes ever since!

2 large or 3 medium sweet potatoes (about 2 lbs. total)
2 to 4 tablespoons tequila
1/4 cup unsalted butter, room temperature
Freshly grated nutmeg to taste
1/2 teaspoon salt (or to taste)
Freshly ground white pepper to taste

Scrub unpeeled sweet potatoes, cut in large chunks and cook in lightly salted boiling water until tender. Then pour off water, cover pan and let potatoes "fluff" about 5 minutes. Quickly peel potatoes; add 2 tablespoons tequila, butter and nutmeg. Beat with an electric mixer or process in a food processor until smooth. Taste and add salt, white pepper and 2 more tablespoons tequila, if desired. Serve warm. Makes 4 to 6 servings.

Mexican Carrots

A tried-and-true favorite in our house, this is one vegetable dish that can be made any time, at a moment's notice—since almost everybody keeps carrots and onions on hand. The Mexican flavor goes nicely with any type of entree.

> **4 large carrots**
> **2 tablespoons olive oil**
> **1 large onion, very thinly sliced, separated into rings**
> **Generous pinch of ground oregano**
> **Freshly ground black pepper to taste**

Thinly slice each carrot on the diagonal, rolling carrot a quarter-turn after each slice. Set aside. In a large, shallow skillet or a wok (or on a griddle), heat oil over medium-high heat. Add onion and cook briefly; add carrots, oregano and pepper. Stir-fry 8 to 10 minutes or until vegetables are tinged with brown. Serve hot. Makes 4 servings.

Zucchini Fritters

A soothing side dish that's plenty welcome with some of the super-hot specials I've included in this book. Quick and easy to make, these fritters are also very appealing even to those who aren't terribly inclined to eat squash of any kind. (If you want to spice up the fritters, just include the optional green chiles.)

> **4 small to medium zucchini**
> **1/2 cup finely chopped onion**
> **2 cloves garlic, minced**
> **2 eggs, beaten**
> **Salt to taste**
> **1/4 cup parched (see page 9), peeled, chopped fresh New**
>   **Mexico hot green chiles, if desired**
> **2 tablespoons olive oil (or more, as needed)**

Using a food processor or a hand grater, grate zucchini. Then, in a bowl, combine zucchini, onion, garlic, eggs, salt and chiles, if desired. Heat oil in a large, shallow skillet until hot. Drop spoonfuls of zucchini mixture into hot oil, making 2-1/2- to 3-inch patties; cook until browned on bottom, then turn and brown on other side. Add more oil to pan as needed. Serve hot. Makes 4 to 6 servings.

Garbanzos

Freshly cooked garbanzos are so much better than the canned type that you won't mind spending a little extra time preparing them. Once cooked, they can be marinated in vinaigrette or any oil-and-vinegar-based salad dressing; added to vegetable dishes, soups or stews; or even deep-fried for a crunchy appetizer.

10 ounces (1-1/2 cups) dried garbanzos
1 stalk celery, cut crosswise in quarters
1 onion, cut in quarters
1 carrot, cut in quarters
1 bay leaf
1 sprig fresh thyme or 1/2 teaspoon dried leaf thyme
5 sprigs parsley
1/4 pound ham end, 1 pork bone or 3 slices bacon
Salt to taste

Sort and rinse beans, then place in a large pot, add enough water to cover by 2 inches and soak 8 to 10 hours. Drain and rinse. Tie vegetables, bay leaf, thyme and parsley in a cheesecloth bag. (If you don't have any cheesecloth, just add vegetables and herbs "loose.") Place bag in large pot with beans, ham end, pork bone or bacon and enough water to cover. Bring to a boil; reduce heat, cover and simmer 1 hour, skimming occasionally. Add salt and continue to cook about 30 minutes longer or until beans are just tender. Drain garbanzos and discard cheesecloth bag and ham. Adjust seasonings. Makes 4 cups.

Eben's Ever-Special Baked Stuffed Tomatoes

Jon Eben and my husband Brennan have been friends since their bachelor days, when they both sharpened their culinary skills. Jon created these luscious, pretty stuffed tomatoes as a side dish for veal scaloppine, but they're just as good alongside most any grilled meat.

4 medium (2- to 3-inch-diameter) tomatoes
1/4 teaspoon garlic powder
4 (1-inch) cubes Cheddar cheese
4 teaspoons Dijon-style mustard
1/2 cup chopped onion
4 dashes Worcestershire sauce
1 teaspoon dried leaf basil or oregano (or to taste)
4 thin (1/2-oz.) slices Swiss cheese, each approximately 3" x 6"
1 tablespoon chopped chives or parsley

Cut a thin slice from top of each tomato; then hollow out tomato, cutting out flesh to leave a shell with sides about 1/4 inch thick and a top opening about 2 inches wide. Chop tomato flesh. Layer garlic powder, Cheddar cheese, mustard and onion (in that order) in shells; top onion with as much chopped tomato as will comfortably fit, then season with Worcestershire sauce and basil or oregano. Fold each Swiss cheese slice in half; top each tomato with a folded slice, letting some of it hang over edges. (At this point, you may cover tomatoes and refrigerate up to a day.) To bake, preheat oven to 350F (175C). Line a baking pan with foil to keep clean-up to a minimum. Arrange tomatoes in pan; bake 15 minutes or until cheese is bubbly and lightly browned. Serve hot. Makes 4 servings.

NOTE: Any leftover chopped tomato can be used in a salsa or as a garnish for burgers, omelets or salads.

Elote con Queso

I was introduced to this corn custard in childhood by my Mexican Aunt Virginia; it was almost always part of our holiday dinners. The recipe is special in that it's made from fresh corn cut from the cobs—in fact, *elote* means "corn cut from the cob." The custard is delicate, yet rich with cheese and cream and lightly spiced with a hint of green chile.

> **About 1 tablespoon unsalted butter, room temperature**
> **2-1/2 cups corn kernels, cut from about 5 ears fresh or frozen**
>   **corn**
> **1 tablespoon baking powder**
> **8 ounces Monterey Jack cheese, diced**
> **8 ounces Cheddar cheese, diced**
> **4 fresh mild green chiles, parched (see page 9), peeled, seeded;**
>   **or 4 canned whole green chiles**
> **3 tablespoons sugar**
> **9 eggs**
> **3 cups whipping cream**
> **1 tablespoon salt (or to taste)**

Preheat oven to 350F (175C). Butter a 3-quart baking dish. In a food processor, combine corn, baking powder, cheeses, chiles and sugar; process just until corn kernels are broken down. In a very large bowl, whisk together eggs and cream. Add corn mixture and stir to combine, then stir in salt. Pour into buttered baking dish. Bake 45 to 55 minutes or until custard is just set and a knife inserted in center comes out clean. Serve immediately. Makes 12 servings.

Chuckwagon Baked Beans

The hearty, satisfying flavor of this dish belies its ease and speed of preparation. It's great with picnic foods or simple grilled meats of any kind, especially when you don't have time to start from dried beans. (If you prefer to cook the beans yourself, boil 1 pound dried white navy or pea beans in about 2 quarts water with 1-1/2 teaspoons salt until soft—usually about 3 hours.)

> 2 (16- to 18-oz.) cans pork and beans (or 1 pound dried beans,
>   cooked as directed above)
> 1 cup packed brown sugar
> 1 teaspoon dry mustard
> 1/2 pound salt pork, cut in strips
> 1/2 cup ketchup
> 1/2 cup chopped green onions (including some green tops)

Preheat oven to 350F (175C). Combine all ingredients and pour into a 2- to 3-quart casserole. Bake, uncovered, 2 to 2-1/2 hours or until sauce is thick and beans are dark and crusty on top. If time is short, you may decrease the cooking time to 1 hour, but the beans will not be as tasty. Makes 8 servings.

Quelites (Mexican Greens)

Quelites is traditionally made with native greens, such as lamb's quarters. Some cooks actually make quite a fuss about using only wild greens, but I've always enjoyed making the dish with spinach or Swiss chard; they're more readily available and taste perfectly delicious. Whichever greens you use, the technique is the same: just stem the leaves, then stir-fry them in bacon drippings (or other flavorful fat) with onion, garlic and a hint of caribe. I like to stir in cherry tomatoes at the last for a colorful accent.

3 tablespoons bacon drippings or lard
1/2 onion, chopped
2 cloves garlic, minced
3 pounds fresh spinach, rinsed well, stemmed
1 teaspoon salt (or to taste)
1 pint cherry tomatoes
1 teaspoon caribe (crushed Northern New Mexico red chile)

Heat fat in a large skillet. Add onion and garlic; stir-fry about 5 minutes or until light golden. Add spinach and stir-fry just until limp. Stir in salt. Remove spinach from skillet with a slotted spoon; keep warm. Add tomatoes to skillet and cook until skins begin to burst. Return spinach to skillet, mix with tomatoes and stir in caribe. Adjust seasonings and serve immediately. Makes 12 servings.

Cavolfiore alla Medusa

Claudia Medusa spent her childhood in Italy, where she developed a lifelong love affair with Italian cuisine. And what a love it has been—she has turned her knowledge and culinary skill into a successful restaurant and catering company in Woodstock, New York. Claudia says, "The hot, slightly sweet, nutty, crunchy and tender elements in this cauliflower dish create *una festa per la boca*—a party for your mouth. Leftovers are a great snack, too!"

> **1 large, perfect head cauliflower**
> **1/4 cup olive oil**
> **2 large cloves garlic**
> **1/2 cup piñon nuts (pine nuts)**
> **1 teaspoon pequin quebrado or Italian crushed hot red pepper**
>   **(or to taste)**
> **1/2 cup golden raisins**
> **Salt to taste, if desired**

Set aside some of the light green leaves from base of cauliflower for cooking later. Then cut cauliflower into florets (cut rather then breaking to get more uniform pieces). Heat oil in a shallow 10- to 12-inch skillet over high heat. Add cauliflower florets; cook until golden brown in some spots. Add garlic and piñon nuts and cook until golden brown. Then add pequin or crushed red pepper, raisins and salt, if desired. Gradually stir in a bit of water, adding just enough to steam cauliflower to the *al dente* stage—tender but still firm to bite. When cauliflower *is al dente*, reduce heat, toss in reserved leaves, stir and cover. Continue to cook just until cauliflower stems are tender when pierced and leaves turn brighter in color. Serve hot or cold. Makes 6 to 8 servings.

Chile-Cheese Onions

Keep the recipe a secret and no one will ever guess how easily you created this wonderfully spicy side dish.

2 cups (about 1 lb.) small white boiling onions
1 cup Chile con Queso, page 20

Slice root and stem ends from each onion. Rinse onions, then cook in boiling water about 15 minutes or until just tender. Drain. Pop each onion of its skin. Rinse cooking pan with hot water, then add peeled onions and Chile con Queso; heat through and serve. Makes 4 to 6 servings.

Snappy Snow Peas

Stir these up any time you want to complement a dish that needs additional color or texture— snow peas have an abundance of both.

4 green onions
3 tablespoons vegetable oil
2 cups fresh snow peas, ends and strings removed
1 (1-inch) piece fresh ginger, peeled, very finely minced
1/4 to 1/2 green bell pepper, cut lengthwise in slivers
1/4 to 1/2 red bell pepper, cut lengthwise in slivers
1/4 to 1/2 yellow bell pepper, cut lengthwise in slivers
2 teaspoons light soy sauce
1 teaspoon ground pure New Mexico hot red chile (or to taste)

Sliver green onions Japanese-style: trim roots and any wilted tops from onions, then cut each in 2-inch lengths. Cut onion pieces lengthwise in thin slivers. Set aside. Heat oil in a wok or large, shallow skillet; add snow peas, green onions, ginger and bell peppers. Stir-fry a few minutes; sprinkle with soy sauce and continue to cook until hot and just barely tender-crisp. Sprinkle with ground chile, stir to mix and serve hot. Makes 4 servings.

Spicy Calabacitas

Try this dish in the summer, when you can find teensy, tiny finger-sized summer squash, still with blossoms attached. You'll love it!

> 1/4 cup unsalted butter
> 1/2 cup chopped red onion
> 2 cloves garlic, minced
> 4 cups baby summer squash (yellow crookneck and zucchini with blossoms attached), rinsed, patted dry
> 2 large red-ripe tomatoes, peeled, cut in wedges
> 4 fresh New Mexico hot green chiles, parched (see page 9) peeled, seeded, chopped
> 2 tablespoons caribe (crushed Northern New Mexico red chile)
> 1 teaspoon salt (or to taste)
> 1/4 teaspoon ground oregano, preferably Mexican
> 1/4 teaspoon ground cumin
> 3/4 cup coarsely grated Monterey Jack cheese
> 3/4 cup coarsely grated full-cream Cheddar cheese

Melt butter in a large, heavy skillet, then add onion and garlic. Cook until lightly tinged with brown. Add squash and tomatoes; stir-fry rapidly, sprinkling with chiles, caribe, salt, oregano and cumin. Cook just until squash are tender-crisp to bite and brighter in color. Sprinkle with cheeses, turn off heat, cover pan and let cheeses melt. Then serve immediately. Makes 4 to 6 servings.

VARIATION

For an entrée version, add 2 cups warmed browned ground beef, taco meat or roast beef slivers and toss together.

Hot Green Beans Vinaigrette

Fun to serve as a salad or vegetable with just about any entree! I sometimes substitute tiny new potatoes for half the beans. (It's not necessary to peel the potatoes entirely—just pare a strip around the center of each potato.)

> 1 pound fresh green beans
> 2 cups water
> 1/2 teaspoon salt
> 2 tablespoons extra-virgin olive oil
> 1 tablespoon wine vinegar
> 1 tablespoon Jalapeño Jelly, page 149, or mild or hot purchased
>   jalapeño jelly
> 1 teaspoon fresh lime juice

Snap off ends of beans; leave beans whole. In a saucepan, bring water and salt to a boil; add beans, cover and cook 5 minutes or until brighter in color and tender-crisp to bite. Drain, then immediately add oil, vinegar, jelly and lime juice. Stir to coat, then serve. Makes 4 servings.

Triple-Mustard-Coated Potatoes

Brennan and I first tasted these in Atlanta, at the home of our good friend Nathalie Dupree. They are delicious served with chicken or almost any other meat—and they'll hold for hours in the oven (the flavor even seems to improve on standing). You can alter the recipe to suit your taste by using different types of mustard.

> **2 cups (about 18) tiny new potatoes, scrubbed**
> **1/4 cup unsalted butter, cut in small pieces**
> **Freshly cracked black pepper**
> **2 tablespoons hot Dijon-style mustard**
> **1 teaspoon dry mustard**
> **3 tablespoons mustard seeds**
> **2 tablespoons minced parsley**

Peel off a thin strip of skin around center of each potato. Cook potatoes in boiling water until tender. Drain, return to cooking pan and add butter. Cover pan and let stand 5 minutes or until butter is melted. Stir potatoes to coat with butter; add pepper, Dijon-style mustard, dry mustard and mustard seeds and mix lightly. Place in an ovenproof dish; keep warm in a low oven until serving. Sprinkle with parsley before serving. Makes 4 servings.

Wild Rice Baked with Almonds & Mushrooms

This recipe was given to me by the chef at a famous resort in Ruidosa. It's extremely easy to prepare and goes well with red meats and all types of game. If you don't have almonds or mushrooms, just substitute other nuts or vegetables of your choice.

1/2 cup unsalted butter
1/2 pound fresh mushrooms, thinly sliced
1 clove garlic, finely minced
1 tablespoon minced green bell pepper
1/2 cup slivered almonds
1 cup uncooked wild rice
3 cups chicken broth
1 teaspoon salt
Freshly ground black pepper to taste

Preheat oven to 350F (175C). Melt butter in a large saucepan. Add mushrooms, garlic, bell pepper, almonds and rice; cook, stirring, until mushrooms are soft. Pour mixture into a large, shallow baking dish; stir in broth, salt and pepper. Cover and bake about 1-1/2 hours or until rice is tender. Makes 6 servings.

Beverages

Cooling beverages offer the perfect relief for hot days and hard work, and the perfect start for a spicy meal. I've selected an assortment of my favorite drinks here, some newly created, some tried and true. You'll find coolers such as Summer Heat, featuring vodka and Midori; the Vicious Vaquero, a high-octane blend of tequila, caribe, Chartreuse and ice; and classics like Margaritas and Silkies. When tequila is called for, the best ones to use are those distilled from all-natural agave plants—check the label.

If you're looking for soothing after-dinner drinks, you'll find those, too—try a creamy Pink Mermaid or perhaps Phenomenal Party Eggnog. And to warm up chilly days, my own New Mexican Hot Chocolate can't be beat. It's spicy, frothy, extra-special—almost rich enough for dessert!

One note of caution: Don't make the mistake of drinking lots of cold beverages to cool your scorched palate *during* a spicy meal. You'll just prolong the pain. Instead, turn to the comfort of dairy fats: sour cream, butter, cheese and the like.

Maria's Martinis

So easy! Just prepare your favorite martini recipe—and heat up the garnish.

2 ounces or more top-quality gin or vodka
Dry vermouth to taste (most people like a sparing splash)
4 ice cubes
1 pickled jalapeño chile

In a cocktail shaker, combine gin or vodka, vermouth and ice cubes. Shake until thoroughly chilled. Strain into a stemmed cocktail glass or serve on the rocks in an old-fashioned glass. Garnish with jalapeño. Makes 1 serving.

Dante's Downfall

A flaming after-dinner drink that's delightfully different from the usual cordials and liqueurs.

1 ounce Grand Marnier
6 whole pink, white or black peppercorns

Pour liqueur into a heatproof snifter or Irish coffee mug. Add peppercorns. Heat by tilting and rotating over a candle or gas flame until the first bubble forms, then carefully ignite with a match and serve flaming. Makes 1 serving.

Mexico City Madman

After two or more, you'll hear mariachis in the distance!

Ice cubes
1-1/2 ounces light tequila
1-1/2 ounces 151-proof rum
Splash of green Chartreuse
1 lime wedge

Fill a double-old-fashioned glass with ice cubes, then add tequila, rum and Chartreuse. Stir. Squeeze lime wedge over drink, stir and serve immediately. Makes 1 serving.

Dona's Death

Brennan's sister, Dona, likes these—but warns, "be careful!"

1 ounce green Chartreuse
1 ounce light tequila
1 ounce Triple Sec
4 ice cubes
1 thin lime slice

Combine Chartreuse, tequila, Triple Sec and ice cubes in a blender and process until well blended. Pour into a stemmed cocktail glass. Cut lime slice to center; hang on edge of glass. Makes 1 serving.

VARIATION
Pink Thing: Add 1 ounce crème de almond.

Summer Heat

So soothing on searing, sizzling summer days—especially after long hours in the office or a morning's maneuvers on the tennis court.

>   **1 cucumber spear or mint sprig**
>   **Ice cubes**
>   **2 ounces vodka**
>   **1/2 ounce Midori**
>   **1 lime wedge**
>   **Club soda**

If using cucumber spear, prepare by cutting a large cucumber in half; then cut a wedge from cucumber half. Pare off peel in a single flap very close to flesh, peeling halfway up wedge. Set aside. Fill a tall, slender 12-ounce glass to the rim with ice cubes, then add vodka and Midori. Squeeze lime wedge over drink and drop into glass, then add club soda to fill. Stir with a swizzle stick. Hang cucumber spear over edge of glass or garnish drink with mint. If desired, serve with tall, thin straws. Makes 1 serving.

Blanco Burro

This luscious drink is as beguiling as a burro. Though it looks very gentle, it can really deliver a kick!

>   **Ice cubes**
>   **1 ounce Cointreau**
>   **1 ounce green Chartreuse**
>   **1 ounce whipping cream**
>   **6 candy red hots**

Place 6 to 8 ice cubes in a cocktail shaker, then add Cointreau, Chartreuse and cream. Shake well, then strain into an old-fashioned glass. Add ice cubes to fill glass; sprinkle with red hots. Makes 1 serving.

Son of a Bitch's Delight

If you like stingers, you'll like this good-tasting drink. Watch out, though—it's strong.

Ice cubes
1-1/2 ounces brandy
1-1/2 ounces bourbon
1-1/2 ounces vodka
3/4 ounce white crème de menthe
1 mint sprig

Fill a double-old-fashioned glass to the rim with ice cubes. Add brandy, bourbon, vodka and crème de menthe; stir vigorously. Garnish with mint. Makes 1 serving.

Gulf Stream Gulp

Sea green, foamy and refreshing as a newly beached wave. You might be tempted to gulp—but you're best off sipping.

About 1 cup shaved ice
1 ounce Sambuca
2 ounces green Chartreuse

Fill a cocktail shaker with ice and pour in Sambuca and Chartreuse. Vigorously stir or shake until foamy, then serve in a snifter or pony glass. Makes 1 serving.

Pink Mermaid

Cooling, pretty, creamy, and wonderful for after-dinner drinks. If no blender is handy, just crush the ice, then shake or whisk the ingredients together.

>   **2 ounces whipping cream**
>   **1 ounce vodka**
>   **1 ounce crème de almond**
>   **4 to 6 ice cubes**
>   **1/2 ounce brandy**

Place cream, vodka, crème de almond and ice cubes in a blender; process until ice is completely crushed and mixture is frothy and light pink. Pour into a glass and top with brandy. Makes 1 serving.

Tracy's White Trash

This drink has become popular, especially during winter, at Churchill's—a chic pub on New York's Upper East Side. It was invented by Tracy, one of the pub's veteran bartenders.

>   **6 ounces milk**
>   **2 ounces Frangelico**

Heat milk until steaming. Place Frangelico in an 8-ounce mug and pour in milk. Makes 1 serving.

Silkies

So special that friends have called me from halfway 'round the world just to get the recipe. These are great brunch drinks—just be prepared to supply lots of refills!

10 ice cubes
1/2 cup frozen orange juice concentrate
1 ounce fresh lime juice
4 ounces gold tequila
6 ounces light cream
2 egg whites
3 tablespoons sugar (or to taste)

Place ice cubes, orange juice, lime juice and tequila in a blender; process until slushy. Then add cream, egg whites and sugar and process on highest speed until very foamy. Serve in stemmed glasses. Makes 4 servings.

Guadalajara Guzzler

A tall, refreshing cooler that's easy to make. The colorful garnish adds to its festive look.

Ice cubes
1 ounce light tequila
1 ounce Campari
About 8 ounces club soda
1 thin orange slice
1/2 thin lime slice
Thin twist of lemon peel

Fill a tall 12-ounce glass with ice cubes; pour in tequila and Campari, then fill with club soda. Cut orange slice from edge to center; lay half-slice of lime opposite cut and twist the 2 slices together. Attach fruit slices and lemon twist to the end of a wooden pick; garnish drink. Makes 1 serving.

Vicious Vaquero

A winner with our friends! It's an unusually good, spicy takeoff on the margarita, truly fit to be associated with the Mexican cowboys.

2 ounces light tequila
1/4 teaspoon caribe (crushed Northern New Mexico red chile)
1 ounce green Chartreuse
6 ice cubes

Combine all ingredients in a blender and process until slushy. Serve immediately. Makes 1 serving.

VARIATION
Vicious Vaquero Martinis: Garnish each drink with a jalapeño-stuffed olive.

Caspar's Cooler

A treat from the Old South. Caspar, a devilish Dutchman, gave us the recipe. He concocted this specialty for his close friends; now he's pleased to share his secret formula with you.

1 ounce Southern Comfort
1 ounce vodka
1 ounce gin
3 ounces fresh grapefruit juice
1 ounce fresh orange juice
Splash of Grenadine
1 cup crushed ice
Splash of club soda
1 orange slice, cut just to center
2 green grapes

Combine Southern Comfort, vodka, gin, grapefruit juice, orange juice, Grenadine and ice in a cocktail shaker or jar; shake well, then pour into a tall, slender 12-ounce glass. Fill glass with club soda. Twist orange slice, place grapes in center of slice and secure with wooden picks; garnish drink. Makes 1 serving.

Fen's Fang

Fen, a sophisticated Canadian stockbroker friend of ours, specializes in this Polynesian cooler with a south-of-the-border influence. It's a pretty melon color, with the true taste of the tropics.

4 fresh or canned pineapple chunks
1 tablespoon cream of coconut
1 (2-inch) piece fresh ginger, peeled, if desired
1 ounce light tequila
1 ounce light rum
1/2 ounce crème de almond
1/2 tablespoon frozen orange juice concentrate
About 1 cup cracked ice or 6 to 8 ice cubes
1 fresh daisy or other flower, if desired
1 maraschino cherry

Combine 2 pineapple chunks, cream of coconut, ginger (if desired), tequila, rum, crème de almond, orange juice and ice in a blender. Process until foamy. Pour into a glass; garnish with a flower (if desired), remaining 2 pineapple chunks and a maraschino cherry. Makes 1 serving.

Margaritas

The most favored drink of all for sipping before a spicy-hot meal. The recipe below is our very favorite formula, perfected over the years and guaranteed to net rave reviews. The drink is best made with juice from Mexican or key limes—the small, thin-skinned, yellow-green ones. Substitute the larger, dark green Persian limes if you must, but *never* use bottled or prepared juice.

> **2 or 3 Mexican or key limes**
> **Coarse salt, if desired**
> **2 ounces Cointreau or Triple Sec**
> **6 ounces light tequila**
> **1 egg white**
> **6 to 8 ice cubes**

Roll limes under your palm briefly to bring out the juice, then cut in half and squeeze to make at least 2 ounces (1/4 cup) juice. Cover and refrigerate juice. Rub lime rinds around rims of 2 glasses, preferably stemmed or old-fashioned glasses. Then dust rims with salt, if desired, and freeze glasses at least 30 minutes to frost them. To make margaritas, combine lime juice, Cointreau or Triple Sec, tequila, egg white and ice cubes in a blender; process until frothy. Serve immediately in frosted glasses. Makes 2 servings.

VARIATION

Margarita Punch: To serve a crowd more easily and save time, I often mix up this punch, made with frozen concentrated limeade. Though the flavor is compromised a bit, you'll still have a much better drink than any commercial mix will yield. Amounts for 6 servings are 10 ounces tequila; 5 ounces Cointreau or Triple Sec; 3-1/2 ounces frozen limeade concentrate; and 8-1/2 ounces fresh lime juice.

Voodoo Punch

Straight from the Caribbean, this punch is perfect for large parties. Make it when you want the atmosphere to be special—perhaps even a little crazy!

3/4 cup packed light brown sugar
1 (3-inch) piece fresh ginger, peeled, thinly sliced
2 tablespoons whole black peppercorns
1 tablespoon whole allspice
4 cinnamon sticks
2 cups water
1 large ice block or ice ring (made by freezing water in a
  2-quart container of your choice)
1 (750-ml.) bottle dark Caribbean rum
1 (750-ml.) bottle vodka
2 cups fresh or reconstituted frozen orange juice (or to taste)
1/2 cup pineapple juice (or to taste)
10 white or pastel daisies, hibiscus or other flowers
10 thin lemon slices
Ice cubes

In a 1-quart saucepan, combine brown sugar, ginger, peppercorns, allspice, cinnamon sticks and water. Bring to a boil; then reduce heat and simmer, uncovered, 30 minutes. Strain, discarding spices; cool. If made ahead, set aside until ready to use. To prepare punch for serving, place ice block or ring in a large punch bowl. Add cooled syrup, rum, vodka, orange juice and pineapple juice. Taste and add more juices, if desired. Poke stem of each flower through center of a lemon slice; float lemon slices atop punch. Serve each drink over ice cubes. Makes about 32 servings.

Phenomenal Party Eggnog

Our family-favorite holiday treat, top choice with hot, spicy foods all year round. It's rich, so a little goes a long way—but any extra can certainly be frozen. (Whisk after thawing to restore a fluffy texture.)

12 eggs, separated
1 cup sugar
4 cups whole milk
1 cup rye whisky
1 cup light rum
4 cups whipping cream, whipped until stiff
Freshly grated nutmeg to taste

Using an electric mixer or a large whisk, beat egg yolks until thick and lemon-colored. Gradually add sugar, beating constantly. Slowly beat in milk, making certain to mix well. Stir in whisky and rum. Beat egg whites until they hold stiff peaks; fold into milk mixture. Then fold in whipped cream. Pour into a punch bowl. Ladle into glass or silver cups; top each serving with a few grates of nutmeg. Makes 20 servings.

Hot New Mexican Chocolate

Traditional Mexican hot chocolate is made with Mexican bar chocolate—a mixture of chocolate, sugar, ground almonds, cinnamon and cloves, formed into round cakes. My adaptation of the traditional recipe tastes much like authentic Mexican chocolate, but has a better texture: Mexican bar chocolate doesn't melt smoothly, always leaving little flecks of chocolate floating atop the drink. To present your hot chocolate Mexican style, beat it at the table with a *molinillo*—a carved wooden stirrer made just for this purpose—and serve it in heavy earthenware mugs. Molinillos are available at specialty kitchenware stores; they're lots of fun to use, adding a bit of showmanship to your presentation!

> 1/3 cup unsweetened cocoa powder
> 1 tablespoon all-purpose flour
> 1/3 cup sugar
> Pinch of salt
> 3/4 teaspoon ground cinnamon
> 1/4 teaspoon ground cloves
> 1 cup water
> 2 cups light cream
> 1 cup milk
> 1-1/2 teaspoons Mexican vanilla extract or 2-1/4 teaspoons
>   regular vanilla extract
> 1 cup whipped cream
> Freshly grated nutmeg to taste, if desired
> 6 cinnamon sticks

Combine cocoa, flour, sugar, salt, ground cinnamon, cloves and water in a heavy 2-quart saucepan. Stir or whisk until very well blended, then heat just until bubbly around edges and barely beginning to simmer. Gradually add cream, then milk, in a very thin stream, beating constantly with a molinillo, whisk or rotary beater. Heat until hot but not boiling; keep warm at least 5 minutes. Stir in vanilla. Just before serving, beat chocolate again with molinillo until frothy. (For a dramatic presentation, do this at the table.) To serve, rinse out 6 mugs with boiling water, then ladle in hot chocolate. Top each serving with a dollop of whipped cream and a grate of nutmeg, if desired; jab a cinnamon stick into cream. Serve immediately. Makes 6 servings.

Sweet Endings

Everybody loves dessert! And if you like it hot, you probably know how satisfyingly soothing sweet desserts can be. Each of the favorites in this chapter is a perfect crown for a super-hot meal. The classic close for a spicy dinner is ice cream, of course—like my Fresh Peach Ice Cream, Strawberry Ice Cream and dramatic Christmas Cardinale Bombe. Sweet and rich in butterfat, these luscious treats cool overheated palates in a hurry. But you'll find warm desserts, too—Butterscotch Peach Crisp, velvety Dessert Fondue, Steve's Skillet Cake and more.

The collection in these pages includes old family favorites as well as recent inspirations. Devil's Food Cake with Fudge Frosting has been in my files since I was nine years old, but Sumptuous Chocolate-Walnut Soufflé, topped with cognac-laced whipped cream and red raspberry sauce, was created just for this book.

Devil's Food Cake

Who wouldn't take the devil's dare when it comes to eating this fudge-topped treat? I've never found another cake as all-around good as this one. I've had the recipe since I was in third grade, when a one-room schoolhouse near my father's farm held a fundraiser. Among the events was a cakewalk—and I won three cakes that night! My mother let me keep just one, and this was the one I chose. It was so wonderful that I asked the baker, Phoebe Schwartz, to share the recipe with me.

> **6 tablespoons unsweetened cocoa powder**
> **1 cup boiling water**
> **1 teaspoon baking soda**
> **3/4 teaspoon Mexican vanilla extract or 1 teaspoon regular**
>   **vanilla extract**
> **1/2 cup solid vegetable shortening**
> **2 cups sugar**
> **3 eggs**
> **2 cups all-purpose flour**
> **1/2 teaspoon salt**
> **1/2 cup buttermilk or sour milk**
> **Fudge Frosting, see below**
> **Chopped nuts, if desired**
>
> *Fudge Frosting:*
> **2 cups granulated sugar**
> **1 cup packed brown sugar**
> **3 tablespoons unsweetened cocoa powder**
> **1-1/2 cups light cream (or more, as needed)**
> **3 tablespoons light corn syrup**

Preheat oven to 350F (175C). Grease and flour-dust 2 round 9-inch baking pans or a 9" x 13" baking pan. In a bowl, mix cocoa and boiling water until smoothly blended. Stir in baking soda and vanilla; set aside. In large bowl of an electric mixer, cream shortening and sugar on medium speed. Increase mixer speed to medium-high; add eggs, 1 at a time, beating until smooth after each addition. Combine flour and salt; add to creamed mixture alternately with buttermilk or sour milk, beating with mixer on low speed after each addition. Then beat on medium speed until smooth and well blended; add cocoa mixture and beat until blended. Pour into prepared pans. Bake 35 to 45 minutes or until a wooden pick inserted in center of cake comes out clean. Cool layers in pans 5 minutes, then turn out onto cooling racks to cool completely. (Cool sheet cake in pan.) Prepare Fudge Frosting; fill and frost cake. Sprinkle frosted cake with nuts, if desired. Makes 1 (9-inch) layer cake or a 9" x 13" sheet cake.

Fudge Frosting:
Mix sugars and cocoa in a saucepan; stir in cream and corn syrup. Bring to a boil over medium heat, stirring. Boil without stirring until mixture reaches soft-ball stage (234F to 240F, 112C to 115C at sea level); then remove from heat. Beat vigorously, adding more cream as needed to make a creamy, spreadable frosting. Frost cake while icing is still warm.

Jam Cake

Norma Jean Ross shared this traditional Tennessee recipe with me, saying her family almost always prepares it at holiday time. It's a rich, spicy cake that's excellent with coffee, milk or eggnog.

4 cups all-purpose flour
2 teaspoons baking soda
1/2 cup unsalted butter, room temperature
2 cups sugar
6 eggs, separated
2 teaspoons ground cloves
2 teaspoons ground nutmeg
2 teaspoons ground allspice
2 teaspoons ground cinnamon
2 cups seedless blackberry jam
1 cup sour milk or buttermilk
Filling, see below

Filling:
1/2 cup unsalted butter
2 cups sugar
2 cups milk

Preheat oven to 375F (190C). Grease 3 round 9-inch or 4 round 8-inch baking pans; line pans with waxed paper. Lightly grease paper. Sift together flour and baking soda; set aside. In large bowl of an electric mixer, cream butter and sugar on medium speed. In small bowl of mixer, beat egg yolks well; blend into creamed mixture along with cloves, nutmeg, allspice, cinnamon and jam. Then add flour mixture alternately with sour milk or buttermilk, beating until smooth after each addition. Beat egg whites until they hold stiff peaks; fold into batter. Pour batter into prepared pans. Bake 35 to 40 minutes or until a wooden pick inserted in center of cake comes out clean. Cool in pans 5 minutes; turn out of pans onto cooling racks, peel off paper and cool completely. To assemble cake, prepare Filling; stack layers, spreading hot Filling between layers and on top of cake. Makes 1 (8- or 9-inch) layer cake.

Filling:
In a medium saucepan, combine all ingredients. Cook over medium heat, stirring, 15 to 20 minutes or until mixture begins to thicken. Use while still hot.

Poppy Seed Torte

A Hungarian lady living in Albuquerque gave me this recipe. A terrific cook, she inherited the recipe from her mother, who always made poppy seed cake for special occasions. The contrasting textures of crunchy poppy seeds and smooth, soothing custard make the dessert a real delight.

3/4 cup poppy seeds
1-1/4 cups milk
About 1 tablespoon unsalted butter, room temperature
2-3/4 cups all-purpose flour
1-1/2 teaspoons baking powder
1/4 teaspoon salt
1/2 cup unsalted butter, room temperature
1-1/4 cups sugar
4 egg whites
Custard Filling, see below

Custard Filling:
1/2 cup sugar
1/4 teaspoon salt
1 tablespoon cornstarch
1-1/2 cups milk
4 egg yolks, well beaten
3/4 teaspoon Mexican vanilla extract or 1 teaspoon regular
    vanilla extract
1/2 cup coarsely chopped black walnuts

Soak poppy seeds in milk several hours or overnight. Preheat oven to 375F (190C). Butter 3 round 8-inch baking pans, then line with waxed paper. Lightly butter paper. Sift together flour, baking powder and salt; set aside. In large bowl of an electric mixer, cream 1/2 cup butter and sugar on medium speed. Add poppy-seed-milk mixture to creamed mixture alternately with flour mixture, beating until well blended after each addition. In small bowl of mixer, beat egg whites until they hold soft peaks; fold into batter. Spread batter in prepared pans. Bake 25 to 30 minutes or until a wooden pick inserted in center of cake comes out clean. Cool in pans 5 minutes, then turn out of pans onto cooling racks, peel off paper and cool completely. Meanwhile, prepare Custard Filling. To assemble cake, stack layers, spreading filling between layers and on top of cake. Makes 1 (8-inch) layer cake.

Custard Filling:
In a saucepan, stir together sugar, salt and cornstarch. Gradually stir in milk, then egg yolks. Cook over medium heat, stirring constantly, until thickened. Cool slightly, then stir in vanilla and black walnuts.

Steve's Skillet Cake

So easy, you won't believe it! This cake is a 5-minute wonder and truly delicious for dessert or brunch. Steve Bryant, a restaurateur, often makes it with huckleberries from his yard—but other fruits are equally good.

1/2 cup unsalted butter
1 cup milk
1 cup sugar
1 cup all-purpose flour
Freshly grated nutmeg to taste
1/2 teaspoon salt
1 teaspoon baking powder
2 cups fresh fruit, such as berries, sliced peaches or sliced apricots
1/2 cup dairy sour cream, if desired

Preheat oven to 375F (190C). Set butter in a heavy 9-inch skillet with an ovenproof handle; set skillet in oven until butter is melted. Meanwhile, in a bowl, beat together milk, sugar, flour, nutmeg, salt and baking powder with a whisk until smooth and free of lumps. Stir melted butter into batter, then pour batter back into skillet. Place fruit in center of batter and bake about 30 minutes or until top of cake is browned and fruit is tender. Serve warm, with sour cream, if desired. Makes 6 to 8 servings.

Pink Adobe French Apple Pie

The very best apple pie I've ever tasted—rich, spicy, embellished with raisins and pecans and topped with creamy Rum or Brandy Hard Sauce. Rosalea, owner and founder of the famous Pink Adobe Restaurant in Santa Fe, created this recipe ages ago; it has proved so popular she can hardly keep up with the demand. Regular patrons frequently order it when they first arrive at the restuarant or even when they make their reservations, just to be sure they'll have a piece! Once you sample this recipe, you'll be preparing it often. The pie freezes beautifully, so always make at least two at a time.

Pastry for a double-crust 9-inch pie
1 pound cooking apples, peeled, cored, sliced
2 tablespoons lemon juice
1/2 teaspoon ground nutmeg
1/2 teaspoon ground cinnamon
1/2 cup granulated sugar
1/4 cup raisins
1 cup packed light brown sugar
2 tablespoons all-purpose flour
2 tablespoons unsalted butter, cut in small pieces
1/2 cup pecan halves
1/4 cup milk
Rum or Brandy Hard Sauce, see below

Rum or Brandy Hard Sauce:
1/2 cup unsalted butter, room temperature
1-1/2 cups powdered sugar
1 tablespoon boiling water
1 teaspoon rum or brandy

Set oven rack in lowest position. Preheat oven to 450F (230C). Roll out half the pastry and use to line a 9-inch pie plate. Place apples in pastry shell, mounding them toward center. Sprinkle with lemon juice, nutmeg and cinnamon. Reserve 2 tablespoons granulated sugar for sprinkling on top crust; spread remaining 6 tablespoons granulated sugar and raisins evenly over apples. Mix brown sugar, flour and butter until well blended, then spread over apples. Sprinkle with pecans, then with most of milk, reserving a little milk for brushing top crust. Roll out remaining pastry and place on pie; seal and flute edges and cut steam vents. Brush top crust with reserved milk; sprinkle with reserved 2 tablespoons granulated sugar. Bake 10 minutes, then reduce oven temperature to 350F (175C) and continue to bake 30 minutes longer or until crust is golden brown and filling is bubbly. Meanwhile, prepare hard sauce. Cool pie briefly, then cut in wedges and serve on warmed plates. Top each slice with hard sauce; let stand a few minutes before serving, so sauce has time to melt down into filling. Makes 1 (9-inch) pie.

Rum or Brandy Hard Sauce:
Cream butter until fluffy, then add powdered sugar and boiling water and beat until well blended. Beat in rum or brandy.

Orange Blossom Blueberry Pie

Fragrant and tangy with fresh orange and orange liqueur, this spicy pie is one of our family favorites. We like it served plain, but you might also try it with a scoop of rich vanilla ice cream melting over each slice.

Rich pastry for a double-crust 9-inch pie (substitute orange
    juice for the liquid called for in your recipe)
5 cups fresh blueberries
1-1/2 cups sugar
1/3 cup all-purpose flour
1 navel orange, unpeeled, thinly sliced
1/4 cup Grand Marnier
1/2 teaspoon ground cinnamon
Freshly grated nutmeg to taste
2 tablespoons unsalted butter
2 tablespoons milk

Set oven rack in lowest position. Preheat oven to 425F (220C). Roll out half the pastry and use to line a 9-inch pie plate; fill pastry shell with blueberries. Reserve 1 tablespoon sugar for sprinkling on top crust; combine remaining sugar with flour and sprinkle evenly over berries. Cut each orange slice in half, then arrange half-slices uniformly around edge of pie. Pour Grand Marnier evenly over top; sprinkle with cinnamon and nutmeg. Dot with butter. Roll out remaining pastry; place on pie. Seal and flute edges; cut steam vents. Brush top crust with milk, then sprinkle with reserved 1 tablespoon sugar and a few grates of nutmeg. Bake 15 minutes, then reduce oven temperature to 375F (190C) and continue to bake 30 minutes longer or until crust is lightly browned and filling is bubbly. Serve warm. Makes 1 (9-inch) pie.

Christmas Cardinale Bombe

So gorgeous to look at and yet so easy to make—this beautiful dessert seems almost too good to believe! It's perfect for parties, especially those with a Mexican theme, since it sports Mexico's national colors—red, white and green (traditional for festive occasions). The Raspberry Sauce that tops each slice is good on plain ice cream, cakes and pies, too.

1 quart vanilla ice cream
1-1/2 pints pistachio ice cream
1 pint raspberry sherbet
1/2 cup shelled unsalted pistachio nuts, coarsely chopped (see Note below)
Raspberry Sauce, see below
Fresh raspberries and mint sprigs, if desired

Raspberry Sauce:
2 (12- to 14-oz.) packages frozen unsweetened raspberries, thawed, undrained
1/4 cup sugar
1/3 cup Framboise or kirsch

A day or so before serving, put a 3-quart bombe mold or metal bowl in freezer at least 30 minutes. Remove vanilla ice cream from freezer; set in refrigerator until soft but not melted. Using a spatula and working rapidly, line frozen mold or bowl evenly with vanilla ice cream. Immediately return mold or bowl to freezer; freeze until vanilla ice cream is firm. Meanwhile, place pistachio ice cream in refrigerator until soft but not melted. Smooth a uniform layer of pistachio ice cream over firm layer of vanilla, then immediately return to freezer until firm; meanwhile, place sherbet in refrigerator until soft but not melted. Fill center of mold with sherbet and return to freezer at least 3 hours. Also freeze a serving plate or platter until very cold. To unmold, dip mold or bowl in hot water to rim; invert on frozen plate or platter. Lift off mold. Carefully stud bombe with pistachios, being sure to cover outside surface uniformly. Immediately return to freezer until ready to serve. Meanwhile, prepare sauce. To serve, heat a knife in hot water; dry off, then cut a slice of bombe. Continue to slice, heating and drying knife before each cut. Drizzle each serving with Raspberry Sauce and garnish with raspberries and mint, if desired. Makes 10 to 12 servings.

Raspberry Sauce:
In a saucepan, combine all ingredients. Bring to a simmer; simmer over low heat 3 minutes. Pour into a food processor and process until smooth. Then push through a fine sieve. Makes 2-1/2 cups.

NOTE: If you can't find unsalted pistachios, simmer salted pistachios briefly in plenty of water, rinse thoroughly, and dry well.

Fresh Peach Ice Cream

Almost too easy to be so good! Double-rich and flavorful, this has been our family's favorite peach ice cream for as long as I can remember.

4 cups milk
1 (14-oz.) can sweetened condensed milk
1 (12-oz.) can evaporated milk
1 cup whipping cream
2 teaspoons Mexican vanilla extract or 1 tablespoon regular
vanilla extract
3 cups mashed fresh peaches or thawed, drained frozen
sweetened peaches
1 cup sugar, or to taste (if using frozen peaches, start with 1/2
cup sugar)
Crushed ice
Rock salt

Thoroughly combine all ingredients except ice and salt in freezing can of an electric or manual ice cream freezer, adjusting sugar to taste. Cover can and position in freezer. Pack ice and rock salt in alternating layers around can, using 8 parts ice to 1 part salt. Freeze until ice cream is frozen soft. Remove dasher from can; pack ice cream down and cover with wax paper. Replace cover and fill dasher opening with cork. Repack freezer with ice and salt, using 3 parts ice to 1 part salt; cover with heavy paper or cloth and let ripen until ice cream is firm. Serve immediately, or pack in plastic cartons and store in freezer. Makes about 1 gallon.

Strawberry Ice Cream

A great way to celebrate summer all year round. Surprisingly, fresh strawberries aren't as full-flavored as this combination of frozen strawberries and strawberry gelatin. (The gelatin gives the ice cream a much better texture, too.)

> 1 (16- to 20-oz.) package frozen sweetened strawberries
> 1 (3-oz.) package strawberry-flavored gelatin
> 1 cup very hot water
> 1-1/2 cups sugar (or to taste)
> 2 eggs
> 1 (12-oz.) can evaporated milk
> 1 cup whipping cream
> 3/4 teaspoon Mexican vanilla extract or 1 teaspoon regular
>   vanilla extract
> Crushed ice
> Rock salt

Thaw strawberries according to package directions, but do not drain (you should have about 1-2/3 cups). Set aside. Empty gelatin into a large bowl, pour in hot water and stir until gelatin is completely dissolved. Immediately add sugar and stir until dissolved. In another bowl, beat eggs with an electric mixer on high speed until thick, fluffy and lemon-colored. Blend in evaporated milk, cream and vanilla with mixer on low speed. Fold egg mixture into gelatin mixture, then stir in strawberries. Fill freezing can of an electric or manual ice cream freezer 2/3 full with ice cream mixture. Cover can and position in freezer. Pack ice and rock salt in alternating layers around can, using 8 parts ice to 1 part salt. Freeze until ice cream is firm. Remove dasher from can; pack ice cream down and cover with waxed paper. Replace cover and fill dasher opening with cork. Repack freezer with ice and salt, using 3 parts ice to 1 part salt; cover with heavy paper or cloth and let ripen 2 to 3 hours. Serve immediately, or pack in plastic cartons and store in freezer. Makes 2 quarts.

Rose's Mousse au Chocolat

Rich, wonderful and romantic. Rose Levy Beranbaum created this luscious, velvety mousse for me and Brennan on one of our anniversaries. Brennan had teasingly challenged Rose to create a mousse as good as the one he remembered from years ago; she said she could not only match it, but probably improve on it!

> **3 eggs, separated**
> **1-1/2 tablespoons water**
> **2 tablespoons cognac or Kahlua**
> **4 ounces good-quality extra-bittersweet or semisweet chocolate, melted**
> **1 cup whipping cream**
> **1-1/2 tablespoons superfine sugar (omit if using Kahlua or semisweet chocolate)**
> **Chocolate curls, if desired**

In a heavy saucepan over very low heat or in a double boiler over simmering water, whisk egg yolks and water until mixture begins to thicken. Whisk in cognac or Kahlua; continue to whisk until mixture has thickened to the consistency of Hollandaise sauce. Remove from heat and whisk in melted chocolate. Set aside. In a small bowl of an electric mixer, beat cream just until it holds soft peaks. If chocolate mixture has stiffened, heat gently over very low heat, whisking constantly, until slightly softened. Transfer mixture to a large bowl; whisk in 1/2 cup of the whipped cream. Fold in remaining whipped cream with a large whisk or spatula, then cut through with a spatula or curved fingers to eliminate large air bubbles. Set aside. Beat egg whites until they hold soft peaks. Beat in sugar (if used) just until mixture holds stiff peaks. Stir a small amount of the egg whites into chocolate mixture to lighten it; then fold in remaining egg whites. Spoon into a serving bowl or 8 small charlotte molds. Refrigerate at least 4 hours or until firm. Garnish just before serving with chocolate curls, if desired. This is best eaten the same day as prepared. Makes 8 servings.

Belgian Dessert Waffles

These delicious waffles make a super ending for a spicy meal. Serve them with two toppings: Ice Cream Fluff, a luscious blend of whipped cream and vanilla ice cream, and rosy Strawberry Sauce.

Strawberry Sauce, see below
1 cup sifted all-purpose flour
2 teaspoons sugar
1 teaspoon baking powder
1/4 teaspoon baking soda
1/4 teaspoon salt
1 egg, separated
1 cup dairy sour cream
1/2 cup milk
3 tablespoons unsalted butter, melted
Ice Cream Fluff, see below

Strawberry Sauce:
1 cup hulled fresh strawberries or frozen sweetened
   strawberries (thaw frozen berries slightly, then pull apart
   with a fork)
1 tablespoon sugar (omit if using frozen berries)
2 tablespoons brandy, if desired

Ice Cream Fluff:
1 cup whipping cream
1 cup vanilla ice cream

Prepare Strawberry Sauce and set aside. Preheat a waffle baker to medium-high. Sift together flour, sugar, baking powder, baking soda and salt; set aside. In small bowl of an electric mixer, beat egg white until it holds very stiff peaks. In large bowl of mixer, beat egg yolk, sour cream, milk and melted butter until blended. Blend flour mixture into egg mixture, beating with mixer on low speed. Increase mixer speed to medium-high; beat until smooth. Fold in beaten egg white. Bake batter in preheated waffle baker until waffles are golden brown and crisp. When waffles are almost done, prepare Ice Cream Fluff. To serve, top each hot waffle with Ice Cream Fluff, then with Strawberry Sauce. Makes 2 (10-inch) waffles.

Strawberry Sauce:
Combine all ingredients in a blender. Process on low speed a few seconds or just until berries are coarsely chopped. Let stand about 1 hour at room temperature or heat over low heat about 15 minutes. Makes 1 cup.

Ice Cream Fluff:
In large bowl of an electric mixer, beat whipping cream on high speed until thickened but not stiff enough to hold its shape. Add ice cream, a spoonful at a time, beating just until smooth after each addition. Serve immediately. Makes 2-2/3 cups.

Butterscotch Peach Crisp

Crunchy, gooey and wonderful! The spicy crystallized ginger really adds to the flavor. You can substitute other fruits for the peaches—try apricots, any kind of berry, plums or rhubarb. If you can handle the calories, top the crisp with whipped cream or ice cream.

About 1 tablespoon unsalted butter, room temperature
1 cup packed brown sugar
1 cup all-purpose flour
1/4 teaspoon ground cinnamon
1/8 teaspoon ground nutmeg
1/4 cup finely diced crystallized ginger
1/2 cup solid vegetable shortening or unsalted butter
2 cups fresh or frozen unsweetened sliced peaches or other
fruit (thaw frozen fruit just until mushy, then pull apart with
a fork)

Preheat oven to 375F (190C). Butter an 8-inch-square baking dish. Combine brown sugar, flour, cinnamon, nutmeg and ginger; cut in shortening or butter until mixture resembles coarse crumbs. Spread fruit in buttered baking dish; sprinkle with crumb mixture. Bake, uncovered, 35 to 40 minutes or until fruit is soft and crumb topping is brown. Makes 4 to 6 servings.

Sumptuous Chocolate-Walnut Soufflé

Hot from the oven, this luscious, fudgy soufflé is first sparked with flaming cognac, then topped with spoonfuls of whipped cream laced with cognac. For truly outrageous indulgence, drizzle raspberry sauce prettily over the cream. (For best flavor, be sure to use a good-quality cognac such as Courvoisier in soufflé, cream and sauce.)

1 to 2 tablespoons unsalted butter, room temperature
1-1/2 cups coarsely broken English walnuts (*not* black walnuts)
3/4 cup whole milk
1 teaspoon Mexican vanilla extract or 1-1/2 teaspoons regular
   vanilla extract
4 egg yolks
Dash of salt
6 tablespoons sugar
2 tablespoons plus 1 teaspoon unsalted butter, melted
6 ounces unsweetened chocolate
5 egg whites
1/4 teaspoon cream of tartar
3 tablespoons cognac
1 teaspoon rum
1 teaspoon whisky
Cognac-Laced Whipped Cream, see below
Red Raspberry Revel Sauce, see below, if desired
1/4 cup cognac

Cognac-Laced Whipped Cream:
1 cup whipping cream
1/4 cup sugar
1 tablespoon cognac

Red Raspberry Revel Sauce:
2 cups fresh raspberries or frozen unsweetened raspberries,
   thawed, undrained
1/4 cup sugar
2 tablespoons unsalted butter
1 tablespoon cognac

Generously butter a 10-inch Bundt pan, using 1 to 2 tablespoons butter. In a bowl, combine walnuts, milk and vanilla. Set aside. Place egg yolks in a blender, food processor or large, deep bowl. Add salt and sugar; process or whisk until well blended. Add melted butter and process or whisk again until blended. If using a blender or food processor, add milk-nut mixture to yolk mixture and process until well pureed. If using a whisk, grind milk-nut mixture in a food mill, then whisk into yolk mixture. Set aside. In a heavy saucepan over very low heat or in a double boiler over simmering water, carefully melt chocolate, stirring constantly. Remove from heat. Preheat oven to 350F (175C). Beat egg whites with cream of tartar until they hold very stiff peaks. Fold melted chocolate into yolk-nut mixture, then fold in egg whites, being careful to maintain volume. Gently fold in 3 tablespoons cognac, rum and whisky. Turn mixture into buttered pan. Bake 30 minutes or until a knife inserted in center comes out clean. Meanwhile, prepare Cognac-Laced Whipped Cream and Red Raspberry Revel Sauce, if desired. When soufflé is done, cool a few minutes, then carefully turn out onto a platter. Heat 1/4 cup cognac in a small saucepan; carefully flame and drizzle over soufflé. Serve soufflé very hot, topping with cream and raspberry sauce, if desired. Makes 8 servings.

Cognac-Laced Whipped Cream:
In a chilled bowl, beat cream until foamy; gradually add sugar in a thin stream, beating constantly. Then add cognac and continue to beat until cream is very stiff. Cover and refrigerate.

Red Raspberry Revel Sauce:
In a small, heavy saucepan, combine raspberries, sugar and butter. Cook, stirring, about 5 minutes or until raspberries are hot and juice is sweet. Then turn off heat and stir in cognac. Hold at room temperature until serving.

Dessert Fondue

A delightful ending for any meal, this sweet fondue also makes a convivial midafternoon or late-evening snack. Just dip your choice of fruit and fresh baked goods in a rich, easy-to-make sauce. The only secret is to watch the cooking temperature closely; any heat above medium-low will cause the chocolate to "bind" (clump up).

> **6 ounces unsweetened chocolate**
> **1 cup light cream**
> **1-1/4 cups sugar**
> **1/2 cup unsalted butter**
> **2 teaspoons Mexican vanilla extract or 1 tablespoon regular vanilla extract**
> **Fruits and/or cakes of your choice, such as strawberries, fresh or canned pineapple wedges, banana slices, apple wedges, orange segments, pound or butter cake cubes, angel food or sponge cake cubes or slices of ladyfingers**

Place chocolate, cream, sugar and butter in a heavy saucepan or fondue pot. Stir constantly over medium-low heat until smoothly melted; continue to cook, stirring, about 5 minutes or until thickened. Stir in vanilla. To serve, attractively arrange mounds of fruits and cakes on a tray. Let guests spear fruits and cake cubes with long fondue forks or dinner forks, then dunk each morsel in chocolate. Makes 6 to 8 servings.

MAIL ORDER SOURCES FOR MEXICAN INGREDIENTS

Adobe House
127 Payne Street
Dallas, TX 75207

Casados Farms/Dos Ves, Inc.
Box 1269
San Juan Pueblo, NM 87566

Casa Moneo
210 West 14th Street
New York, NY 10011

El Molino Tamales
117 South 22nd Street
Phoenix, AZ 85034

Jane Butel's Pecos Valley Spice Co.
500 East 77th Street
Suite 2324
New York, NY 10162

La Semillera Horticultural Enterprises
P.O. Box 810082
Dallas, TX 75234

Mexican Connection
142 Lincoln Avenue
Santa Fe, NM 87501

Sasabe Store
"Hot Stuff"
P.O. Box 7
Sasabe, AZ 85704

Simon David Grocery Store
7117 Inwood Road
Dallas, TX 78207

Taos Chili Company
Turley Mill Building
Box 1100 B.A.
Taos, NM 87571

Tia Mia
Department BA 03
Sunland Park, NM 88063

Metric Chart

Comparison to Metric Measure

When You Know	Symbol	Multiply By	To Find	Symbol
teaspoons	tsp	5.0	milliliters	ml
tablespoons	tbsp	15.0	milliliters	ml
fluid ounces	fl. oz.	30.0	milliliters	ml
cups	c	0.24	liters	l
pints	pt.	0.47	liters	l
quarts	qt.	0.95	liters	l
ounces	oz.	28.0	grams	g
pounds	lb.	0.45	kilograms	kg
Fahrenheit	F	5/9 (after subtracting 32)	Celsius	C

Liquid Measure to Liters

1/4 cup	=	0.06 liters
1/2 cup	=	0.12 liters
3/4 cup	=	0.18 liters
1 cup	=	0.24 liters
1-1/4 cups	=	0.3 liters
1-1/2 cups	=	0.36 liters
2 cups	=	0.48 liters
2-1/2 cups	=	0.6 liters
3 cups	=	0.72 liters
3-1/2 cups	=	0.84 liters
4 cups	=	0.96 liters
4-1/2 cups	=	1.08 liters
5 cups	=	1.2 liters
5-1/2 cups	=	1.32 liters

Liquid Measure to Milliliters

1/4 teaspoon	=	1.25 milliliters
1/2 teaspoon	=	2.5 milliliters
3/4 teaspoon	=	3.75 milliliters
1 teaspoon	=	5.0 milliliters
1-1/4 teaspoons	=	6.25 milliliters
1-1/2 teaspoons	=	7.5 milliliters
1-3/4 teaspoons	=	8.75 milliliters
2 teaspoons	=	10.0 milliliters
1 tablespoon	=	15.0 milliliters
2 tablespoons	=	30.0 milliliters

Fahrenheit to Celsius

F	C
200—205	95
220—225	105
245—250	120
275	135
300—305	150
325—330	165
345—350	175
370—375	190
400—405	205
425—430	220
445—450	230
470—475	245
500	260

INDEX